GUILT IN HIDING

POISON TOE PRESS

GUILT IN HIDING

DONALD LEVIN

A MARTIN PREUSS MYSTERY

This is a work of fiction. All of the characters, establishments, events, locales, and organizations portrayed in this novel are either products of the author's imagination or are used fictitiously and are not construed as real. Any similarity to real persons, living or dead, is coincidental and not intended by the author.

ISBN: 0997294108
ISBN-13: 9780997294101

Cover and interior by Publish Pros
www.publishpros.com

First edition published 2016
Printed in the United States of America

For Sue

Policemen, he came to believe, were just the journalists of evil; they described it with reports, photos, videos, forensic reports; they were to their horror what the historians and biographers were to the Holocaust and Hitler.

—*Richard Flanagan, The Unknown Terrorist*

Innocence is often just guilt in hiding.

—*William McIlvanney, Strange Loyalties*

Prologue

She was the last one to see them before they disappeared.

The office manager for the orthopedic surgeon held the elevator door for them. The aide pulled the young man in the wheelchair into the elevator car backwards so the leg rest supporting his casted leg wouldn't bump into the rear wall.

"First floor?" the woman said, and the aide, a pretty young woman with long hair parted down the middle of her head, nodded her thanks.

They rode down to the lobby from the sixth floor of the Providence Hospital Medical Office Building in Southfield. The office manager followed them outside and said, "Can I give you a hand?"

The aide smiled, shook her head, and pushed the wheelchair across the busy side street toward the parking lot.

The minibus from the group home where the young man lived was in one of the handicapped spaces. From where she stood the office manager could see the aide go through the complex process of getting the wheelchair on board. She locked the wheels and pressed a button on her key fob. The side door of the minibus opened and a metal platform unfolded and lowered to the ground. The aide unlocked the wheels of the chair and pushed it onto the platform, then locked the wheels again and drew a safety belt around the bottom of the chair.

She pressed a button on the control pad that dangled from the side of the minibus and the platform rose.

1

She climbed into the vehicle and unlocked the wheelchair and pulled it inside.

Then the office manager's cell phone rang and she turned away to speak with one of the doctor's patients.

When she disconnected and looked again, the minibus was gone.

Monday, June 7, 2010

1

"Sorry," the woman said. "I'm a wreck."

Her name was Peggy See and she was the house manager, thin and pale and trembling with nerves. "Nothing like this ever happened before."

"That's okay," said Martin Preuss. "Take it slow." He and Reg Trombley from the Detective Bureau of the Ferndale Police Department sat on the sofa in the living room of the group home. They waited for her to continue.

She passed a shaky hand over her forehead. "He's twenty-three. He has Fragile X Syndrome, with moderate retardation and some visual impairment. Also anxiety behavior and delayed language skills. For now he's also non-ambulatory. He took a tumble down the stairs last month and broke his leg so he's in a wheelchair."

"Do you have a photo?"

She retrieved a snapshot from a bulletin board outside the room off the kitchen that served as her office. The photo was a group shot of all the residents. "That's him. Zach Warranow." She pointed to a serious young man with a long narrow face, thick glasses, rosy cheeks, and a full head of curly black hair. He was wearing khaki shorts and a blue polo shirt. One of the aides had her arm around him.

Preuss said, "Good looking kid."

"Sweet, too," Peggy said. "The woman beside him, that's Elizaveta Kertész. The one who's also missing. She was taking Zach to his orthopedist's appointment. It was at three. They should have been back by four-thirty, five at the latest."

It was then almost seven.

"When I didn't hear from her by six I called the doctor's office but it was closed for the day. I left a message and the office manager called me back and told me Elizaveta left with Zach around quarter after four. That's when I called the police."

"What's the aide's story?"

Trombley read off from his notes. "Thirty-two, divorced, mother of an eleven-year-old girl, lives in southwest Detroit. She's worked here for almost three years."

"Any trouble before this?"

"Never," Peggy See said. "She's totally trustworthy. That's why I think she must have had trouble on the road. An accident or something. I called her cell about a dozen times. Everything went to voicemail and she hasn't called back."

"Gail Crimmonds is out retracing the route," Trombley told Preuss.

Preuss said, "My son lives in a group home and they have a rule that a driver and an aide both have to be in the vehicle whenever a resident goes anywhere."

"It's the same here. But we were short-staffed for the day shift. I didn't want him to miss his appointment so I made a judgment call to let them go by themselves. Elizaveta's never let me down."

"Have you tried the boy's parents?" Preuss asked. "Maybe the driver took him home for some reason."

"I spoke with his mother. She hasn't seen him since the last time she came to visit. She was not pleased to hear from me. Said she's going to sue the agency for losing her son."

"She may reconsider when we find him," Preuss said.

"I hope you're right." She shook her head. "She lives in Bloomfield Hills," she said, as if that explained it.

Preuss and Trombley shared a look. Family in the moneyed northern suburb put a different face on the disappearance.

"I'll need her number," Preuss said. "And her address, if you have it."

"I'll get them. I can't believe Elizaveta would have done anything with that young man. You can see from that photo, she adored him. There must be some other explanation."

That other explanation was what we're afraid of, Preuss thought.

"What do we know about the aide?"

Preuss stood with Trombley on the sidewalk. The street was quiet. Patrol Officer Gail Crimmonds had returned and sat in her scout car in front of the group home. The other night shift patrol cars were searching the city for the minibus, a white high-cube vehicle with room for six wheelchairs. A BOLO had gone out to the Michigan State Police and the Ohio State Highway Patrol.

"Not much more than I told you," Trombley said. "There's nothing on her in any of the systems. Her car's still parked in front of the house, that Escort over there. Keeps to herself. Nobody seems to know much about her personally, but from what the house manager told me she's an ideal employee."

"Can we get somebody to check her place in Detroit in case she went there?"

"I'll see who's available."

"Where's Bellamy?"

"Can't raise him. Dispatch can't find him either."

"Who else do we have? What about Ed Blair?"

"We can try him, but I doubt he's available. His wife's at Karmanos again. The cancer's back."

7

"I heard. Why don't you give him a call, ask him if he can get away and swing by the driver's house. If he can't do it, tell him not to worry, we'll find somebody else."

Trombley went off to make the calls and Preuss started down the sidewalk. It was a neighborhood of two-story homes off Hilton and Woodward Heights in the Detroit suburb of Ferndale. He remembered when this home opened a little over three years ago. As with the residence where his son lived, the neighbors complained about retarded and handicapped people in their neighborhood. For a while the department got calls every night about a ruckus from the house, even though the group home residents were incapable of making the kind of commotion they were blamed for.

Once the neighbors got to know them and saw how harmless they were—especially after one of the women who lived in the house baked a cake for the block party one year—the complaints ended and the residents were welcomed into the neighborhood.

He paused at the end of the block. It was a warm evening and the June night was fresh and calming, the sky grey tinged with violet. A perfect night for baseball. His son Toby should be at the game by now. They were loading up for the trip down to Comerica Park to see the Tigers play the White Sox when Trombley's call came. Preuss had been looking forward to going with Toby on this outing. A night game had everything his son loved . . . bright lights, action, the constant buzz of crowd noise, the crescendos of cheers . . .

Toby was in his wheelchair and they were waiting in the driveway for his turn to be loaded onto their minibus. He had on a blue Tigers cap and over his white Tigers jersey with blue pinstripes and Old English D he wore a bib that said, "Spit Happens."

When Trombley got hold of Preuss, he explained what was going on and apologized for ruining his evening.

"No worries," Preuss had said. "You did the right thing. Be there in fifteen minutes."

Preuss told his son he was sorry but there was an emergency and he had to get back to work. He'd come over later to wish him goodnight.

Toby couldn't speak or tell his father how he felt but he was expressive in other ways, and Preuss carried his son's look of disappointment all the way down Woodward Avenue from Toby's group home in Berkley to this one in Ferndale.

"Martin?"

Trombley trotted up behind him. "Ed says he can't leave. His wife took a turn for the worse and they rushed her into surgery. The duty officer says there's nobody to spare right now."

"Okay. Let me see what I can do."

Trombley returned to the house and Preuss stood thinking about all the times Toby went out in his group home's minibus. What would he do if something like this ever happened to his son? Toby was the only one left of his family and the most important person in his life. Losing him was unthinkable. How would he go on?

He returned to the group home. Instead of waiting around for something to happen, he decided to go into Detroit himself.

2

Elizaveta Kertész lived in the top floor of a two-family home within sight of the Ambassador Bridge to Canada in southwest Detroit. There was no sign of the minibus on the street or the alley that ran alongside the house, a brick foursquare with a turret topped by a cupola on the left side and two full porches, one up and one down. Taped to the mailbox on one of the two doors on the bottom porch was an index card with *Kertész and Furlong* in careful printing.

He rang the bell and banged hard on the door. In a few seconds the other door was opened by a woman with deep brown, almost black eyes and skin the color of coffee with milk and a headful of wavy black hair just beginning to go grey. Early- to mid-forties. An inch or two over five feet, slender in a billowing peasant blouse over Levis. Birkenstocks. She made a hand gesture inviting him to state his business through the top glass of the outside door.

He held up his badge and introduced himself. "I'm looking for Elizaveta Kertész," he said through the glass. "Do you know if she's home?"

"She lives upstairs. But she hasn't come home from work. Is everything okay?"

"That's what I'm trying to find out. She hasn't been seen since she left with one of the residents of the group home where she works this afternoon."

"Maybe you better come inside."

Because of the age of the house and the neighborhood, he expected older furnishings but the living room the woman led him into was decorated in steel and chrome and leather. On the walls were framed posters of Mexican art, Frieda Kahlo's self-portrait, a reproduction of an elaborate Day of the Dead mural, and an edenic scene with two nude figures standing in a lake surrounded by a forest, all heavy in reds and greens.

She held a hand out to a chair and he sat.

Preuss said, "What's your relationship to Elizaveta?"

"I own the house. Rosa Martinez. She's been my tenant upstairs for the past three years. But we've also gotten to be friends."

"When was the last time you saw her?"

"This morning, when she left to take her daughter to school. Then she was off to school herself."

"She didn't say anything about being late tonight?"

"Not to me."

"Where is her daughter now?"

"Doing her homework down here in the kitchen. On days when Elizaveta works, Rachael stays with me till her mom gets home."

"Can I speak with her?"

The girl sat hunched over a math workbook at a massive wooden table in the kitchen. She looked up when Preuss and Rosa Martinez approached the doorway from the dining room. She gave Preuss a clear-eyed appraising look. She had high cheekbones and white, almost transparent skin.

Rosa said, "Rachael, this is Detective Preuss. He's a policeman and he wants to ask you some questions."

"Hello Rachael," Preuss said. "Did your mother say anything to you about being late today? Maybe if she had errands to run?"

"No." Rachael's voice was small and soft, making her sound even younger than she was.

"Have you heard from her at all today?"

"No."

"Did she seem worried about anything? Or talk about any problems she was having, maybe somebody she was worried about?"

Rachael shook her head. "Why are you asking me these questions? Did something happen to her?"

Rosa Martinez put her arm around the girl. "This afternoon your mom left work with one of the people she takes care of, and she hasn't come back yet. Detective Preuss is making sure she's okay."

Rachael stared at her as though that couldn't possibly be the truth.

"There are lots of possible explanations, honey," Rosa said. "She might have had car trouble. Maybe her phone lost its charge so she couldn't call us. Maybe the boy she was driving got sick and she had to take him to the hospital."

She glanced at Preuss for validation of these. He said nothing. They had all been checked.

"All right, Rachael, thanks," said Preuss. "The minute I hear anything, I'll let you know, okay?"

"Are you going to find my mother?"

"We will," he said, as the voice in his head told him not to make promises he couldn't keep.

Preuss stood and Rosa kissed the girl on the top of her head and told her she'd be right back. She followed Preuss into the living room.

He said, "Is there any other family?"

"There's a sister somewhere in Ohio. Otherwise that's it."

"Has she ever brought home any of the people she takes care of?"

"Never. That would be against the rules, no?"

"People do break the rules."

"Not Elizaveta."

"Do you know if she's seeing anyone?"

"Not that I know of. I don't think she has many friends. She doesn't have time. When she's not with her daughter she spends every minute working or going to school."

"Where is she a student?"

"Wayne State. She's studying vocal music."

"Is Rachael's father in the picture?"

"I've never seen him or heard either of them talk about him."

He thanked her for her time and gave her one of his business cards. "If you hear from her, or if she shows up, could you call me right away? My cell number's on there, too."

She walked him toward the door. He noticed a photograph on the table in the hallway by the door. It showed Rachael with Elizaveta on Belle Isle; the silver tubes of the Renaissance Center stood gleaming in the background.

This was a better image than the photo Peggy See showed him. Elizaveta and her daughter had their heads together. She was an attractive woman with medium-length honey-colored hair parted down the center of her head and hanging in a relaxed fall to her shoulders, with prominent freckled cheekbones. She had brown eyes that angled down at the outside corners, giving her an air of perpetual sadness even when she smiled, as she did in the photo.

Preuss said, "Can I hang onto this? I'll make copies and get it back to you."

"Of course. I have to say, you're not leaving me with a good feeling."

"Let's just take one step at a time. I'll be in touch."

"Do you want to come in? There's a fresh pot of coffee," Peggy See said. They stood together in the front hall.

"No, I'm good, thanks," Preuss said. "I'm not going to stay. I just wanted to check in."

"The other detective left a little while ago."

"I told him he could go. He said he wanted to get out looking for them. An officer's parked outside in case there's any news."

He heard the commotion of loud voices up on the second floor as aides got the residents ready for bed. In the living room Rachel Maddow was on the television talking about the massive spill of oil bleeding into the Gulf of Mexico from the Deepwater Horizon oil rig collapse. Then she went into the car bomb plot in Times Square from the previous month. The crazy world seemed to be spinning out of control.

He forced himself to think about the problem in front of them. "I went to Elizaveta's place in Detroit, but her daughter hasn't heard anything from her and neither has the woman who owns the house."

Peggy See sighed. "None of this would have happened if I hadn't let her go out by herself."

"There are lots of eyes out there looking for them."

"I hope they find them." After a moment she said, "You said your son lives in a group home?"

"He does."

"Where?"

"Berkley."

"It's not run by Angels of Mercy, is it?"

"It is."

"I know that place. I worked there for a little while before I came here. Who's your son?"

"Toby Preuss."

"Oh, sure. I remember him. Everyone talked about what a sweet boy he is. We heard his dad was a policeman. So you're the one."

"I'm the one."

"This place is similar to his, except our consumers are older, and they're ambulatory."

Preuss hated the term "consumers." The staff at Toby's house used it, too. He never understood why they didn't just say "residents," which is what the people who lived in these places were. These houses were supposed to give a home-like setting to people with handicaps to keep them out of institutions, yet "consumers" made it sound like a financial arrangement.

Of course, like everything else, that's what it all came down to. But it would be nice to pretend otherwise.

"I take it Zach's mother never came?"

"No, she said she was in a business meeting she couldn't leave."

Peggy See looked thoughtful for a moment, then said, "I guess that's more important than her missing son."

The front door to Toby's group home was locked for the night, but Connie, the respiratory therapist on duty, answered his knock right away. She was a buxom woman with elaborate floral tattoos over her upper arms and the slice of chest that was visible above the low-cut opening of her tee shirt.

"That transport ever turn up?" she asked.

"Bad news travels fast."

"Always does."

"It's still missing," Preuss said. "Along with the driver and one of the residents. Everybody here's accounted for?"

"Of course. Soon as I heard about it I called Melissa at the game and made sure everybody was safe."

"How's Toby?"

"Melissa said he had a blast."

As though on cue, he heard Toby's foghorn voice rolling down the hall from his room.

"I guess so," Preuss said.

"Gonna be a while before he calms down enough to sleep. He sure loves going out."

He has a far more active social life than I do, Preuss thought as he walked down the hall to Toby's room. Because of his cerebral palsy Toby could not articulate words, but Preuss was never at a loss for knowing what his son carried in his mind and heart. Now, for example, before he even reached the doorway, from the ruckus Toby was making Preuss knew his son was giving his own exuberant play-by-play of the game to his aide.

Preuss stood in the doorway and saw his son lying in bed with one of his trademark crooked grins. It was impossible to distinguish words but there was no doubt Toby was telling his aide about his outing, his vocalizations undulating from cheerful falsetto to deep bass.

He still wore his Tigers jersey. His Tiger's cap had fallen onto the pillow as he wagged his head in excitement.

His aide Melissa noticed Preuss standing there and opened her mouth to say something but he put his finger to his lips before she could get anything out.

He stood watching his son for a few more seconds, then when Toby paused to take a breath he said, "Hey, noisy guy. What's all this commotion?"

It took Toby a second to process his father's voice. It didn't seem possible but his smile broadened, and he began to scream even louder.

"Toby," Preuss said, "people are trying to sleep around here."

He entered the room and leaned over the bed to kiss the boy on the side of his face and wrap him in an enormous hug. Toby gave in to the deep pressure of his father's arms and Preuss could feel his son's tight muscles relaxing.

Holding his son had the same effect on Preuss . . . it unlocked the stresses that built up from the world he lived in day after day. Preuss inhaled Toby's sweet smell, a mixture of straw-berry shampoo, lilac soap, and the boy's own yeasty scent, like baking bread.

He helped Melissa undress his son and as always he gave the boy's body a quick check for signs of mistreatment. All was fine. He eased his son's arms, stiff with contractures, through the arm-holes of the Ferndale Police Department tee shirt that was Toby's nightshirt and then maneuvered it over his head.

Preuss stayed for another hour, sitting in the chair beside the bed rubbing his son's knobby back and reading the daily note from his teacher at school. That day therapy dogs had visited his classroom and his teacher wrote how Toby suffered the dogs lick-ing his face as long as he could stand (he hated to have his face touched) and then used his computer-assisted communications device to say the pre-recorded message, "Let someone else have a turn."

Vintage Toby, Preuss thought. He wished more people could appreciate the boy's subtle capabilities, especially his humor. Preuss knew too many looked at Toby and saw nothing more than a potted plant and missed the richness of his true personality.

Their loss.

Toby wound down. His vocalizing became occasional hums with a chirp of glee every now and then, and his breathing evened out and he fell asleep, curled like a comma on his right side. Preuss watched the boy's peaceful slumber for a while longer, then straightened Toby's head on the pillow so he wouldn't get a crick in his neck, tucked the sheet and light blanket around him, and kissed him goodnight.

On the way home he called Peggy See but she told him Zach and Elizaveta were still missing.

Tuesday, June 8, 2010

3

Preuss awoke a little after three, restless and uncomfortable. His first thought was of Zach Warranow . . . so aware of Toby's vulnerability, he felt the missing young man's fear and disorientation as a terrible quivering in the pit of his stomach.

The vanished woman, Elizaveta Kertész, disturbed him too. If she were as conscientious as everyone said, she would not have left her daughter. He had an awful feeling about how this would turn out.

Knowing he'd never get back to sleep, he took a shower and dressed and went downstairs to make a pot of coffee. He called the station but there was no overnight news about the minibus.

He stood at the kitchen counter drinking his coffee and gazing out the window into his back yard. The day brightened.

By six he was at his desk at the Eugene Shanahan Law Enforcement Complex on Nine Mile in Ferndale. He spent the first hour reading through incident reports from the previous day and evening. He did this every day to keep up with activity in Ferndale but now he paid particular attention to anything that might suggest what could have happened to the minibus. There was nothing.

For the next hour he wrote a report on a case he had been investigating, a series of holdups at knifepoint in the early morning hours during the past two weeks around the overpass from Detroit on Woodward Avenue at Eight Mile Road. He had put together a decoy operation and sent a plainclothes patrolman out for a few nights in the vicinity of the holdups and sure enough the villains made their move on the decoy.

It turned out to be a father and son working together. The father had a long record for larceny and assault but the son's jacket had been clean to that point.

So nice to see the older generation handing down their knowledge, Preuss thought.

He saved the report to the case file and returned his attention to Zach and Elizaveta. Assuming no movement on the missing vehicle this morning, he would need to pay a visit to the boy's home and speak with his mother, not just because of a possible kidnapping but there may be familial issues that weren't apparent to the staff at the group home.

"What are you doing here?"

Startled from his thoughts, Preuss looked up to see the duty sergeant, Paul Horvath, standing in his office doorway.

Preuss said, "Contrary to what you might have heard, I'm a member in good standing of this public safety force."

"I mean didn't you get the message?"

"What message?" Preuss looked to see if there was a blinking red light on his office phone, checked his cell for a text, his desktop for an email. "Nothing."

"From the chief. An email went to everybody in the Bureau."

"What can I tell you, Paul. I didn't get anything."

"He wants us all in the conference room. He's got something to tell us."

Reg Trombley, Hank Bellamy, the Bureau's administrative assistant Tanya Corcoran, and Horvath and Preuss were crammed into the chief's tiny conference room. Missing were Janie Cahill, the detective assigned to the Youth Bureau who would be on vacation for another week, and Nick Russo, the Detective Bureau chief who was out for the rest of the month. In Russo's absence, Preuss as senior detective was acting head.

"Don't tell me we're getting a replacement for Tony," Bellamy said. He was balding and pear-shaped with a wispy mustache like a wooly bear caterpillar on his upper lip.

Tony Tullio had been the most senior detective in the Bureau until he retired the year before. In the aftermath of the national financial crisis in 2008, Ferndale's finances still didn't allow for a replacement so the Detective Bureau had been operating with an open position for almost a year.

"I doubt that's what this is about," Horvath said.

Preuss said, "You know something?"

"I've heard rumblings."

"What kind of rumblings?"

Before Horvath could explain, the tall, spare form of Chief William Warnock entered and took his seat at the head of the conference table. As always while on duty he wore his blue dress uniform with crisp white shirt.

"Good morning," he said. The group mumbled their good mornings.

"I know you're all busy so I'll get right to it. You're going to hear some news today but I wanted to bring you into the loop first."

He looked from one face to the other.

"As most of you know, except for my time in the navy I've served with the Ferndale PD for my entire adult life. I worked my way up from patrolman and for the past six years I've been privileged to be your chief. I don't regret a second of it and if I had the chance to do it over again I'd do the exact same thing. I love this place. I love the people. I love the community we serve."

Preuss shifted in his chair. He sensed where this was heading and it wasn't good.

"But today I'm putting in my papers for retirement," Warnock said.

He paused to let that sink in.

Damn, Preuss thought.

Damn damn damn.

The others around the table shared a look of disbelief.

"My wife and I have been talking it over for the past few months and we're both agreed we want to enjoy a different kind of life while we're still healthy."

"What will you do?" Trombley asked.

"Travel. Spend time with the grandchildren. Do what all retired people do: eat dinner at four o'clock and go to bed at nine."

A murmur of nervous laughter.

"But seriously, this past year I've been thinking more and more about how short our lives are, how little time we have to draw breath. I decided I didn't want death to be my retirement plan so I'm going to make the best use of the time I have left without having to worry about going out to crime scenes in the middle of the night in January."

When no one said anything else, Warnock said, "My plan is to leave at the end of next month. I've already talked with the mayor and the City Council. Today I'm going to announce it to the department and the community. I wanted to tell you first because I came up through the Detective Bureau and I still feel like this is my departmental home. It's been a privilege to serve with every one of you."

He looked around one last time, nodded, and was up and gone.

Leaving them to sit staring at each other.

Trombley said, "I'm in shock."

He had followed Preuss into his office and now sat in the visitor's chair. Preuss wished the younger detective would go back to his cubicle so he could be alone to process Warnock's bombshell but Trombley sat there trying to figure this development out and Preuss didn't want to kick him out of the office.

"First Tony," Trombley said, "now the chief."

"Lots of changes."

"You've probably seen your share of coming and going over the years. I'm still a relative newbie."

"There've been a few. Since I've been here Warnock was advanced to chief, Russo was promoted to chief of the bureau, you and Janey came in, Tony left, two or three others have retired—but for the most part this has been a stable group. The detective's shield is a career goal for a lot of cops."

"Me included."

"So once they're here they tend to stay. Unless they get tapped for something else, like Bill."

"I gotta say, you're taking this with remarkable calm."

"He seems comfortable with the decision so I'm happy for him. It's terrible for me, of course. Warnock's been a good friend and he's helped me negotiate Russo's crazy vendetta."

"That's right. And now he won't be here."

"No."

"That blows."

"It does."

Besides being the chief of the Detective Bureau, Nick Russo was also Preuss's ex-father-in-law. He was responsible for Preuss becoming a policeman. Preuss married Russo's daughter Jeanette, and when she died one night seven years ago when a drunk driver t-boned her on her way to her mother's in Traverse City after loading their two boys into the minivan and walking out on Preuss, Russo held him responsible for her death and had never forgiven him. As much as he could, Warnock intervened whenever Russo's hatred of Preuss threatened to get out of hand.

But now Warnock would be gone.

"And you know what the big question is," Trombley said. "Who's going to be his replacement? He didn't say anything about that."

"It's not his job to handpick his successor."

"Hey, why don't you go after it?"

"Oh please."

"I'm serious. You'd be phenomenal."

"I'd rather staple my eyes shut."

Trombley sat up, warming to the notion. "No, do it, Martin."

"Out of the question."

"Why not?"

"Do you have any idea how precarious my situation in the department is? And you think they'd jump me over Nick?" He shook his head. "Never happen."

"Lot of people'll support you. At least think about it?"

"No."

"'Martin Preuss, Chief of Police.'" Trombley held up his hand and swept it across the words as though underlining them on an office door. "Don't you like the way that sounds? It has what you call a ring to it."

"No," Preuss said. "The thought is so awful it makes me want to puke."

"Just tell me you'll think about it."

"I won't." Preuss stood. "Forget it. But I would like to do some actual police work. If that's all right with you?"

Trombley raised his hands in surrender and Preuss immediately regretted snapping at him.

"Sorry. I guess I'm not taking this so calmly after all."

4

The house was at the end of Vaughn Crossing, a cul-de-sac near a pond off Long Lake Road in Bloomfield Hills. It was a sprawling post-modern monstrosity that began as an arts and crafts bunga-low but traveled through decades of twentieth century styles to end as a concrete and glass Bauhaus box with cantilevered ter-races overhanging the wooded back yard. In the front yard was a Zen water feature, a round concrete ball that gurgled as though choking on the architecture.

They parked in front of the house and walked up to the front door. The doorbell sounded inside like a Japanese gong.

The woman who answered was skeletally thin with a face that was taut and shining. She wore an impeccable ecru linen suit and held a cell phone in one hand.

"Ms. Warranow?" Preuss said. He introduced himself and Trombley and before he could get anything else out she inter-rupted him.

"Hansen," she said. "Marcia Hansen. I dropped the Warranow when I was divorced."

"May we come in? We're here about Zach."

"Have you found him?"

"We haven't."

She turned away. "I suppose you better, then," she tossed back over her shoulder.

Heels clattering on the slate floor, she led the way into a sunken living room that was on the modernist end of the home's mix of architectural styles. She held out a hand toward a couch that Preuss and Trombley sat on. It was as uncomfortable as it looked. She perched in a chair that looked as if it had been made of sharp-angled glass.

"I take it you haven't heard from Zach," Preuss said.

"I don't know what those idiots at the group home told you," the woman said, "but my son is nonverbal. I wouldn't be able to 'hear from him' even if he were here in this room with us."

"I meant have you heard anything about him."

"Not since the house manager called me last night."

"When was the last time you saw him?"

"I was down there the weekend before last. This past weekend Harvey and I went to New York. Harvey's my partner."

"Is he around?"

"He's in Chicago."

"So just to be clear," Preuss said, "you haven't seen your son for almost two weeks?"

"I feel no need to be one of these helicopter parents hovering over their handicapped children. Those people at that group home are paid to take care of him. I trust them to do their jobs. And until now they have."

"What about the woman who was driving the minibus, Elizaveta Kertész. Do you know her?"

"Never heard of her."

She made a show of checking the time on the phone she carried. "Is this going to take much longer? I have a meeting with GM management at the RenCen in forty-five minutes."

"What do you do, ma'am?"

"I'm an events planner. I put together fund-raising parties, employee recognition celebrations, weddings, you name it . . . I take care of everything from floral design to invitations to venue rental. I run my own company."

"Your son and his driver went missing at a little after four yesterday," Preuss said. "Where were you at the time?"

"Oh please. You can't possibly think I had anything to do with this."

Preuss waited her out.

"For heaven's sake. I was at a business meeting at the Acura dealership in Troy. Do you want the names of the people I was meeting with? It lasted all afternoon, from three till eight. During which time I got the call informing me my son was missing."

"Can you account for your partner's whereabouts?"

"Right, because we're both engaged in a conspiracy to kidnap my own son."

Again he waited.

"As I said, he's in Chicago for a business meeting. He's an attorney specializing in governmental malpractice." She flung the last statement like a threat.

"Ms. Hansen, we still don't know what happened to Zach," Preuss said, "so we have to look at every possibility. Can you think of any reason why someone you know might want to hurt him? A business acquaintance maybe, or someone with a grudge against you?"

"I can't think of any reason why anyone would want to harm my son." Preuss caught the note of contempt in her voice, aimed not at him but at Zach. "He's harmless. He wouldn't hurt a fly, and couldn't even if he somehow could form the notion to. Which he couldn't."

"Kidnappers don't pick their victims by the amount of harm the victims themselves can do."

"Are you saying my son was kidnapped?"

"There's no indication of that, but we have to consider every-thing right now. It's not out of the question that your son is being held somewhere."

"I suppose they just see we live in a fancy house and think we'd pay anything to get our loved one back."

"And what about your partner? Any enemies that you know of?"

She thought for a few seconds. "He's an attorney," she said, "so I'm sure he has enemies. But he has his own children. Anybody who wants to get back at him for something would go after them and not Zach."

Trombley said, "Does Zach's father see much of him?"

"He lives in Hawaii," she said with a toss of her head. "When Zach was an infant, as soon as it was clear there was something wrong with him his father took a large powder out of our lives."

"When was the last time you saw or heard from him?" Preuss asked.

"Not for years."

"Does he have a phone number where I could reach him?"

"What do you need that for?"

"We'll need to speak with him," Preuss said. "We have to rule him out as a suspect in Zach's disappearance."

She gave a harsh and humorless cackle, as though she were skating on the thin edge of hysteria. Then she got up and went over to a table by the wall. She opened a drawer and retrieved a small notebook. She copied down a number on a sheet of lined paper that read "From the Mind of Marcia" and tore it out and handed it to Preuss.

"Rule away," she said. "But you should know my ex-husband never had any interest in his son, and when I knew him never had the gumption for a kidnapping scheme. Or getting out of bed, for that matter. He comes from inherited money, so when God passed out ambition he must have been off getting high."

She took another look at her phone. "We almost done here?"

Preuss looked at Trombley, who nodded. "For now," Preuss said. "We'll find your son, Ms. Hansen."

She turned up the corner of her mouth in a gesture of near-total disdain for Preuss and everything he represented.

Neither man said anything until Preuss negotiated the Explorer back onto Woodward and they headed south toward Ferndale. Then Trombley let out his breath in a rush, as if he had been holding it this entire time.

"Damn," he said. "For a second I thought you were going to haul off and smack her. Especially with that whole 'my son is nonverbal' thing."

"The thought may have crossed my mind."

"And she hasn't seen him for two weeks? What's that about? You see your boy every day, don't you?"

"Sometimes two or three times a day."

"That's what I'm saying. Nope. Something wrong here."

Preuss drove for a few minutes in silence, then said, "People react to having a special needs kid in different ways. Some get angry, some take it as a personal failure. I've seen parents who never get over that anger. I think we just met one of those."

Trombley shook his head. "Rich folks, man. They're not the same as you and me."

"No," Preuss said. "They have more money."

Back at the Shanahan Preuss sat in his office with a cup of coffee and worked his way through the phone numbers Marcia Hansen gave him. Her partner Harvey Bauer had law offices on Telegraph in Franklin but Preuss couldn't get past his secretary, who told him Mr. Bauer had been in Chicago since Friday. Preuss asked for the number of the hotel in Chicago, and when he called it they confirmed Bauer was there.

The ex-husband was harder to get in touch with. Hawaiian time was six hours earlier than Michigan's so the ex was sound asleep but Preuss asked the woman who answered the phone to wake him up.

"I'd rather not, if it's all the same to you," she said. "He just got out of the hospital and he needs his rest."

"What was the matter with him?"

"Exhaustion."

"What hospital?"

"Can I ask what this is regarding?"

"He might be involved in a crime I'm investigating here in Ferndale."

"He hasn't been in Ferndale for over twenty years."

"The name of the hospital, please?"

She mulled that over, then said, "New Horizons Recovery. In Honolulu."

"That doesn't sound like a hospital. That sounds like a drug rehab program."

"Look. He asked me not to tell anybody this, but you're right. He's been in rehab for a meth problem for the past thirty days. He's doing really well, but I'm trying to protect him until he's stronger."

"When did he get out?"

"Two days ago."

He got the name of the rehab institute. It would take more time to check on the program since they didn't give out information on their clients, so he'd need to go through channels. But for now Preuss didn't believe the man was involved in Zach's disappearance and was content to scratch him off the list.

Amazing, he thought, how some people with the worst habits aways find the most loyal protectors. His brother was the same way . . . before his drug habit killed him, he always found some-one to love and defend him, no matter what he did.

Reg Trombley appeared in the doorway.

Preuss said, "What's up?"

"I just got a message from Dispatch. You're going to want to hear this."

5

Martin Road Park in Ferndale covered several city blocks on the east side of Woodward Avenue north of Nine Mile Road. A wooded area lined the west and south ends of the park, which contained a baseball diamond, basketball hoops, an in-line skating rink, play structures and swing sets, soccer fields, park benches and pavilions and concession stands, and a sledding hill and walking trail. Bordering the park were the Detroit Curling Club on the south end and Webb Elementary School and the Ferndale Cornerstone Community United Lutheran Church to the north.

With its mission of social justice, the church was a member of both the South Oakland Shelter, an agency providing services to the homeless in Oakland County, and Forgotten Harvest, which sent donated food to a free soup kitchen the church ran every Tuesday and Thursday year-round from 11:30 a.m. till 1:30 p.m. Volunteers staffed the soup kitchen and created meals out of the donated food.

Leonard Costigan, the church's Director of Adult Ministries, oversaw the project. He was a man whose passion for social justice was one of the characteristics that most appealed to the search committee that had hired him two years before.

The lunch service was full on this particular Tuesday, and Costigan was busier than usual keeping the serving trays filled with the baked chicken, mashed potatoes, green beans, German potato salad, mixed vegetables, green salad, rolls, Jell-O, and cherry pie that comprised the menu.

So it was not until near the end of the lunch period that Costigan had the leisure to sit and survey his flock. A lean man in his early fifties with intense eyes and a crisp salt-and-pepper mustache, he had started up the soup kitchen as soon as he began work at the church, and knew most of those attending. They represented not just the homeless of Ferndale, but the elderly, the young, and the poor . . . anyone who needed a nutritious hot meal was welcome.

He watched them now, keeping a rough tally of who was here and who wasn't. He liked to think this program was ensuring they would all get a good meal at least twice during the week, and was helping to keep them safe. Whenever any of the regulars didn't show up for a few days, he went around asking after them to satisfy himself they were well and not sick or dead. If nobody knew what was happening with people who had stopped coming, Costigan called in Oakland County Social Services.

He kept a special eye out for one woman he knew only as Sheila (she refused to tell him, or anyone, her last name). All he knew besides her first name was that she was homeless and lived during the warmer months in Martin Road Park behind the church. He was standing out behind the church one day and saw from a distance that she maintained a sort of camp for herself among the trees at the south end of the park. She spent her days at a park bench, and by night she unrolled her sleeping bag so she could sleep under the stars. In bad weather she slept under a tattered pup tent, both stashed safely during the day with her other belongings behind the concession stand.

Costigan thought she was in her thirties, though it was difficult to tell with people who were homeless because their years on the street wore them out prematurely. She was a tall woman with honey-colored hair that hung to the middle of her back. She must have washed it often because it was always shining clean and curled along its entire length as if it were corrugated. She was not so careful about her other hygiene and many times Costigan had to suggest she use one of the church bathrooms to clean up.

She did not give off the crazy vibe that some of the other homeless men and women radiated, but she kept to herself, never spoke when she would come to get her meals, and responded to Costigan's efforts to engage her in conversation with either a shy smile or a blank stare.

One other thing Costigan noticed about her was that she ate little. If anyone could be said to live on air, it was Sheila. Where others piled their plates high, she was sparing in what she took . . . she never ate meat, chicken, or fish. She took veggies when they were offered, or else the green salad that was always plentiful.

So when he saw she had piled her plate high on this day with all the offerings from the lunch, he was intrigued.

He went behind the table where the hot food steamed in large aluminum foil containers. "Have you seen Sheila today?" he asked Vivian, one of the older women who served up the food.

Vivian scanned the room and said, "Over by the window."

"What I mean is, have you seen what she's eating?"

"I did. I doled out a little spoonful of veggies she always asks for. But I was surprised she kept wanting me to add more food to the plate." Vivian imitated Sheila's gesture, a rolling of her hand.

From across the room they watched the quiet woman nibbling green beans one by one as though trying to make each one last even though she had a mound of food on her plate.

"That's unlike her," Costigan said.

"Maybe she developed an appetite."

"Maybe."

"Lord knows she's thin enough. She could use some weight on those bones."

Costigan hung back as Sheila left the Fellowship Hall with her loaded tray when she thought nobody was looking. Visitors to the food pantry weren't allowed to take food with them but he stopped Vivian from saying something when they saw her leaving. He let her get up the stairs to the main floor before he followed her.

She left by the rear doors bearing the tray in front of her. She crossed the parking lot behind the church and went through the gate in the fence separating church property from the broad meadow that formed the central area of the park. She didn't look back so she didn't see Costigan trailing behind her. There were no structures for him to hide behind so he kept to the trees that formed the western border of the park and rushed to keep up with her as she hurried through the center of the meadow, skirting the grassy hump of the sledding hill.

She went straight back to the wooded area behind the inline skating rink, where the trees were thickest. There she kept her belongings.

All she had were a surplus army pup tent, a sleeping bag, a half-dozen tattered plastic carry bags containing her worldly goods, and an orange five-gallon Home Depot tub that served as a seat, a carrier for her clothes and other belongings when she needed to transport them, a storage unit to keep her food safe from the critters she lived among, and a tub whenever she washed her hair.

Costigan watched her slender back as she bore the tray piled high with food through the trees and approached the park bench that served as her base of operations, which was not visible from the park meadow because of the sledding hill.

She set the tray down on the bench. Costigan saw her bend forward but couldn't tell what she was doing. He circled around behind her and came as close as he dared. He saw a young man in a wheelchair parked in the dirt on the far side of the park bench.

Costigan thought he was young, maybe in his teens, with curly hair. One leg stuck straight out in a cast.

From his hiding place Costigan heard the boy making a gentle humming sound as his head waggled on his neck.

Sheila straightened him in his chair. A pillow was scrunched between his leg and the side of the wheelchair. She took the pillow and inserted it between his left arm and the curved back of the wheelchair so he would sit up straighter.

Then she took a piece of chicken from the plate on her tray and separated a small piece with her fingers and offered it to him. She said something Costigan couldn't hear, but it sounded like she was calling the boy Tom.

The young man waggled his head with more force and turned his face away from the food. The hum in his throat modulated into an unhappy whine. He brought his arms up in front of his face as though protecting himself against the food she was offering.

His mouth hung open and Costigan saw a thin filament of saliva droop from it and arc as the breeze through the trees caught it. The whine became a cry of distress.

Sheila set the chicken down and reached forward to grab a handful of the young man's bib and tenderly wiped the drool off his chin.

6

"That's where I saw them," Leonard Costigan said, and pointed through the trees.

Preuss and Trombley and three blue-and-whites had converged in front of the school bus garage at the Webb Elementary School that abutted the park next to the church. Another blue-and-white was parked down the block from the south end of the park.

Preuss stood at the side of the garage searching the trees through binoculars in the direction Costigan had pointed. "I don't see anything."

Costigan said, "Look to the right just behind the skating rink."

Preuss adjusted his view but shook his head. "Sledding hill's in the way."

"No, look to the right."

Trombley gave an impatient huff. "Why are we even doing this? Let's just come up behind them and grab them."

"You don't understand," Costigan said. "This woman is very fragile. Very unstable. There's no telling what she'd do to the child if she saw a group of police approaching her."

"What's she doing with him in the first place?" Preuss asked.

"I don't know." Costigan explained how she raised his suspicions with all the food she was taking. "I don't know who he is or how he got here. All I heard was her saying 'Tom.'"

"She called him Tom?"

"Yes."

"If it's the boy we think it is, his name is Zach Warranow and he's been missing since yesterday." He scanned the park again through the glasses.

"I don't see anybody," he said. "All I see are empty park benches. No wheelchair, no Zach."

He handed the binoculars to Trombley. "See what you can find. Look past the right side of the skating rink, behind the play set."

Trombley looked, said, "Just what you saw. Nothing."

"All right." Preuss raised the two-way radio. "Unit Ten, come in."

"Ten responding."

"There are benches in the stand of trees behind the playground on the Orchard Avenue side. Move in, see if anybody's around."

"Roger that."

"Don't go in all gangbusters. If you find a young guy in a wheelchair, we need to keep him safe."

"Roger."

"Let's go," he said to Trombley.

Trombley and Costigan followed him into Preuss's Explorer. He led the scout cars out of the school bus parking lot and onto Woodward Heights. They turned left and blew through the stop sign and took another left onto Bonner Street and sped down Bonner to make a left on Lewiston. Lewiston ended at the Detroit Curling Club parking lot where Preuss stopped and he and Trombley piled out and quick-walked across the park into the woods. One uniformed officer stood beside a park bench on which stood an empty orange Home Depot bucket.

"Nobody home," he said to Preuss and the others.

Preuss looked at Costigan who came trotting up behind them for an explanation.

"She was here," he said. "With the boy. I saw them and went inside to call you."

"Could she have seen you?"

"I was careful."

"Well," Preuss said, "whatever you saw before, they're gone now."

"They can't have gotten far," Trombley said, "if they were here."

"Let's get everybody looking for them. Do a grid search starting from the park. She can't get far pushing a wheelchair."

* * *

A lady held the door and smiled at them both as they entered the chilly air conditioning of the Hilton Road Party Store. Whenever she had a little money Sheila would come down here to buy snacks or personal items. Today she didn't have any money but she hoped she could convince the owner to let her have what she needed on credit.

"Sheila," the man behind the counter said.

"'Lo, Mr. Habib."

"New addition to the family?"

"Oh, he belongs to a friend of mine. I'm just taking care of him for a little while."

"That so."

"Yup."

"What's his name?"

"Tom."

Mr. Habib came around the counter and knelt down on cracking knees to get face-to-face with the young man.

"Hello there, Tom."

Habib snapped his fingers a few times but the young man didn't blink or notice what Mr. Habib was doing. "Doesn't look like he can see very well even with those glasses."

"He sees just fine," Sheila said. "Don't you worry about him."

Habib examined the young man for another few moments. He had been whining since Sheila brought him into the store. "Doesn't seem so happy, either. You say he belongs to a friend?"

"Yes."

"How long are you watching him for?"

"My friend told me I could watch him for as long as I wanted to."

"Is that so."

"Yup." She straightened the young man in his wheelchair by propping him up with pillows.

"I don't have any money today, Mr. Habib. So I wonder if you'll let me have some things on credit. For Tom."

Habib stood up. "Credit," he said, turning the word over in his mouth as though it had an unfamiliar taste.

"I can pay you whenever I get some money."

"What kind of things do you need?"

"Some diapers for one, because he's starting to smell bad."

"Your friend who's letting you borrow him didn't give you enough diapers?"

"She was in such a hurry, she must have forgot."

"What else do you need for him?"

"Some infant formula."

"Isn't he a little big for formula?"

"No, Mr. Habib. He just looks mature for his age."

"Which is how old?"

"I think my friend said he was five or six."

"Now Sheila," Habib said, "you know this fella's older than five or six. Look how big he is. He looks like he's in his teens at least."

"Oh, I don't think so. I think he's young. That's why he's in a wheelchair, because he can't walk yet."

"I'd say that cast on his leg has something to do with that. And why's he banging his head like that?"

Sheila looked at the boy she called Tom, and realized he was stiff and convulsing against the back of his chair.

"Looks like he's having a fit," Habib said.

"No, it's just because it's so much colder in here than it is outside. He's just cold, that's all. And hungry. I tried to feed him before and he didn't want to eat anything. But I know he's hungry because he hasn't had anything to eat since yesterday and that's why I thought some baby formula would hit the spot for him. And he's also sort of stinky, which is why I need the diapers."

Mr. Habib inhaled and wrinkled his nose. "I'll say."

"But I can't afford to pay, Mr. Habib, and so that's why I need you to extend me some credit."

Mr. Habib thought for a few seconds, then said, "Why don't you go over there and pick out some diapers and wipes and formula for him, and I'll give them to you. On the house."

"Thank you so much! I knew I could count on you, Mr. Habib."

She pushed the wheelchair over to the aisle where the store sold baby supplies.

When she was hidden from his sight, Habib stepped back behind the counter and dialed 911.

Though he tried to get her to linger, she had been gone from the store for more than fifteen minutes with her supplies in a plastic bag hanging from the handles of the chair by the time Martin Preuss got the message from Dispatch.

7

When she left the party store she turned right on Hilton, intending to stroll toward East Lewiston and from there head back to the park. Flashing lights caught her eye and when she looked up she saw a police car heading down the street full-tilt-boogie toward her. Sheila placed her body between the road and Tom in the wheelchair and pushed him into the parking lot of an electrical supply company next to the party store. She ducked out of sight behind an SUV.

The police car continued down Hilton without stopping. But she had a bad feeling. Her mother used to say she had second sight, and every once in a while in her life it was as if a voice in her head told her what was going to happen next, and then that thing happened. It had saved her life many times before. Right now that voice was telling her the Ferndale police were looking for her.

Her, and Tom.

Tom must have felt it too because he was getting more and more agitated. He was banging his head against the headrest of his wheelchair and his entire body would get stiff and he would make a scary noise as if he were being strangled. The fit would pass and it would leave him limp for a while, until it happened again. These were happening more and more since he woke up this morning.

"There, there," she told him, patting his shoulder. "It's going to be all right, Tom. I've got some food for you and some clean diapers and as soon as we get settled someplace you'll feel a lot better."

He looked up at her with his beautiful blue eyes through pop-bottle lenses and she ran a hand through his curls. Sheila was certain he believed her. And she was certain things were going to work out fine, in the end.

She peeked out from behind the SUV and saw the street was clear. "Hang on, Tom," she said. "I've got a lot more tricks up my sleeve."

She pushed the wheelchair across Hilton Road and turned right on the first side street, Goodrich. This entire section was all light industry. She saw workmen unloading trucks or grabbing a smoke outside.

"Okay, Tom," she whispered in the boy's ear, "I'm going to throw a cloak of invisibility over us so no one will see us." She stopped and mimed throwing a garment over them both. "How's that feel? Now nobody can see us, I guarantee it."

As though she had been telling the truth, not one of the workers bothered to throw a glance her way as she pushed Tom up the street. At the corner of Woodward Heights she turned left and rushed across the street to Grayson, where she turned right. The neighborhood became residential. At the end of the long block of neat one-story bungalows she came to Mapledale, where she took a quick jog left and crossed over into Harding Park, another large city green space.

"Okay, Tom, now we're safe," she said. "I know this park almost as well as I know my own." She was huffing as she got the words out. "In fact, sometimes I like to come over here and spend the night when I want a change. Change is good, isn't it, Tom?"

She headed for the stand of trees in the northeast corner of the park, bumping the wheelchair over grass and uneven ground and causing Tom even more distress.

"Sorry," she whispered in his ear, "sorry. We're almost there."

Tom began screaming incoherent words.

"No," she said, patting his shoulder. "No no no no no. Please. Keep your voice down. We have to be quiet, Tom. Please be quiet. We're safe now. We're safe."

In her haste to get to the security of the trees she moved faster, and as she went she jostled Tom even more. And he got even more upset.

Fortunately at that moment a wood chipper started up at the end of the park and made a terrible racket. Tom's crying couldn't compete.

Sheila didn't realize that before the wood chipper amped up, the woman who lived in a house bordering the park had heard Tom's crying and looked out her kitchen window to see a young woman right up in the face of a boy in a wheelchair who was screaming bloody murder. She dialed the police and hung up from them just as the wood chipper started.

This time Preuss got the message right away. He and the others converged on the park before the wood chipper had fallen silent.

8

She took off running as soon as she saw them, but didn't get far. With his long legs Reg Trombley caught her with ease. He had her handcuffed before she even stopped moving.

Zach Warranow wouldn't stop crying so Preuss called an ambulance and asked one of the uniformed officers to accompany the young man to the hospital. His second call was to Peggy See to let her know he found Zach and he seemed to be all in one piece. Preuss told her he directed the ambulance to Providence Hospital, and she said she would meet them there.

"I don't know how to thank you, Detective Preuss."

"I'm just glad it turned out okay for him. You might want to let his mother know he's back."

"And what about Elizaveta? How's she doing?"

"I'm afraid there's no sign of her. A different woman had Zach."

"I don't understand."

"Apparently it was a homeless woman who's known around here. I'm about to find out how she and Zach crossed paths."

"So how is she connected to Elizaveta?"

"That remains to be seen."

Preuss placed Sheila in the large interview room. He suspected she would be more comfortable there than in the smaller of the two rooms, which was no bigger than a closet and even he got claustrophobic in it.

He got her a bottle of water and let her sit by herself for a while with a uniformed officer standing out of sight outside the door. She seemed calmer after the storm of hysterical crying after Trombley collared her. Preuss asked if there was someone she wanted him to call for her but she just shook her head.

"Am I under arrest?"

"You're not, Sheila. But until we figure out what's going on here, I'm going to ask you to stay with us for a little while. Is that okay?"

In reply she laid her head on the table.

Now he sat with her worn plastic bags on his desk.

"I'm not sure she understands the kind of trouble she might be in," Trombley said.

"Neither do we. We don't know if she's even done anything against the law, right? Until we find out what happened, we don't know how to proceed with any charges."

"So what are you going to do?"

"First I'm going to talk with her and see if we can find out what happened with Zach."

"She doesn't strike me as someone who's entirely competent."

"No." Preuss considered that and said, "Can you call over across the street and see if anybody's available to sit in with us?"

Across the street from the Shanahan was the building that housed the 43rd District Court.

"Carnahan?"

"No, definitely not the ADA. I want somebody who can make sure her rights are protected."

"Got it."

Trombley went off to find an attorney. Preuss didn't think there would be any charges for the woman, but Trombley was right, he didn't know if she was competent to understand what was happening so it would be best if she had some legal assistance and he didn't want to wait for legal aid to find somebody.

He gloved up and emptied the bags onto his desktop. What spilled out were the typical small objects that someone without a home collected and carried around: trinkets and souvenirs that seemed worthless but held personal, even magical value to their owners . . . reminders of the normal lives they used to have or souvenirs of events whose significance was known only to themselves.

Now he sorted through Sheila's wrinkled clothes and socks, tattered and well-thumbed books of poetry by Rainer Maria Rilke and Sylvia Plath, an empty glass bottle of Coke, a comb with missing teeth, a Raggedy Ann doll, a dog's leash, a man's wristwatch with a broken crystal, a single infant's shoe, a series of faded photos from an instant camera showing a young woman who may or may not have been Sheila with a baby and then a toddler of indeterminate gender, one adult-sized sandal made out of an old car tire, torn and crumpled papers that were so old and weatherbeaten the pages were impossible to read, dried-out tubes of lipstick and cakes of face powder and other makeup, a variety of smelly rags, leathery oak leaves and maple helicopter seeds, and smaller plastic bags of different sizes.

He opened one of the small bags and found more papers. He laid these out on his desk. One was an expired driver's license from Nevada in the name of Sheila Hawkins with an address in Henderson. She was thirty-eight. The picture from the Nevada DMV was faded but showed a younger version of the woman in the interview room, smiling into the camera. It expired ten years ago and the fraying around the edges showed that it, like the woman herself, had lived a rough life in the intervening years.

He found discharge papers honorably releasing Sheila from her service with the US Marines.

Christ on a bike, Preuss thought, another homeless veteran. He led an investigation last year into a shooting that involved a homeless vet. The owner of the bakery where the shooting took place was named Matt Lewis and he helped out vets in trouble whenever he could, though he got himself into some hot water all on his own. Preuss hadn't been in touch with the family since the investigation closed so he didn't know if the bakery owner still helped out veterans but he would remember to ask. This woman might get some help out of this, if she wasn't too far gone to accept it.

He returned Sheila's things to their bags and threw his gloves into the wastebasket. He left his office and walked down the hall to the large interview room. Through the glass wall he saw her sitting at the table with her head down.

"Want me to stay?" the uniformed officer outside the door asked.

"Hang out for another few minutes. I'll let her rest for a while longer."

"I've seen her around town," said the officer, whose name was McGinley. "Here and there."

"The closest she has to a fixed abode is the park where she stays."

"I heard you picked her up with that missing kid."

Preuss nodded. Zack wasn't a kid but he let the comment pass.

"I wouldn't figure her for something like that. She always seemed harmless. Kept to herself."

"We don't know what was going on. Looked like she was trying to take care of him."

He returned to his office and sat down and stared at her plastic bags. The baby shoe, the photos of the child . . . it made sense that she didn't mean harm to Zach Warranow. But was she trying to replace a child she may have lost or had taken away from her? Was she trying to protect him from something or somebody? Though with someone like Zach there might not be anything in particular . . . his handicaps alone would trigger protective impulses.

But how did she find him? What was he doing there?

And what happened to the minibus that carried him?

And where is the woman who was driving?

He was pondering these when Trombley returned. He brought along a short older man whom Preuss didn't know. He looked to be in his late sixties, with a substantial paunch, a lawyer-ly pinstripe suit, silvery hair, and glasses drooping down his nose.

Trombley made the introductions. The man's name was Max Halperin. He was an attorney specializing in wills and estates who was retired but who took on a case every now and then to keep his hand in. He had been over at the 43rd filing some papers when Trombley came looking for an attorney.

"I explained what we needed," Trombley said, "and Mr. Halperin said he could help out."

Preuss said, "The woman we're going to talk with we're treating as a witness and not a suspect, but when you see her you'll know why we need you in the room."

"Your colleague explained it to me. As it turns out, one of my nephews is schizophrenic so I'm versed on legal issues related to mental health. Sounds like you just want a responsible adult in the room when you interview the young lady."

"Exactly."

"My compliments. Many wouldn't be so concerned about a homeless woman."

"She was found with a young man who went missing last night from a group home for adults with disabilities. I don't think she was involved with his disappearance, but I need to find out what she knows. The minibus he was in and the woman who was driving it are still missing."

"Got it. Lead on."

9

Preuss opened the door to th̶ ̶ ̶ ̶ ̶ew room and Sheila Hawkins jerked her head up.

They seated themselves with Halperin next to Sheila, and Preuss and Trombley across the table. After introductions, Preuss said, "Sheila, I'm going to be taping our conversation, if that's okay with you?"

She shrugged.

"I need you to answer out loud, okay?"

She cleared her throat and said, "Yes, it's okay with me if you tape our conversation."

"Thank you. Would you state your full name?"

"Hawkins. Sheila."

"Do you have a fixed address?"

"Yes."

He waited, said, "Could you tell me what it is?"

"The planet Earth."

He searched for a glimpse of irony in her look but she stared back at him straight-faced. "Any particular spot on the planet Earth?"

"My park."

"Martin Road Park?"

"Yes."

"So you don't have anyplace with an address? Like where you get mail?"

"I don't wanna *get* any mail."

"What about SSI or your veteran's benefits? Where do those come?"

"I don't have any."

"You don't have any government benefits?"

"No. Then they'll know where I am, and they'll find me. So far I've kept away from them, but if I'm someplace where mail comes they'll plant a transistor in my government check and then use that to track me and send me messages!"

Max Halperin placed a calming hand on her shoulder and murmured, "Shhh. Nobody's going to do that, Sheila. Not here, not today. We won't let them."

She said, "You can't stop them, you know. They're too powerful."

Halperin glanced at Preuss and Preuss took that as his cue to move along. "Sheila, do you know why you're here?"

She thought about that and as she did Preuss considered how her looks had changed from the young woman who gazed out of the driver's license photo with such hope and promise. It was the same woman put through the wringer, fifteen years of heartbreak and violence and living on the street. Missing teeth, deeper parentheses along the sides of her mouth, roughened skin from exposure to the elements.

He repeated his question, and she shook her head, then remembered she needed to reply out loud and said, "No."

"It's about the young man you had with you."

"Tom?"

"That's what you call him?"

"He reminds me of Tom Hanks. You know, with all that curly hair and one of those happy smiling faces like Tom Hanks has. So I call him Tom."

"What can you tell us about him?"

"He's my friend."

"I could see that. He seems to like you a lot."

"We're good buddies."

"How did you meet him?"

She put a hand on her head and scrunched up her hair as though she could pull the answer out by the roots. "I can't remember."

Preuss looked at Max Halperin, who placed a hand on Sheila's shoulder and said, "Sheila, I just want you to know you're not in trouble here. You understand that, don't you? Nobody's accusing you of anything. The detective just wants to find out what you know about the boy you call Tom, and you're helping them. Do you understand?"

She gave him a wan smile. "Yes."

"That's good," Halperin said. "So did you meet Tom for the first time last night?"

"Yes."

Halperin nodded to Preuss. "I think we're all on the same page."

"Sheila," Preuss said, adopting Halperin's tone, "could you tell us where you met Tom?"

She rubbed her eyes with her knuckles like a sleepy child.

"Sheila?" he prompted.

"In the parking lot."

"What parking lot?"

"Of the church."

"The church where you go to the food bank?"

"Uh-huh."

"What was he doing there?"

"Just sitting. In his wheelchair."

"How did he get there?"

"They dropped him off."

"Who?"

"These men."

"Did you know them?"

"No."

"How many were there?"

"I think I saw three. No, wait. Just two." She counted them on her fingers. "Two," she decided.

"Did you see a woman?" Trombley said.

"No. Just men."

Preuss said, "How did they get there?"

"One came in a van and the other came in something bigger, like a bus."

"Do you remember what time it was when all this happened?"

"I don't know. I don't have a watch that works because I never need to know what time it is."

"Was it dark out?" Trombley said.

"No, it was still light."

"What were you doing? I'm wondering how you could have seen all this."

"I was walking around the park, like I do at night. There wasn't anybody there last night so I could walk around without anybody bothering me. Sometimes when there are teenagers hanging around they give me a hard time."

"I bet they do," Preuss said.

"Once," she began, and grew quiet. Remembering something unpleasant, Preuss could see.

When she didn't say more, he said, "Did you see them come, the men in vans?"

"I was walking around, and I heard the first van come. I hid in the trees because I didn't want anybody to see me. Then after a little while the second one came."

"Okay," Preuss said, "let's get to the part when they dropped Tom off. Tell us about that."

"I heard loud voices like they were angry and I got scared. I didn't come out till I heard them leave and when I looked out I saw Tom sitting by himself in the middle of the parking lot. He looked like he was scared so I pushed him back to where I stay at night so he wouldn't be afraid and I could keep him company.

And I stayed with him. I tried to stay awake in case the men came back but I fell asleep. In the morning I knew he must be hungry because I was hungry, and it was one of the days for lunches at the church so I went to get us some food but he didn't want what I got him. And I could smell the mess he made in his pants so we went to the party store on Hilton and I got some food for him and also some diapers and baby wipes from Mr. Habib. He gave it all to me for free because I don't have any money today."

She ran a hand through her crinkly hair, pulled it straight. "Or hardly ever, if you want to know the truth."

10

"Could you call the pastor at the church," Preuss said, "and see if there's any CCTV of the parking lot?"

"Will do," Trombley said.

"You should be so lucky, my friend," Max Halperin said. The three men sat in Preuss's office. "These things don't work more than they do."

"Still, we might catch a break," Preuss said. "If there's any video, I want to get it fast before it gets recorded over. What she just told us is huge. Video would fill in the gaps and show us the players."

"I'll try Costigan right now."

Trombley left to make the call.

"Thanks for your help, Max," Preuss said. "You intervened at just the right times."

"Happy to help. What are you going to do with her now? Not going to charge her with anything, I hope?"

"I'm more convinced than ever she was trying to protect the kid. But she's an important witness and I don't want to lose track of her. I'm worried she doesn't have a place where we can find her again if we need her. I have a feeling she's going to melt away."

"I don't think she's as out-there as she pretends to be. A lot of that is her defense against the world. Still, she's traumatized from being homeless. And who knows what else is going on with that poor girl's mind. 'The pure products of America go crazy,' as the poet said."

"I'll hook her up with a shelter for the night and maybe tomorrow they can find her a placement somewhere. She could also do with a physical. And maybe meds on top of that. I want to find that driver. A young woman named Elizaveta Kertész."

"Most Americans mispronounce that last name," Halperin said. "It's not Ker-TEZH, it's CARE-tase. It's Hungarian. Means 'gardener.' Is she Hungarian?"

"I don't know."

"With a name like that, I bet she is. I might be able to help. I know somebody who's connected with some of the European émigré communities in the area. If you want, I can ask him to do some checking, see if anybody knows anything."

"That would be helpful, thanks."

Halperin slapped his thighs and stood. "About our friend Sheila I'm sure you'll do the right thing, Detective." He took a card from his jacket pocket and handed it to Preuss. "Call me if you need anything else."

"I'll try to pry some payment out of the city for your trouble."

"That would be lovely but if not it was my honor to help."

"Good news," Trombley said. He met Preuss in the narrow hall on the way back to the interview room. "Costigan said the church does have CCTV of the parking lot. The bad news is, he's not sure it was turned on last night."

"What use is CCTV if you don't turn it on?"

"My very words to the good reverend. He's going to call me back in a few minutes and let me know."

Sheila Hawkins had fallen back asleep. This time she didn't wake up when Preuss and Trombley came into the room and took their seats on the other side of the table from her.

"If she stayed up most of the night with Zach she must be exhausted," Trombley said.

Preuss said, "Sheila?"

No response.

He reached out to tap her arm and she jumped awake and pulled back from him as though she'd been bitten by a snake.

"Easy," Preuss said. "Everything's okay. You're safe."

She looked around the room, her breath amped up and her sleepy eyes wide with fear.

"Where's the man who was here before?"

"He had to leave," Preuss said. "But everything's okay, we're going to take care of you."

"Can I go home now? I want to leave."

"Of course. You're not under arrest."

"You'll take me back to the park?"

"I have a friend who works for South Oakland Shelter. I'm going to ask him to arrange for a room for you for the night."

"But I want to go back to the park. That's where I stay."

"It's not safe enough. Not after what you've been through and what you've seen."

Preuss leaned forward. "Sheila, you did a good deed with the boy you call Tom. His real name is Zach, and thanks to you he's safe and sound and he's being taken care of."

"Can I see him?"

"He's going to spend tonight in the hospital so the doctors can watch him. And he needed his medicine so they're going to get him stabilized."

"I didn't have any medicine for him. If I did, I would have given it to him."

"Nobody's blaming you. You saved the day, remember? We can go see him tomorrow."

"Really?"

"Yes. If he's all right they'll let him out of the hospital and I'll take you to see him."

"You'd do that?"

"Sure. But you have to promise me something in return. You have to promise me you'll stay in the room we're going find for you. At least for a couple of days. Will you do that for me?"

She considered that.

"You'll take me to see Tom?"

"I will."

She looked from Preuss to Trombley.

"You promise?"

"I promise."

"Then so do I."

11

The director of South Oakland Shelter on Twelve Mile Road in Lathrup Village greeted Sheila Hawkins with warmth and let her stretch out on a cot in the back room while he searched on his laptop for a place for her. His name was Jim White and he looked homeless himself with a bushy unkempt grey beard and limp hair that hung to his shoulders. He was the husband of the lead singer for the Birmingham Brawlers, one of the local bands that Preuss's group, the Flynns, often shared a bill with. Preuss had gotten friendly with him while chatting at their gigs.

Preuss thanked him and told Sheila he would see her the next day.

Back at the Lutheran Church in Ferndale, Trombley had cued up the monitor in the closet-sized security room.

"It's a four-camera digital system," he said. "Two cameras surveil the parking lot and one watches each of the entrance doors, front and back. They're set for motion detection. They record on an SD card with time and date stamps."

"All the cameras record on the same card?"

"There's a quad screen, so all four cameras record on the same image. Your basic Office Depot rig. They installed it last year when they had a run of car break-ins during services. Costigan says they sometimes forget to turn it on so we're lucky it was working last night."

They crammed two chairs into the tiny room and Trombley clicked the mouse attached to the keyboard wired to the monitor.

"There's a sound capability too," he said, "but that's never turned on."

"Can't have all the luck."

The quad monitor hissed into life and showed the four scenes visible through the cameras. Because they were driven by motion detection, they came on when there was activity. In the morning they stayed on as the church staff arrived for the day, and then they clicked on and off throughout the day as people came and went for church business.

The images from the early evening got their attention.

"There!" Trombley said.

They watched the group home minibus pulling into the lot. The time stamp was 5:26 p.m. There was someone in the driver's seat but Preuss couldn't tell if it was Elizaveta or not, nor if anybody was in the passenger seat.

The minibus was stationary for a few minutes and the lack of motion shut down the cameras. They clicked on again at 6:47, when a white commercial van with lettering on the side that Preuss couldn't quite make out pulled up beside the group home minibus.

"Can you see what that says?" Preuss asked.

Trombley leaned forward and paused the image. "Resolution sucks."

"Cheap system," Preuss agreed.

"It looks like that second word is 'Painting.' Hard to tell, though."

"That first word could be 'Advantage' with a few A's in front."

"Yeah, 'AAAdvantage Painting.' So they can be first in the phone book."

"People still use the phone book?"

Trombley looked around for one but there wasn't one in the closet. "Never mind," Preuss said, "we'll look it up later. Let's keep going."

Trombley set the image in motion again and they watched a man exit the commercial van and go over to stand at the driver's side window of the minibus. He was a big guy but he wore a hoodie over a baseball cap pulled low so they couldn't see his face.

"Can't even tell what race he is," Trombley said.

They watched the man open the driver's door of the minibus and pull someone out from behind the wheel. It wasn't Elizaveta. It was another man, tall and slender and dressed in what looked like plaid shorts and a tie-dyed tee shirt. His face wasn't visible either because the man from the commercial van was swinging him around by his long hair.

"What's that on his arm?" Trombley asked.

"Left forearm's wrapped with something. Looks like a cast."

Hoodie flung Tie-Dyed to the ground. He scrambled to his feet and Hoodie came at him and popped him right in the face. Tie-Dyed hit the ground again.

"Too bad the sound isn't on," Trombley said.

"Or at least the subtitles."

"Also too bad they're not wearing signs with their names on them."

"Better still."

Preuss watched Tie-Dyed get up holding his shirt to his nose to stanch the blood from it. Hoodie knocked him down again and kicked him in the pit of his stomach, then stomped away in disgust.

Tie-Dyed lay on the ground for a bit longer, then raised himself to his knees and Hoodie rushed over and lifted his head and popped him in the face again and he went over sideways.

"Ouch," said Trombley.

"Poor guy's getting his ass kicked."

Tie-Dyed struggled to his knees again and from there to his feet. Hoodie shoved him toward the commercial van, then got behind the wheel of the minibus and shut the door. Tie-Dyed got into the passenger seat of the commercial van and it pulled away and left the parking lot. They never got a look at the van's driver.

Hoodie in the minibus turned toward the rear compartment.

"Enter Zach," Preuss said.

They watched the man bolt out of the vehicle and shout after the commercial van. "He's like, 'Hey!'" Trombley said. "Don't need subtitles for that."

Hoodie jumped back into the minibus and fishtailed out of the lot. Preuss and Trombley watched as Sheila Hawkins entered the scene and looked around.

Then she turned and ran off. A few seconds later the minibus zoomed back.

The side door slid open and a platform emerged and lowered Zach in his wheelchair. Hoodie jumped down and unhooked the chair and pushed it off the platform, then raised the platform and as soon as the side door slid closed he jumped back into the minibus and sped out of the lot.

Trombley said, "What kind of bastard leaves a handicapped kid by himself in a wheelchair in the middle of a vacant parking lot."

They watched Zach begin to cry. He brought his fists up to his eyes and rocked back and forth in the wheelchair. He raised his face twisted with fright to the sky.

"Look at him," Preuss said. "He's petrified."

They watched as Sheila Hawkins entered the frame again and edged toward Zach's chair. She examined Zach and then looked around to see if anybody might be coming back for him. She looked to be talking with Zach and trying to calm him down. She stroked his head and patted his shoulder. He rocked faster.

"It's not working," said Trombley. "He won't calm down."

"Too afraid."

After a minute Sheila pushed his wheelchair out of the camera frame. "Taking him to her camp," Trombley said.

The image was static for another five minutes and then went to black. It kicked on again in the early morning hours according to the time stamp in the corner of the screen. It remained on for five minutes and neither man saw anything in the parking lot.

"Some woodland critter on the prowl," Preuss said.

There was nothing until a little after eight when the motion detector clicked on and they watched a number of people, including Leonard Costigan, park their cars and enter the church.

Then later in the morning the cameras picked up the comings and goings of people driving up in beaters and pushing shopping carts for the food pantry. One of those walking in was Sheila Hawkins. The camera over the back door picked her up exiting the building, followed by Costigan.

"That pastor seems unusually interested in her," Trombley said. "Think there's something funny going on?"

"Hard to tell with these religious guys, where their concerns start and stop."

He was thinking of the preachers he had run into during the last couple of years, but when he glanced at Trombley he saw a troubled look on the younger detective's face. He remembered Trombley was a devout Catholic and decided not to say anything more about clerical foibles.

One of the other cameras picked up Sheila and Costigan crossing the parking lot and going through the gate at the rear of the lot into the park proper. Preuss and Trombley watched Costigan reenter the church and then exit it again a short time later.

"That's when he called us," Preuss said.

The two detectives watched themselves meet with Costigan in the parking lot, and then Preuss said, "I think that's enough.

Can we take this memory card? I want to see if we can get the images of the guys enhanced. License plate of the commercial van too."

"The State AV unit might be able to work on it. If we're lucky we'll get it by Christmas, gift-wrapped nice and tidy."

"Will you follow it up?"

"Sure."

"So at least three men, including the driver of the paint truck whose face we never saw."

"There might have been others in the back of that van," Trombley said.

"Maybe. But the main players were the guy driving the minibus and the passenger from the painting van. Be nice to know what they were fighting about."

"Something didn't go right."

"No. It looked like Hoodie didn't want the bus. Maybe he wasn't expecting it. Or was expecting a different kind of vehicle."

"If it's a hot car ring, he might have ordered a regular van and was pissed when Tie-Dyed showed up with that big monster."

"Good possibility," said Preuss.

"I'll check the hot sheets, see what else might be missing."

"Meanwhile I'll work on tracking down the paint truck. And I still want to know what happened to Elizaveta Kertész." He pronounced her last name as Max Halperin had.

"The minibus got jacked and she was dumped somewhere?"

"But then where is she? I want to get people out checking every square foot between Providence and the group home."

"If she's there," Trombley said, "we'll find her."

But Preuss was not so certain.

12

Trombley's contact at the Michigan State Police Audio Video Analysis Unit told him they were reeling under budget cuts like everybody else and were short-handed. But they'd work on the video as soon as they could.

Which, Trombley thought, might well mean Christmas after all.

So he called one of his buddies from Wayne State who now ran a photography studio. His buddy said he could enhance a video right away. Trombley packed up the memory card and took it to his friend's studio.

Preuss spent the next hour in his office typing up his notes from the session with Sheila Hawkins and his observations from the church's security card. He saved it to the case folder and went to refill his coffee cup from Tanya Corcoran's coffee machine but the administrative assistant had gone home for the day and the machine was empty. He glanced at his watch and realized it was after six.

He didn't feel like suffering through the canteen's version of machine coffee so he returned to his desk with his empty cup. He stared out the window at Nine Mile Road, clogged by the usual summer obstacle course of orange and white construction barrels. On the sidewalk in front of the station a young Asian woman was taking selfies with a small boy who was mugging for the camera. Both wore overlarge sunglasses, and the Asian woman wore short shorts and high platform shoes. The boy was posing with a two-fingered hip-hop salute and a broad smile.

Mother and son? They had the same features, and were about the right ages.

Preuss watched the boy with envy for his youthful zest. Preuss knew he had many fine qualities but zest was not among them and hadn't been for a number of years. Even before Jeanette died he felt as though he had turned into an almost hopeless old man. He came to believe that was what he was trying to self-medicate with alcohol—the pain that all his possibilities from his own youth had expired.

Though of course drinking made things worse in every way.

He had stopped after Jeanette died but was still waiting for his zest to return. He was afraid that had flown forever.

You might not have *joi de vivre*, he told himself, but you have *joi de Toby*.

Toby, with the inexhaustible gusto of perfect innocence.

He watched as the pair outside kept taking selfies from different angles, and as the woman teetered on her platform shoes he remembered he and Reg hadn't found a phone book at the church. He left the woman and boy to their fun and hauled an Oakland County phone book out of his bottom desk drawer and looked up AAAdvantage Painting.

There was a number for a company with that name in Royal Oak Township, a tiny suburb of Detroit whose mostly poor, African American population occupied half a square mile north of Eight Mile. He punched in the number on his desk phone and got a woman's brassy voice sounding like Edith Bunker letting him know the office was closed for the day and inviting him to leave a message. The beep came and he hung up.

He would try them in the morning. With luck, he could run out there and take a giant step toward solving at least one of the mysteries that were starting to clog this investigation.

Outside the mother and child had gone. Preuss cleared his desk for the night, organizing his files into stacks. As he sometimes remembered to do, he scrawled a list of outstanding items he needed to take care of the next day.

He looked them over and decided to take care of one right now.

Rosa Martinez answered on the third ring. He could tell she was disappointed it was him and not Elizaveta.

"Still no word?" he asked.

"None. It's been twenty-four hours. Can we file a missing persons report now?"

"Because the young man she disappeared with is disabled, we started looking right away. How's Rachael holding up?"

"Not well, as you might expect. She didn't want to go to school today because she didn't want to miss her mother in case she came back. I stayed home with her."

"There's one bit of good news. The young man she was driving showed up today."

"But not Elizaveta?"

"No. Nor the minibus."

"Is he all right?"

"Seems to be. He was being taken care of by a local homeless woman."

"How did that happen?"

"It's not clear at this point."

"But he's okay?"

"They're keeping him overnight at Providence for observation. He's lucky the woman was there. Otherwise he'd be in bad shape."

"That's one good thing," she agreed.

"Did you connect with Elizaveta's sister in Ohio?"

"I did. She hasn't heard from Elizaveta either. I'm very worried. She wouldn't just leave her daughter like this."

"She wouldn't be the first mother who walked out on her children," Preuss said.

"It's not something she'd ever do."

You think you know people, Preuss thought, but you never do.

They were both quiet. Then he said, "You'll keep me posted if you hear anything?"

She said she would, and he said he would do the same.

He crossed that task off his list and Hank Bellamy stuck his head in the doorway of his office.

Oh please, Preuss thought. Not you. Not now.

Bellamy said, "Working late again? Don't you have a life?" Only semi-kidding.

"Don't you listen to your messages? I've been trying you since last night."

Bellamy dropped into the visitor's chair. "And here I am."

"Where have you been? Why haven't you answered?"

"I was working my cases, *boss*." He hit the last word with un-subtle irony. "My plate's full, as you know."

Bellamy had a reputation around the Detective Bureau as being Russo's eyes and ears and he was not a friend to Martin Preuss.

"What can I do for you?"

Preuss filled him in on the missing minibus investigation.

"Well, good luck with it." Bellamy made to stand.

"Hold it. I need you to do something."

Preuss wrote something on a sheet of paper and handed it to Bellamy. "I'd like you to retrace the minibus's route. Start with the doctor's office all the way to the group home. That's the doc's address in the Providence Medical Building. See if you can find somebody along the way who remembers seeing it, or remembers anything about the missing woman. Get some uniforms to help."

Bellamy took the paper with hesitation. "So what, I'm supposed to stop at every house along the way?"

"It's called detective work."

"What about my other cases?"

"What are you working on that's more important than this?"

Bellamy ticked them off on his pudgy fingers. "There's a roofing scam that's hitting older residents. A robbery at the CVS on East Nine Mile. A spate of stolen bikes. A garage break-in with over a thousand bucks in tools taken. A theft of property, auto—"

Preuss held his hand up. "Stolen bicycles are more important than a missing woman?"

"You asked me what I'm working on and I'm telling you. Plus I'm working midnights."

"Put on hold whatever can wait. Reg and I are meeting in the morning at nine . . . plan to be there."

"I won't be able to get this done before tomorrow."

"Do the best you can."

Bellamy looked at the page Preuss gave him, shrugged, and left.

"On second thought," Preuss muttered to Bellamy's afterimage, "try to do better than that."

13

Except for the young woman across the hall from Toby's room—bedridden and bound to a ventilator—no one was around at his son's group home.

There was no one in the kitchen or in the living room watching the television where one of the *Pirates of the Caribbean* movies played. Except for the medical equipment in the bedrooms, the one-story home off Twelve Mile Road in Berkley was set up as much like a regular house as possible for the technology-dependent young people who lived here. This was a pilot program, and as far as Preuss could tell it was working out fine.

He left the station intending to take his son for a walk around the neighborhood but there was no sign of Toby. He heard a shout of laughter from the patio off the living room. He peeked through the curtains on the door to the back and saw the residents and staff and many of the residents' family members. He remembered with a stab of annoyance at himself that the house was having a barbecue tonight, and he had been invited to it. And asked to bring some dessert.

They welcomed him, empty-handed as he was. One of the aides said, "Hey Toby, look who's here!"

And he saw his sweet boy sitting in his wheelchair out of the late-afternoon sun, the space between his two front teeth visible in his beatific smile. As always when he saw his son at the end of a difficult day, Preuss felt as though he were coming home to the place he had always wanted to be after a long journey. Toby was propped up on the seat of his wheelchair by pillows, and his knobby legs were cushioned on the footpad by the pillow Jeanette had gotten him the year before she died, the one that read "We're Good Friends, My Dad and Me."

"Hey sweetheart," Preuss said, and planted a wet kiss on the side of his son's head on the flat part of the temple between his hairline and the swell of his stubbly cheek. Preuss made the sucking sound that he called an elephant pulling his foot from the mud, and it sent Toby into a paroxysm of laughter. His beautiful face beamed.

"He's been waiting for you," Melissa the aide said. "We told him you were coming and he's been waiting patiently."

"Sorry I'm so late," Preuss said. He didn't want to admit he'd forgotten, though he had to fess up to not bringing dessert.

"Not to worry," Melissa said, "there's plenty of food. We have ice cream and watermelon and cherry pie."

"And I brought brownies and chocolate chip cookies," Connie the tattooed respiratory therapist said. She was taking care of business at the barbecue grill, spatula in hand. "Are you hungry?"

He realized he was starving. He hadn't eaten all day.

"Choices are chicken, hamburgers, and hotdogs," Connie said. "There's also a veggie burger if you're into that."

"A hamburger would be great," Preuss said.

"Salads too? Garden and potato."

"Perfect."

Connie served the food up in a paper plate and he pulled a chair beside Toby. Toby couldn't eat regular food but he was hooked up to his feeding tube and his liquid nutrition was being pumped into the g-tube button in his tummy so he was eating right along with everyone else. The pump made its soft intermittent whirr as the formula flowed into him.

"I heard the missing young man from the Ferndale house turned up," the house manager of the home said. Her name was Deb Hilbert and she was a short stocky woman who radiated calm.

"He did," he said. "Safe and sound."

"I heard you found him," Melissa said.

"Oh, that's right," another of the parents said, "you're the policeman."

"Toby's dad is a detective," said Melissa. "Isn't that right, Toby? Just like on *Law and Order*. Your dad's a detective like Lennie Briscoe."

In more ways than one, Preuss thought.

"Toby's favorite show," Melissa said. "We watch it all the time, don't we, T-boy?"

Toby hummed and chortled. Preuss loved to see him this buoyant. For the past few months he had stayed healthy, no scares or hospital visits.

He balanced his paper plate of food on his lap and ate his burger with his left hand while he rubbed Toby's forearm with his right. For the moment Preuss was as happy as his son.

Enjoy every sandwich, Warren Zevon had said. Toby understood.

Melissa went inside the house to check on the young woman across from Toby's room and came back out with a boombox. She tuned it to an oldies' station that was doing a marathon of Beatles' songs and they all sang along to "Hey Jude," "She Loves You," "Do You Want to Know a Secret," and "Obla Di Obla Da." Toby squealed with joy. He loved to sing, and added his deep foghorn growl to the mix.

When it grew too dark and buggy to stay out, Preuss helped get all the residents inside and gave Toby his evening bath by himself while the aides got the other children ready for the night.

Stretched out in his pjs in bed, loose and rosy and fragrant, Toby listened as his father talked about his day's events, making small noises of sympathy or distress. Preuss would often offer a comment that he thought Toby might make as his way of having a conversation with his son. He talked about his current case, the successful return of Zach Warranow, and the continuing mystery of what had happened to the minibus and the woman who was driving it. He talked about the surveillance video and what he had planned for the next steps. He talked about the remaining questions: who were the men in the church parking lot and how did one of them wind up with the minibus, and what happened to Elizaveta Kertész and why would she leave her daughter alone for so long.

This was a way for Preuss to connect with Toby, and it helped him get his thoughts together about his investigations. Several of the medical personnel he had run into, and even some of Toby's caretakers and teachers, believed it was wish fulfillment to think Toby had the cognitive ability to understand what was said to him. But Preuss knew in his heart Toby understood everything, and his sounds and expressions were genuine attempts to communicate past the range of conditions that limited him—the cerebral palsy, the visual impairment, the retardation, the microcephaly. There was nothing to be lost and everything to be gained by assuming Toby could grasp it all.

After awhile Toby's eyes began to flutter and he soon fell asleep. In the chair beside Toby's bed, Martin Preuss watched his beloved son sleep for another half hour, and then went home.

As always, being with his son mellowed him out and focused him. It had been a long day—he'd been up for twenty-one hours—and he was tired but not worn out enough to sleep. Too unfocused even to play his guitar once he got home, he wandered around the house, straightening up, loading the dishwasher with plates and silverware from several days' worth of meals, and trying not to listen to the voices of the ghosts who haunted his home and his life and who for some reason were strident this night, as

if to balance with unpleasantness the peace he felt leaving Toby
. . . all the dead or gone, but loudest of all Jeanette, still blaming
him for his faults.

But—listen to me, he thought; we're even arguing after she's
dead—it would be a mistake to think if he had been a better husband the marriage would have been stronger. It was not a good
marriage, no matter which way you looked at it, and he was not
the sole cause of the general unhappiness that contaminated his
home; Jeanette bore some of that blame.

But he also heard the angry ghost of his son Jason, lost somewhere in America (or so Preuss thought—he could be anywhere
in the world by now); the neglectful and heedless ghosts of his father and mother, both long gone but here with him in the linger-
ing effects of the damage their indifference and abuse did to him
over the years; the drug-addled ghost of his dead older brother,
resenting Martin for being the good son while never realizing
how unhappy Preuss was growing up because his brother sucked
all the energy and life from his family; the bully-boy ghost of his
ex-father-in-law Nick Russo, the chief of detectives . . .

He wasn't crazy enough to believe he heard their actual voices in his head, but he felt the collective pressure of their continuing presence in his life, complaining, chastising, berating, resenting the full range of his choices.

Jesus, he thought, moving from room to room and touching
the material things of his world, the chairs and guitars and sofa
and CDs and tables and lamps, their textures and fabrics reminding him what was real—do we ever escape our past?

He laid on the sofa with his arms behind his head, tracing
the cracks in the ceiling. Only Toby seemed to be on his side, offering his foghorn hums in support of his father who was doing
the best he could . . . Toby, who saved his parents' foolish decision
to wed and stay together. Who allowed his father to find and ex-
press his best self.

He closed his eyes and tried to relegate the clamor of his past to a soundproof closet long enough to get some respite from it.

After a while he slept.

Wednesday, June 9, 2010

14

At the Shanahan in the morning Preuss and Reg Trombley waited to start their meeting until Hank Bellamy arrived. When he didn't show by 9:20 they started going over what they knew about the disappearance of the minibus.

A half-hour later Bellamy strolled in carrying an extra large coffee in a brown paper container and blamed the line at Tim Horton's for delaying him.

Trombley opened a folder and passed around stills from the church's security video.

"How'd you get these so fast?" Preuss said.

"I stayed late last night and printed them out. Thing I couldn't do is blow them up or sharpen the focus. I got in touch with a college buddy who runs a photography business and first he said he could do it yesterday but he had a last-minute rush job. So he'll get me something tonight."

"Nice work," Preuss said. He thumbed through the stills. Trombley had printed out three sets of the two vehicles in the surveillance video and several stills of the two men who were visible. The focus was fuzzy, though they would be helpful as a first step.

Trombley had to make an appearance at the 43rd District Court that morning so there wasn't much he would be able to do till later. And Bellamy had his assignments. So Preuss headed out to see a man about a van.

AAAdvantage Painting operated out of a sprawling structure made of concrete blocks painted a weathered purple on Wyoming Avenue in Royal Oak Township across from the community center of the Township's housing project. Preuss remembered passing the building many times. The Township shared a border with Ferndale, and Wyoming was a well-traveled path to Eight Mile, but he had thought it was still an auto repair shop, which it was for many years. There was no sign on the building.

He parked on the off-street apron beside a half dozen cars in various states of destruction from the collision shop next door. He heard a whine of machinery from inside the paint company building and walked through the open oversized doorway to a large space filled with ladders and tarps and five-gallon buckets.

At once he spotted a white van to the right inside the door. He copied down the license plate number and walked around it. It was an older Econoline spotted with dings and rust.

"Van's not for sale."

Preuss turned to find a short barrel-chested man standing before him with a tanned face and wavy steel-grey hair combed all the way back. He had a salesman's wide smile, all teeth and insincerity. The effect was of a matinee idol from the 1950s. Behind him holding a sheath of papers was another man, younger, owlish and serious, in a spotless blue coverall with a paint brush logo around the letters AP on the front pocket.

"I'm not in the market," Preuss said. He showed his ID and said his name. "Who am I speaking with?"

"Al Campanella." He reached out and shook Preuss's hand with a dry, hard grip. "I own the place. This is my assistant manager, Ray Bouchard." Bouchard nodded.

"Are you this vehicle's owner, Mr. Campanella?"

"The business owns the van so I guess that's a yes."

The whine of a paint mixer somewhere in the back made it hard to hear.

Preuss said, "Is there someplace quieter we can talk?"

Campanella flashed a warm smile and said, "Let's go into the office. We'll talk later," he told his assistant.

Campanella led Preuss to a small grubby office at the side of the work area. Two desks filled the room. At one sat a heavy woman hunched over a computer. Preuss nodded to her and she gave him an indignant look in return.

Campanella closed the door and it shut out enough of the noise to allow for a conversation. He took a seat behind the empty desk. There were no other chairs in the room.

"Sorry there aren't any extra chairs," he said. "I'm hardly ever in here. This is mostly a place where Dolores can work on the books out of the commotion."

At the sound of her name Dolores looked at Preuss with a clear dislike. Because her refuge was being invaded, he thought. He wondered if she was the woman whose brassy voice was on the telephone recording.

Preuss handed Campanella a copy of a photo from the surveillance video that showed the van with the company's name. "That printing on the side is this business, correct?"

"Well, that's my company name."

"But not your van?"

"It looks like one of mine but they're all accounted for. Can I ask what this is about?"

"That van showed up on a security camera while another vehicle was being stolen. A man stepped out of this"—he tapped a finger on the white van—"and drove away in the stolen vehicle."

"And you think it's the same van that's parked out there?"

"That's what I want to find out."

Campanella chuckled as if it were the most natural mistake in the world. "That vehicle out there's been parked right where you see it for the past week. Won't even start. I just haven't had time to take it in. Check for yourself if you want. It won't even turn over, let alone drive."

"How about you start it up for me and we find out?"

That smile again, which was becoming annoying.

Campanella opened a drawer in his desk and withdrew a set of keys. "Follow me," he said.

He led Preuss to where the van was parked. He held out the keys and said, "Want to do the honors?"

Preuss took the keys and slid behind the wheel. The cabin of the van reeked of the cigarette butts piled in the ashtray, and was littered with mounds of rank McDonald's and Burger King wrappers and empty Pepsi cans. In the rear was a paint-stained tarp but no other equipment.

Preuss fitted the key into the ignition but Campanella was right, it was dead.

He reached down to flip the lever that opened the hood and got out and tossed the keys back to Campanella. He boosted up the hood and saw all the components in the engine compartment appeared intact.

"Satisfied?"

Preuss looked around on the floor beneath the truck and saw the thick sludge of a major leak from the oil pan. He got down on this hands and knees and saw where the drip came from. The drying leak was stippled with the cottonwood seeds that had been floating in the air for the past few days. Campanella was right, this van hasn't moved for a while.

"I guess in your business you have to be suspicious of everyone," Campanella said.

They walked back into the office and Campanella put the keys back in the desk drawer.

"Is that the only van you own?"

"The only white one. I do have three others. One's green and two are grey."

Preuss handed him copies of two more photos that Trombley printed from the security video. "Do you recognize either of these men?"

Alberto Campanella took then and examined them. "Not very good pictures," he said.

"Best we have right now."

He shook his head. "Nope. Don't know either one."

"They don't work for you?"

"This guy I can say no for sure." He pointed at Tie-Dyed. "Guy in the hoodie, you can't see his face so it could be anybody."

"Mind if I have a look around?"

"Be my guest. Though most of the guys are out on jobs."

When Preuss opened the office door Al Campanella fell into step behind him.

"I can find my way around on my own," Preuss said.

"This is a working shop, I just want to make sure you don't get hurt." He flashed Preuss his movie star smile. "Wouldn't want the City of Ferndale to sue me now, would I?"

Preuss ignored the comment and walked around the entire facility, inside and out, and didn't find another white van. At the back of the work area was a grimy door to the even grimier bathroom, another grimy door that had a padlock, and a door labeling Mixing Room.

He also didn't find anybody who resembled either of the two men in the surveillance video.

"Where are the other vans?"

"Out on jobs."

"Where were they two nights ago?"

"Parked inside here, like they always are. The workers aren't allowed to take them home and you don't want to leave anything parked outside at night around here."

"And where were you Monday night?"

"Where I always am. I left work around seven or eight like always and went straight home."

"Anybody vouch for you?"

"Some of the fellas stayed around till a little after six, so they can tell you I was here. And I live alone, so the rest of the night I was by myself. You know how some people are happily married? I'm happily divorced."

That smarmy smile again.

Preuss let it go by. "I'd like you to get me the registration numbers for the other vans. And the addresses of the jobs they're on."

"Sure thing," Campanella said. He turned to Dolores. "Would you get the detective the information he needs?"

"And I'd like the names of all your employees."

"No problem. Dolores'll see to it. Won't you, hon?"

Dolores sighed.

Back at the Shanahan Preuss set about working through the names Dolores gave him. He visited the job sites—an automotive dealership on Main Street in Royal Oak, a house in Warren, and an empty former dry-cleaner's near Woodward and Six Mile in Detroit—and satisfied himself the other vans weren't the ones he was looking for. Besides being the wrong colors, they had ladder rigs attached to the sides, not the top.

Campanella had six men working for him, both full- and part-time, according to Dolores. Preuss pulled up the records of the vans, along with the DMV photos of the employees. None of the faces of the men came close to matching Tie-Dyed from the surveillance video. Because of his size, Hoodie couldn't have been anybody, as Campanella pointed out, but none of the company's employees seemed to match his body type.

Preuss ran Campanella's name through ICHAT, the Internet Criminal History Access Tool maintained by the Michigan State Police Criminal Justice Information Center, but didn't get any hits. He also checked OTIS, the Offender Tracking Information System, with no results either. He figured there was no point in running all the other names through these systems until they had something definite to look for.

He stood and stretched. If none of the company's employees matched the two scrappers in the church's surveillance video, who had the company van?

A rap on the doorframe interrupted his thoughts. Paul Horvath, the duty sergeant.

"Sorry to bother you, Martin," he said. "I know you're in the middle of something. But we just got a call from one of the uniforms and you're the only one here."

"Reggie still in court?"

"Yeah. And Hank's out. I need you to go up to Beaumont. Got a nasty assault case. A home invasion put a woman in the hospital."

"I wish we'd get a replacement for Tony already. He's been retired almost a year. We need another hand."

"As my saintly Irish grandmother used to say, if wishes were horses."

"We'd all be buried in horse shit."

"Yeah, pretty sure that's not how the proverb ends," Horvath said. "But I get your drift."

15

"Helen Vlastos?"

The woman in the bed by the door pointed toward the window, where he heard a faint "That's me" from behind the drawn curtain.

He announced himself and said, "Okay if I come in?"

"Give me another few minutes to get her settled," said another woman's commanding voice. "Then she's all yours."

He wandered into the hall and stood by the window looking out over Thirteen Mile. He had taken the elevator in the north wing of Beaumont Hospital and as he stood gazing out the window of 7 North, he remembered all the time he had spent here. Whenever Toby had a medical emergency they sped him right to Beaumont; Preuss must have been here a dozen times for Toby alone. His elder son Jason used to damage himself often with his thoughtlessness (or, as Preuss now thought, his self-abuse) on bicycles and skateboards. Jeanette gave birth to the two boys here.

And that didn't count all the times he was here for work. When he was shot in the shoulder by the kid on PCP a few years ago' he was in for a few days. He had spent hours interviewing victims of crimes in Emergency, trying to get through to people who were half out of their minds with shock or grief or adrenaline, victims of shootings or stabbings or MVAs or beatings or drug overdoses . . . victims of the havoc people visit on each other with all the culture's well-developed technologies of violence and greed . . . daily life as wartime.

As it happened, 7 North was where the young man stayed who was wounded in the bakery shootings a year ago last spring. He wondered how that family was making out, and remembered he had meant to get in touch with the father, Matt Lewis, about Sheila Hawkins. He pulled out his iPhone and made a voice note so he wouldn't forget. It would be good to see how they were all doing anyway.

He remembered he had also told Sheila he would take her to see Zach today . . . he made another note about that.

Pacing now to stave off a wave of hunger (he hadn't eaten anything since the barbecue at Toby's last night . . . he would have to take better care of himself), he walked past a waiting room where a young man with a blood-smeared long-sleeved shirt and cargo shorts with flip-flops sat fidgeting in front of a television that played Fox News. (Why does every institutional television play Fox News, he wondered.)

"Excuse me," Preuss said. The young man glanced up. "Are you here with Helen Vlastos?"

The young man nodded. He had a squirrelly sort of nervousness.

"You're the one who was with her when she was attacked?"

The young man shot to his feet. "Vince Stoneburner."

"Detective Preuss, Ferndale PD. Has anyone taken a look at you?"

"I'm fine," Stoneburner said. He looked down at his shirt. "None of this is mine."

A nurse stuck her head around the corner. "She's all yours."

Preuss raised a hand in thanks and the young man set off with him.

"Please wait here? I need to talk with her alone."

"Oh, okay, sure."

The kid took his seat in front of the television and gnawed a fingernail.

Preuss knocked on the door to Helen Vlastos's room and said, "Ms. Vlastos?"

"Come on in." The same feeble little bleat.

Preuss entered her curtained-off area and found a woman whose frailty matched her voice. She was pale with a gauze bandage under her chin. Her bed had the rails padded. A seizure prevention precaution, he knew, common with people under observation for traumatic accidents.

He introduced himself and said, "Can I sit down?"

"Sure."

He took out his notebook. "I need to verify some information first." He made sure he had the correct spelling of her name, as well as her address on Planavon in Ferndale and her age. She was 23. An infant, he thought. Just a few years older than Toby, around the same age as Jason.

"Do you live there with Vince?"

"It's his apartment. But I've been staying with him, yeah."

"So they patched you up okay?"

"Yes."

"Can you tell me what happened?"

"I told the other policeman."

"If you could tell me too? Officer Vollmer wrote up the incident report but I'm the chief investigator."

She took a deep breath.

"Me and Vince just got home from O'Toole's. In Royal Oak?"

"I know the place."

"And so we met our friend Jeff and we were going to order some pizza and hang out."

He verified Jeff's full name. "Go on."

"And so Vince and Jeff started to watch a game on TV and I went into the kitchen to order the pizza. There's a closet between the living room and the kitchen and I'm passing the closet and all of a sudden this guy in a ski mask jumps out with a knife. Before I can do anything he grabs me and holds the knife to my throat and I'm like pissing myself, I was so scared! I start screaming and I'm like, 'Lemme go! Lemme go!' That must have been when he cut me. Here." She pointed to the gauze under her chin.

"Did you know who it was?"

"Not at first. He had the mask covering his face and he's wearing rubber gloves. So I'm struggling and yelling my ass off and Vince comes running into the kitchen. And then this guy starts hollering about, 'I'm gonna kill you, bitch! I'm gonna cut your heart out!' Soon as I hear his voice I know it's Fred. Fred Samuelson. We dated for about five minutes a couple months ago. Until I broke up with him."

"Was he violent with you before?"

"Never. I always thought he was just this mousy little guy, tell you the truth."

"So he's got hold of you and he's telling you he's going to kill you. Then what?"

"Then Vince runs grabs a knife from one of the drawers and he's trying to stab Fred to make him let me go and I'm seeing blood flying everywhere and all of a sudden I feel this terrible pain in my side and I know I got stabbed."

"Could you tell which one did it?"

"I'm sure it was Fred."

"How? Sounds like things were pretty chaotic."

"No, I know it was Fred because he swung the knife at Vince and Vince backed away for a second and that's when I could feel the blade going in. It felt like the most awful burn I've ever had in my life. I thought I was going to pass out."

"Where was Jeff during all this?"

"Calling 911. After Fred stabbed me he threw me down on the floor and I saw him go after Vince with the knife but Jeff got off the phone and there was a baseball bat in the living room so Jeff grabs the bat and starts beating on Fred and then Vince, he goes after him too. Somehow Fred must of got past them both and ran out of the apartment."

"Must have been frightening."

"You have no idea. And from what I hear, Fred's still out there."

"He is," Preuss said. "We're looking for him."

Helen Vlastos seemed to fold in on herself, and her face collapsed into tears. Which must have caused her stitched up wounds to flare because she writhed in pain.

"Goddamn Fred," she said through clenched teeth. "I hope he dies."

Once he left her room, he found Vince and took his statement, then tracked down Jeff and took a statement from him. It seemed clear what had happened, and that Vince and Jeff saved her life.

On his way back to the station Preuss asked Dispatch for the last known of Fred Samuelson, but there was nobody home when he rang the buzzer at Samuelson's apartment on Thirteen Mile in Royal Oak.

At the Shanahan he called around to the emergency departments at hospitals in the three-county area, but none of them had any record of Fred Samuelson coming in with stab wounds. Preuss put out a BOLO on him and then wrote out the reports of his interviews.

He saved them to the case file and picked up a message Tanya Corcoran left for him. It was from a detective with the Oak Park Department of Public Safety. He had apprehended a suspect for breaking into a vacant house and stealing a washer and dryer and noticed the similarity with one of Preuss's cases, a series of break-ins where appliances were stolen from homes being renovated.

The Oak Park detective didn't realize his guy was already arraigned and had been remanded to the Oakland County Jail before Preuss could get there. So Preuss went out to the County campus on Telegraph in Pontiac and by the time he got to sit down with the guy and satisfied himself he was also the one responsible for the Ferndale break-ins, the rest of the day was shot.

He went to Toby's to take his son on a long walk around the group home's neighborhood and talk about his day. It either made Toby tired or else he was already knackered from his own day at school, so Toby slept for most of the walk after getting over his initial excitement at seeing his father.

Toby's head lolled as Preuss strolled around the quiet suburban neighborhood, nodding to dog walkers who passed him. Every one said hello to Toby. Preuss marveled again how his son knew more people than he did.

As dusk came on, so did the lights in the homes they passed. He looked into living rooms and watched the families going about their lives like actors on stage sets. He knew it was all illusory but Preuss felt a continual stab of envy for the mothers and fathers and sisters and brothers performing their roles as members of average happy families as he and Toby walked by house after house.

He took Toby back to the group home with a somber gratitude for the reality of his son. He bathed Toby and got him ready for bed.

On the way home he picked up an order of General Tso from Hong Kong One on Nine Mile and after picking at it he realized he had no appetite. He packed up the leftovers in the fridge and spent the rest of the night playing his Les Paul with his earphones on and the volume cranked up as loud as he could stand it.

By the time he fell into bed his ears felt like they were packed with cotton and his head rang like a bell.

16

It was late, they were tired and hungry, and all they wanted to do was get the last load off the truck and head home. Or to a bar, whichever came first.

Joe Delancey was especially beat. He had been on the job since early that morning because a series of emergencies at buildings in downtown Detroit pulled him in hours before his shift was supposed to start. As the gang leader for the service crews at the Michigan Elevator Company, Delancey had to manage the situations, which meant bringing in some crews on their days off. They weren't happy about it, and weren't shy about letting him know.

Delancey was not as young as he used to be, as the younger guys never failed to take great joy in pointing out to him, and working these long days wore on him. The fifty extra pounds he packed on over the years didn't help his stamina any (he was pushing 250 these days), even though he was still work-strong and liked to brag he could beat the crap out of any young punk who gave him grief.

His boasting was good natured, but he was on his last nerve tonight and pitied anybody who got in his way.

They just got the last truck emptied and he was about to release his boys when they heard the red phone ring. The red phone was the emergency line in the office of the manager on duty, who happened to be Delancey tonight. One of their elevators in a high-rise apartment building in Franklin was down and needed service ASAP.

His crews pissed and moaned because they thought one of them was going to have to go out on the call, but the last of the repair guys who had been out that day pulled into the company's fenced-in compound on Woodward Heights in Ferndale. Before he even got out of the truck Delancey asked if he could take this run since the other guys had been on the clock since seven that morning.

"Sure," the repair guy, whose name was Cruz, said. "Gimme a minute to tap a kidney and I'll be good to go."

With that news Delancey released his other work crews. When Cruz was ready, Delancey took his usual position out in the middle of the street so he could hold up traffic while the truck backed out of the compound. It was after nine and almost full dark out so he took a flashlight in each hand.

Before Cruz was out, a Ford F-250 came barreling down the street and wouldn't slow down when Delancey waved his arms. "Stop!" he shouted. When the pickup didn't slow he shouted again, "STOP!"

At the last second the pickup squealed to a stop. The repair truck backed out and pulled away.

"Hey," Delaney cried, "whassa matter with you! Didn't you see me standing here?"

The guy in the pickup stuck his head out the driver's side window and said, "Chill the fuck out."

Delancey stood in the center of the road. "What'd you say to me?"

"I said, chill the fuck out, asshole. And get outta my way."

The pickup edged toward Delancey.

Delancey held his ground. No, he thought. I'm too tired to take this right now.

The pickup crept right up to Delancey's substantial belly. Delancey didn't move, and the pickup didn't veer left or right but came straight on.

The driver gunned the engine and the vehicle lurched forward, knocking Delancey back. He kept his feet under him and started around to the driver's side of the truck when it lurched forward again and caught Delancey's hip and spun him around and knocked him right on his ass and out of the truck's path.

The truck kept moving toward the railroad crossing next to the compound.

Delancey scrambled to his feet and flung one of the flashlights at the truck. The light made a star fracture in the middle of the rear window and bounced in pieces into the street.

The truck continued on for a few more feet, then its brake lights flared as it stopped just before the tracks. Moving fast for a big man, Delancey ran toward it. The driver threw the truck into park and scrambled from the cab.

Delancey had time to register how big the driver was before he put his head down and barreled into the guy's chest, knocking him backwards into the open driver's side door. Delancey raised his other flashlight to bring it down on the other man's head but at the last moment the guy moved and the metal tube hit the thick meat of his shoulder instead.

Delancey raised the body of the flashlight to hit him again and the guy shot a big right hand into Delancey's nose. It knocked him backwards and the driver's roundhouse left caught him like a hammer and spun him around.

Before Delancey could recover enough to defend himself, the pickup driver pounced on him and drove him backwards with a flurry of punches. It was all Delancey could do to protect his head and he lost his footing and slid down the backslap of the below-grade tracks. The driver slid down after him and kept at him with fists that felt like bricks, pummeling Delancey into unconsciousness.

When he came to some time later, he found himself face down among spiky weeds and empty liquor bottles at the bottom of the ditch. Everything hurt. He couldn't open one eye and his ribs were killing him. They must have been cracked. He tasted dirt and blood in his mouth and his tongue pushed at loose teeth.

He groaned and tried to get his arms under him but one arm was numb from the shoulder down so he couldn't move it. He got the other arm free but set his hand on a piece of broken glass and cried aloud.

The effort made pain jolt through his head and the world went black again.

When he woke up he was cold, colder than he should have been in the middle of June.

Shivering in the dew-soaked weeds, he noticed a woman on her belly in the ditch staring back at him. Her eyes were wide open a couple yards away.

He blinked his one good eye, tried without success to imagine why she would have been here.

Dizzy, bewildered, he rasped out, "Hey, I'm hurt here." In his confusion he thought she was there to rescue him. "Can you give me a hand?"

She didn't reply.

It took him a while figure out why.

Thursday, June 10, 2010

17

"That your girl?"

Hank Bellamy shone the flashlight onto the face of the woman in the ditch beside the railroad track. Preuss bent down without disturbing the scene.

She was laid out on her front. Her dark tee shirt rode up on her back and her skin was waxen. She was facing him and he recognized the prominent freckled cheekbones, the downturn at the outside corners of her dead open eyes.

"I've never seen her in person," Preuss said, "but I'm sure that's her. That's Elizaveta Kertész," he said because he couldn't think of anything else to say that wasn't a howl to the dark skies.

So much for the hope it wouldn't turn out this way.

If wishes were horses.

They climbed the side slope to the roadbed and Bellamy nodded to Arnold Biederman and his evidence techs so they could start gathering what they needed. The Oakland County medical examiner had already been out and pronounced her dead but Bellamy, who was the detective on duty for the overnight shift, wanted them to leave the body as it was until Preuss could come and identify her.

"Any ID on her?" Preuss asked.

"Nothing," Bellamy said.

"No handbag or wallet?"

"Nope."

"She's badly beaten. What are you thinking, a mugging gone wrong in the course of the vehicle theft?"

"Doubt it," Bellamy said. "She's still wearing a watch, plus a couple rings and a pendant-necklace-type-thing and an ankle bracelet that might be gold. If this was a mugging, all that bling would be gone."

"Unless it was interrupted. But then she wouldn't be laid out with such care."

He shook his head. He so wanted it to turn out differently that he couldn't think straight.

"No witnesses either, I suppose?"

Bellamy said, "Everybody else'd gone home from the elevator company except the guy who found her."

"How'd we find him?"

"One of the repair guys, name of Fernando Cruz, came back late from a call and found the gate wide open and Joe Delancey's car still inside. He looked around and found Delancey and the girl. I took a statement and told him he could go home."

"Looked like marks of strangulation among all the other bruises."

"We'll ask them to fast-track the autopsy, but it's still going to take time. With all the trampling at the scene it's hard to say if she was killed here or not, but Biederman says he doesn't think she was. Way she's laid out, all neat and straight, I'd say the same. ME thinks she's been dead two days."

"She's been here two days?"

"Here or somewhere."

Preuss considered that and went back to the ditch. Bellamy was right, she looked laid out, not as if she fell where she was killed or even dumped. If he was going to dump a body here, he would have hauled it over his shoulder and dumped it in the ditch and she wouldn't wind up in the position she was in.

The ambulance Fernando Cruz had summoned was parked beside the road, lights flashing. Delancey was on board and being attended to.

Preuss said, "What's up with that guy?"

"Road rage victim," Bellamy said. "He took a beat-down from somebody who left him in the ditch. He didn't get much of a look at the guy who did it but he gave us a description of the vehicle. Grey F-250."

"Narrows it down to a couple hundred thousand."

"Yeah, there's that," Bellamy said. "Think there's any connection between your girl and this guy?"

As Chief Warnock would say, everything's connected, Preuss thought. "Hard to say, him or whoever beat his ass. Though I can't imagine somebody would kick the shit out of somebody and then leave him next to a dead girl he killed."

"Stupider things have happened."

"That's a fact."

Preuss walked back to his SUV. He'd have to deliver the bad news to Rachael Furlong and Rosa Martinez. Soon.

As though thinking about the chief summoned him, William Warnock's black Charger pulled up behind Preuss's Explorer. He had his chief's uniform on though it wasn't yet three in the morning. The two shook hands. This was the first time Preuss had spoken to him since his retirement announcement.

"Won't have to do this much longer," Preuss said.

"That's the idea. What do we have?"

"The woman who was driving the missing minibus. Killed."

"Nuts."

"Bellamy caught it. He called me when he saw she fit the description."

"You make the ID?"

"I did."

Warnock nodded. He was a tall laconic man not much given to speaking when there was nothing to say. He rubbed the ancient acne scars along his jaw.

Preuss said, "We'll meet later and take stock of where we are."

"There was a handicapped boy missing too?"

"A young man, in his twenties. But we found him."

"Think he's involved somehow?"

"Hard to say, but my guess is no. I have a scout car keeping an eye on the house just in case. We still haven't located the vehicle, or whoever took it."

"I'd say that's become a priority."

"It has."

Warnock gave him a baleful look. "Martin, you have this in hand?"

"It's under control."

Warnock sighed. "You're not going to like this, but I'm going to call Nick back."

"Bill—"

"I know, I know. But you're too short-handed and there's too much going on right now. You shouldn't have to handle the administrative side as well as this. Besides . . ."

"What?"

"I don't know if you've heard, but he's planning to throw his hat in the ring for my job."

"Please don't tell me that."

"You must have suspected he would."

"I didn't want to think about it."

"Well," said Warnock, "it's true. He called me to let me know right after I announced."

"He found out fast."

"He has channels of information around the department."

And one of those channels is named Bellamy, Preuss thought.

"At least he's in the Grand Canyon," Preuss said. "It'll take him a few days to get home. I might have this wrapped up by then."

"No, the camping trip only lasted a week. He's been home for a while. He'll be in his office in the morning."

Now it was Preuss's turn to sigh. "That's the second worst news I've heard tonight."

"There's a bright side I want you to think about. If he's named department chief, there's going to be an opening for chief of detectives. I want you to apply."

"If Russo's running the department, you think he'd ever appoint me as bureau chief? I'd be lucky to keep my shield."

"I can reason with him. If he's chief he'll have a lot more on his plate than his vendetta against you. I'll talk to the mayor and Donahue on the Council." City Councilman Mark Donahue was a former policeman who still had many ties to the department in the small governmental circles of Ferndale. "You've got a lot of friends on the force and around the city and I'm certain we can line them up on your side. We can make this happen, Martin."

Before Preuss could respond, Bellamy walked up to them and said, "Ambulance is ready to take Delancey to Providence. Want to talk with him first?"

Preuss said, "I do."

"We'll finish this later," Warnock said. "Just think about it for now, okay?"

"Sure."

Joe Delancey was on a spinal board inside the ambulance. The EMT driver stood outside, waiting for Preuss to finish so she could take their patient away.

"How is he?" Preuss asked her.

"Couple broken bones, probably a concussion. Lots of cuts and bruises but nothing major."

Preuss nodded his thanks and climbed inside the ambulance.

"Mr. Delancey?"

The man on the spinal board looked up at him but he was in bad shape. Purple bruises were already up on his face and arms. He had an oxygen cannula in his nose and an IV line snaking up to a clear solution in a bag. The EMT with him held an ice pack to his head.

"I'm Detective Preuss. I want to ask you about the woman you found down there."

"She was there when I came to."

"Do you remember if she was there when you fell?"

Delancey gave a small pained shake of his head. "Sorta had my hands full, wasn't paying attention."

"The guy who beat you, would you recognize him if you saw him again?"

"Maybe. All happened so fast."

"Had you ever seen the young woman before?"

Instead of answering his eyes rolled up in his head.

"Mr. Delancey?" the EMT said. "Stay with us. Are you going to be sick?"

She injected something into the IV line and Delancey closed his eyes. But Preuss wasn't going to get any more from him now. He stuck a business card in the man's pocket and nodded to the EMT.

"All yours," he said.

18

They didn't finish until after four in the morning. Preuss decided he would wait for a few hours before contacting Rosa Martinez . . . let her and Rachael Furlong get the last few hours of peaceful sleep. Rachael in particular would not have many peaceful nights after this.

He went down to the canteen to get a cup of machine coffee and saw Bellamy sitting in the corner with his hands around a can of Coke. For all the problems Bellamy caused him, he could be good police when the occasion required, as it had tonight.

He sat in the bench across from Bellamy and sipped his coffee. As always, it was too hot when it came from the machine. He set it down to cool.

"You didn't get much sleep this night," Bellamy said.

"No."

"Tough, finding her like that."

"It was."

"As long as I'm a cop, I'll never get used to seeing a life snuffed out like this one. Pretty girl, young, her whole life ahead of her."

"She had a child, too. Eleven-year-old girl."

Bellamy sipped his Coke, said, "I guess this is your case now, since you caught the original report."

Preuss said, "Reggie caught the original. He called me in on it."

"So you took it over."

"I suppose I did."

"Tony used to do that, too. Comes with the territory of being senior guy, I guess. And acting chief of the bureau."

"When there's a handicapped kid involved it's hard to keep me away."

"That too," Bellamy allowed. "But it'll pass along to you anyway." Cases the night shift caught flowed to the day detectives.

"Let's meet about this later on," Preuss said. "In a little while I have to go into Detroit and do the notification but then you, me, and Reg'll talk about how to go forward."

"Telling a little girl her mother's dead . . . don't envy you that one."

On the way to Rosa Martinez's he called her to say he was coming. He didn't want to ring her doorbell at six in the morning and spring this bad news on her.

She opened the door to him dressed in tan capri pants and a green WSU tee shirt. She wore her hair pulled back in a headband that had the effect of framing her face. She was an attractive woman.

He could tell by her face she expected the news he was going to deliver. "Come in," she said. "Want some coffee?"

"No, thanks. I'm caffeined-out for the minute."

She led the way through the living room into her kitchen. It was a large room that looked as if it had been remodeled using part of what used to be the living room. Older homes like this didn't have kitchens this big, as a rule. The remodel kept vintage details like oaken cabinets and an island made of a huge slab of butcher block, wavy and scarred from years of hard use.

She poured herself a cup of strong-smelling coffee and they sat at a table covered with a red and white checked oilcloth. She seemed to be gathering herself for what he was about to tell her.

"You don't have good news," she said.

"No. I wish I had something different to tell you. We found Elizaveta's body early this morning."

She lowered her head and took a deep breath in an effort to control herself. "I knew it." She grabbed a handful of paper napkins from the holder on the table and dabbed at her eyes and face.

"Ever since she didn't come home that first night I've been waiting for this. She'd never leave her daughter. Do you know what happened?"

"She appears to have been a victim of violence."

"Oh, poor Elizaveta." She let her head fall onto the back of her hand.

"Can you think of anybody who might want to harm her?"

"I can't. I've been thinking about it since you were here, afraid we'd be having this conversation. But I can't think of anyone who would want to hurt her. Everyone who knew her loved her."

"Not everyone."

"I guess not. I'll have to ask Elizaveta's sister to come up. Rachael should be with her family."

"Of course. Where is she now"

"Upstairs. She's been staying in my spare room. She's still asleep."

She looked around the kitchen, then at Preuss.

"You didn't have to come all this way just to give us the bad news. You could have called."

"No. People get this face-to-face."

"It can't be easy for you."

"It never is."

"When did you find her?"

"Around two this morning. But it looks like she's been dead for a couple of days."

"So since Monday?"

"Looks that way."

"You've been up most of the night?"

"I have."

"Are you sure you don't want that coffee? I put a fresh pot on as soon as you called. You look like you need it."

Without waiting for an answer she was up and at the cupboard getting a mug for him and a small plate. She set down the WDET mug and filled it with coffee.

She retrieved what looked like a sugar-topped croissant from the wooden bread box on the counter and placed it on the plate in front of him. "You look like you need this too," she said.

He stared at it. He had no appetite, but he didn't want to refuse so he took a small bite. To his surprise it was delicious, light and fluffy with a sweet glaze. He took another bite and then he gobbled up the rest of it and washed it down with a sip of coffee, which was rich and strong and as good as the croissant.

"That's called a *cuernos de azucar*," she said. "Sugar horn."

"Tastes almost French."

"Mexican pastries are influenced by the French and Spanish."

"It's lovely. Did you make it yourself?"

"I did. When I'm stressed I bake. Rachael helped. Want another?"

Before he could reply a stirring came from overhead.

"Sounds like Rachael's awake," she said.

"I better go up and talk with her."

"I can handle it if you'd prefer. I'm a medical social worker so dealing with grieving people is my business. And I've got a relationship with her. She should hear it from me."

"I'd appreciate having you there, but the notification is part of what I do."

He followed her back through the living room and up the carpeted stairs to the second floor.

Rachael was sitting on a bed, holding a floppy blue stuffed bear. Rosa sat beside her and put her arm around her and Preuss turned a desk chair around and sat on that.

"Sweetheart," Rosa Martinez said, "you remember Detective Preuss?"

She nodded, still glassy-eyed from sleep.

"He's got something to tell you, *mi amora*."

Preuss leaned forward so his elbows were on his knees. "Rachael, I'm sorry but I have some really awful news. We found your mother this morning, and I'm sorry to say she was not alive."

The girl searched his face as though she didn't quite understand what he was telling her. "No," she said, "you must have made a mistake." She looked to the woman beside her for confirmation.

"It's true, Rachael," Rosa Martinez said. "I'm so sorry."

"No," Rachael said again.

"Oh honey, it's true," Rosa said.

As the girl tried to process the information, her face crumpled and she let out a wail that pierced Preuss's heart. She buried her face into Rosa's bosom, which muffled the cries but didn't stop them.

Preuss exchanged a glance with Rosa, and she nodded toward the door.

"Please let me deal with this," she said to him. "It'll be a while before she has anything to tell you."

He agreed and she reached out to him. He took her hand and she squeezed it before she released it and pulled the sobbing girl closer.

"She's lying down," Rosa said when she returned to the kitchen. "She said she wanted to be by herself for a while."

"I'd like to take a walk through Elizaveta's apartment. If you'd prefer I get a warrant I will, but it would be faster if you could let me in. We've already lost two days."

"Of course. The keys are on my fridge."

She led him out her front door to the vestibule to the building and unlocked Elizaveta's door. "She doesn't have much in the way of furnishings," she said over her shoulder as they climbed the stairs. "Things are sparse up here."

A pair of leaded French doors at the top of the stairs opened into the living room. As she had said, there wasn't much in the way of furniture or decorations: a threadbare sofa, a floral chair, both looking like Salvation Army finds, and an old tubed TV. On the walls were original-looking canvases of Detroit scenes signed by artists Preuss had never heard of. Maybe friends of hers from school.

The dining room had a large table covered with musical scores and other papers on one end and Rachael's school books and worksheets on the other end with more canvases on the walls. A small boom box sat on a wire rack that held a few dozen CDs. Her tastes ran to classical music and indie rock: Franz Ferdinand, Arctic Monkeys, the Hives. There was also a smattering of Top 40 albums—Adele, Taylor Swift, Pink. He assumed these were Rachael's.

A violin case leaned against the wall in one corner beside a music stand and a chair. He opened the case. The instrument was inside, its lovely caramel curves glowing as though from an inner light.

"She plays violin, too?" he asked.

"That's Rachael's."

At the end of a long hallway there were two tiny bedrooms, one a little girl's room and the other Elizaveta's. Both had a dresser and a twin bed but not much else. On the dresser next to Elizaveta's bed there was an old black-and-white photo of a young, dapper-looking man in the 1930s, and the same color photo of Elizaveta and Rachael laughing that Rosa had let Preuss borrow.

He gloved up and went through the drawers in Elizaveta's dresser but found nothing except for women's clothing, all of it casual. Same in the closet . . . hangers filled with Levis and blouses and one or two good pairs of slacks. There was one nice black outfit and a white women's dress blouse, which might have been the outfit she wore for recitals.

He returned to the front of the apartment, where Rosa was seated at the dining room table. He sorted through the papers spread out there. Her bills . . . DTE, Visa, Consumers Energy, gas receipts.

"I'd like to bag these up," he said. "Might be something here that helps us understand where she's been the past few days."

Rosa didn't answer. He saw she was looking down on the music scattered over the table top. Her eyes were shining with sorrow.

"She was so gifted," she said. "This is such a terrible waste of a life."

19

Instead of slaking his hunger, the sugar horn and coffee Rosa Martinez served him had revved it up. He got off I-75 at Nine Mile and pulled into the Tim Horton's on the service drive. He needed to eat something more but he didn't feel like taking the time at a sit-down restaurant . . . he wanted the anonymity of a fast food shop to regroup before facing the rest of his day.

He ordered a breakfast sandwich and a steeped tea and sat in a corner but when he unwrapped the sandwich a trio of young men hunkered in and sat nearby. They were all in their 20s with identical billy-goat chin beards and one wouldn't shut up even as he shoveled donut holes into his mouth nonstop. Preuss tried to tune him out but his voice was an incessant bray as he talked about "dudes" and "chicks" and "holding my dick" and "I didn't want them to think I was gay."

Preuss couldn't stand to listen to him, couldn't stand the confident stupidity of them all—how did they stay so self-absorbed in the face of the unrelenting indifference of the world?—so he gobbled his sandwich in three bites and tossed the container of tea into the trash bin and left.

At the Shanahan he checked in with Tanya Corcoran.

"I heard your missing girl turned up dead," she said.

He fell into the empty chair in her office and rubbed a hand over his face. He felt stiff from fatigue. His missing girl. How did she become his?

"She did," he said.

"Shame."

"Yeah. Hank still here?"

She nodded. "In the chief's conference room."

He walked around the narrow warren of the station's halls to the conference room outside Chief Warnock's office. Through the closed glass door he saw Bellamy sitting with Warnock—and the broad muscular back of Nick Russo.

That didn't take long, Preuss thought. Early bird gets worm.

He left them to their conversation and went to his office. He sorted through his messages. One was from Jim White from South Oakland Shelter.

He punched in the numbers on his desk phone. "Jim," he said.

"Hey Martin. Have you heard from our friend Sheila?"

"No. Why?"

"She disappeared from the motel where we had her. I thought she might have tried to get in touch with you."

"No," Preuss said, "in fact, she promised me she'd stay put."

As soon as he said that, he remembered he promised he would take her to see Zach Warranow yesterday. In all the chasing around he did for the Helen Vlastos investigation and the home burglary suspect it slipped his mind.

He explained his oversight to White.

"Easy to remedy," White said.

"Once we find her."

"Any idea where she went?"

"Pretty sure she'd go back to the park where she was staying. But you know what, we caught a murder last night. There's a connection with the young guy Sheila was with when we found her, in fact. I'll look for her as soon as I can but I can't drop everything right now."

"Well, let me know."

"Will do. Meantime, can you keep the bed open for her?"

"Till tonight, my friend. After that, no promises."

He hung up from White and found the business card Max Halperin left with him. He punched in Halperin's number and soon a secretary put him through to the attorney.

"Detective Preuss. How's our star witness?"

"I was hoping you could tell me. I got her settled in a motel room through SOS yesterday morning, but she took a powder."

"That's not good."

"No. Have you heard from her?"

"Sorry, no."

"Give me a ring if you do?"

"Of course. Any progress on finding your other missing gal?"

"The driver of the group home minibus? Yeah, she turned up."

"Don't like the sound of that."

"She's dead. Somebody killed her."

"Oh, lord, what a terrible thing. I was hoping this would have a happy ending."

"Weren't we all."

"Did you ever hear back from my friend? The one I told you about?"

"No."

"Well, let me check with him again to see if he's heard anything. He's got his fingers in lots of pies in some of the immigrant communities around the area. You never know what he'll turn up."

"That would be great," Preuss said with little hope anything would come of it.

He hung up and Bellamy's pear-shaped figure loomed in his doorway. "Hey."

"Hank. Did you have a chance to go through the route I asked you to?"

"I started, but then the girl's death last night pulled me away."

"Assign some uniformed officers to keep at it. I'd like you to check Elizaveta's Call Detail Records, see if you can put together a timeline of her last few days. And start looking for the driver of the pickup Delancey had the altercation with. Check auto glass companies in the area, see if a truck matching that description comes in for a rear window replacement.

"We need to find out more about her. Reg can start with her background. I'm going to keep at the security video from the church. We'll meet this afternoon at four and figure out where we are. Let's keep each other informed about developments, right?"

When Bellamy didn't reply, Preuss said, "What?"

"Dunno if you heard, but Nick's back in the house."

"So I saw. You two have a nice little chat?"

"Can I sit down?"

Preuss held a hand out toward the visitor's chair on the other side of his desk and Bellamy lowered himself into it.

"I noticed the chief was in with you," Preuss said.

"Nick asked me to brief him on the Kertész case. Seeing as how I caught it."

Preuss said nothing. He could tell where this was heading.

"He wants me to be primary on it."

Preuss considered that, said, "Okay."

"You're good with it?"

"Do I have a choice?"

Bellamy shifted in his chair.

"You still going to be on the lobster shift?"

"Nick is switching me to days for the duration."

"Anybody else going to nights?" Like me, he thought.

"No. We're going to keep the overnight unstaffed for now."

The "we" in that sentence was not lost on Martin Preuss.

"Are there any case files you can give me?" Bellamy asked.

"All my records and notes are in the case file on the server. You filled out the original report so you have the case number."

"Martin," Bellamy said, "Nick also said he wants me to work it without you."

"Really."

"Yeah. His decision, not mine. It was up to me—"

"What about Reggie?"

"Reggie can keep doing what he's doing. I'll give him the message about doing a background on the girl."

"I assume it's all right with everyone if I keep working the missing minibus?"

"Sure."

Expansive now it was clear who was in charge (and it wasn't Preuss).

"Don't worry, Hank," Preuss said. "I find anything pertaining to your case, I'll make sure I keep you all"—for the first time grouping William Warnock in his mind with Russo—"in the loop. That work?"

Bellamy thought about that and pronounced it acceptable.

He stayed seated across from Preuss for another few moments as if trying to think of something else to say.

Preuss had the distinct feeling he was staring into the porcine, mustachioed face of the next chief of detectives.

After Bellamy left he sat for a while thinking about what he'd just heard. No surprises, except in how fast Russo cut him out of the investigation. Probably decided that before his first cup of coffee. The question now was, how big a fuss should he make?

Or rather there were two questions. The second was, should he disregard his conversation with Bellamy and follow his own sense of the case?

As though rehearsing that line of approach, he closed his office door and created a timetable of events on a page of the flip chart that stood in the corner of his office . . . everything he knew from before the group home minibus was reported missing up to the discovery that morning of Elizaveta's body.

When he finished he sat looking over the chart. The answer was here, he knew. Despite the fears the politicians and media cultivated, murder was hardly ever a random crime. People were killed by people they knew.

He tore the page off the pad and taped it on the wall. He stood looking at it until his cell phone rang.

He didn't recognize the number but answered it anyway.

"Preuss."

"Detective," said the voice on the other end. "This is Andre McCray calling from the *Detroit Free Press.*"

Preuss said, "Andre. How can I help you?" McCray was a reporter on the metropolitan desk at the newspaper. In the past Preuss had a few dealings with him and found him to be honest and his stories for the most part accurate.

"Do you have a minute?" McCray said.

"Sure."

"I'm following up on a couple things that came across my desk."

"Okay."

"That missing driver of that group home van . . . I heard she was found dead this morning. Any truth to that?"

"Andre, you're going to have to speak with Lieutenant Russo. I can't comment to the media, you know that."

"Fair enough. What I'm also calling about, I'd like a comment from you on a lead I was given that you've been removed from the investigation."

"Excuse me?"

McCray repeated what he just said and Preuss was choked by a sudden anger. A red mist blurred his vision.

This must be what they mean by seeing red, he thought.

"Detective? Still there?"

"Where did you get that from?"

"You know I can't reveal my sources. Is it true?"

Could Bellamy have leaked it already?

Impossible, he decided. Bellamy didn't have the connections with the local news media, and wouldn't have taken it upon himself to do it anyway. Warnock had no reason to cut his legs out from under him like this, and the only other one who knew what had just happened that morning was Russo.

Who wouldn't have hesitated. It must have been Russo.

"If it's true," McCray said, "this is the second investigation you've been removed from in the past two years. You were also taken off the Kaufman girl's disappearance. Care to comment?"

Preuss forced himself to stay calm. "The Sheriff's Office took over the Kaufman case, Andre. Not the same thing as getting removed from it."

"Can I take that as a confirmation you've been removed from the current case? Any comment?"

"I have neither comment nor confirmation."

"How do you feel about this—"

He disconnected before McCray finished the sentence.

He dropped the phone into his jacket pocket.

He opened his office door, closed and locked it behind him, and went down the hall and around the corner to Tanya Corcoran's office, which was next to Russo's. He stood for a moment in Tanya's doorway, then turned and opened Russo's door without knocking and strode into Russo's office.

Russo was sitting at his desk, working over figures in a report. Without raising his head he stared at Preuss over the top of the eyeglasses he wore for close work.

Russo reddened. "What do *you* want?"

Preuss stood before him and leaned forward, propping his hands on Russo's desk.

"I just had a talk with a reporter from the *Free Press*. No doubt the one you put onto me. And before that, Hank Bellamy. What's the matter, Nick, you didn't have the guts to take me off the case yourself? Or isn't it even worth speaking to me anymore?"

Russo glared at him.

"I'm thinking as soon as you and Warnock and Bellamy met you were on the phone to the reporter making sure word got out you were pulling me off another case."

"You're out of line."

"*I'm* out of line? Last time you pulled this shit Bill talked me out of filing a grievance. Not this time. Now you're trying to discredit me in public. You may not like it but I'm senior detective on this squad and I'm going to sue your muscle-bound ass for harassment. And let's see what happens when *that* goes public. We'll see what it does to your little campaign for chief."

Russo gave Preuss a cold smile. He pulled his glasses off and tossed them onto the desktop.

"You think I'm giving you a hard time, Martin? Okay, maybe I am. Maybe I talked to this reporter, maybe I didn't. You go right ahead, file grievances to your heart's content. But I'll tell you something."

He cocked his head, flexing the muscles in his bull neck.

"It doesn't matter what you do because you're finished. In this department, in law enforcement. I don't care if you're here a hundred years, as long as I'm in this chair you're not going to be more than the dog's breakfast in my eyes. And I'll tell you something else. Bill talked to me about you becoming the chief of Ds once I move into the chief's office—and that's going to happen, trust me on this one—but if you think I'd ever see you promoted to this job in a million years, you're even less connected to reality than I give you credit for. Kiss that job goodbye, Martin. In fact, kiss your entire career goodbye. You're through."

"Is that right."

Now it was Preuss's turn to give the other man a chilly smile. Stay cool, he told himself, and he was surprised that he felt calm, even serene, in the face of Russo's venom.

"Yeah, Martin, that's right."

Preuss shook his head. "You're pathetic, Nick. Seriously. You're a pathetic little man. I feel sorry for you. And I feel sorry for what's going to happen to this department if you take it over."

Russo grabbed his glasses off the desktop and swept them onto his face. "I were you, I'd worry more about yourself. Now get out of my office before I bring you up on charges. Again."

"The thing of it is, you used to be a good detective. But you let your grief over Jeanette turn you into a sad, pitiful shell, and all the threats and bully-boy talk in the world aren't going to change that."

Russo didn't look up but he was getting even redder. Preuss could even feel the heat radiating from Russo's face, as if he were about to explode.

Before that happened Preuss left his office.

He took a deep breath and kept on going out to the parking lot.

That was stupid, he told himself. It was all true, of course, and it felt great to say. But talking to his superior like that was just dumb.

Still, he thought, retrieving the Explorer, he didn't have much to lose now.

He cranked up Stevie Ray Vaughn on the CD player and sang along with "The House is Rocking" as he drove the few blocks up to Martin Road Park. He took another left on Orchard Avenue and parked behind the tiny outbuilding where Sheila Hawkins kept her stash of possessions during the day.

He hoped he could catch her before she disappeared to where ever she spent her days, but there was no sign of her. He checked inside both women's and men's restrooms and called her name, but he didn't spot her or her stuff.

He crossed the field and the parking lot to the Ferndale Cornerstone Community United Lutheran Church. He asked the receptionist if Leonard Costigan was around, and when she said he wasn't he asked if she had seen Sheila Hawkins that morning. The woman said she knew Sheila very well but hadn't seen her yet today. He left a business card with her and asked her to call him if Sheila showed up.

She said she would and he walked back to where his car was parked.

He was in no hurry to return to the Shanahan.

20

He never told anyone on the FPD, but Reg Trombley came close to having another line of work than the police. Once he wanted to be an actor.

He did so well in performances at Cass Technical High School, the magnet school in downtown Detroit, that his teacher Mrs. Frankfurter encouraged him to pursue acting as a career and arranged for an interview with a friend in the Theatre Department at Wayne State University. Mrs. Frankfurter told him he had all the gifts a young man needed to succeed in the business . . . he was handsome with smooth caramel-colored skin stretched taut over killer bone structure, he was tall and athletic and could move well, he had a sweet baritone voice, and he had a natural stage presence that, as Mrs. Frankfurter said, "captured the eye" while he was onstage in student productions as Nathan Detroit in *Guys and Dolls*, Oberon in *Midsummer Night's Dream*, and Professor Harold Hill in *The Music Man*.

He loved performing. He loved the attention, and he loved the way an actor could lose himself inside a part while still putting all of his life experiences (such as they were for a teenager) into the role.

His parents hated the idea of him being an actor, of course. But what soured him on acting was a trip he took to New York City during the fall semester of his third year at Wayne State. One of the theatre professors took a group of students to see a half-dozen plays and visit the graduate theatre program at New York University. There he learned how hard the profession would be (as well as how expensive a graduate degree from NYU was). He talked with actors who waited tables and drove cabs for years after their formal education ended. Their lives consisted not of acting in the great dramatic canon Reg dreamed of performing but of going to auditions and getting rejected. They were all beautiful men and women, and, he was certain, as talented as he was if not more so. Yet everyone struggled. He got an eye-opening understanding that luck and connections were the major determinants of success in acting, not talent. Who you know and who you blow, as one of them said.

When he returned to Detroit he changed his major to criminal justice. His father was a lieutenant in the Detroit Police Department and it seemed a natural move. He never regretted a day of his theatre training because he met his wife Sandy when they were both students in Wayne's Theatre Department, and acting sometimes came in handy on the job when he had to convince villains he was on their side even if all he wanted to do was pummel them bloody.

And there was a part of him that kept the idea of acting in his back pocket, perhaps when he retired and started a community theatre group. Sandy taught English at Ferndale High School and sponsored the drama club, and she always talked about working in community theatre after she retired.

So it was that Reg Trombley knew where the College of Fine, Performing, and Communication Arts was located on the WSU campus in downtown Detroit. The Theatre Department offices were on the third floor of Old Main on Cass Avenue, and the Music Department offices and studios were on the second floor. In the office of the Music Department he introduced himself to the secretary and told her he was looking for anyone who knew Elizaveta Kertész.

At the mention of her name the secretary, a woman named Tawanda Pippen ("No relation," she said, assuming he would know who she was referring to) (he had no idea), gave him a broad, glistening smile. "Everybody knows Elizaveta. We just love her to pieces, she's so sweet."

"I'm looking for someone who knows who she hangs out with, what kind of personal life she might have, like that."

The woman thought for a moment, then said, "I'd try Cherie. Professor Schraeder. She knows her best of all the faculty."

"Is she in?"

"She was earlier." Tawanda raised a slender finger with a bright red talon-like fingernail and pointed out the door. "Her office is down the hall and to the right."

Trombley thanked her and walked down the corridor. This brought back so many memories . . . he wasn't a music student but the sights and smells—and even posters on the walls—were similar to the ones he remembered from the Theatre Department upstairs. Such a long time ago, he thought. So much has changed in his life.

Cherie Schraeder was a short pretty white woman with a mass of curly honey-colored hair and a strong jawline that looked like it could cut glass. Trombley thought she could be a tough customer if a student crossed her or missed rehearsal. She was dressed all in black: black vest over a black turtleneck and black silk pants. Except for her shoes, which were red Keds.

She invited him into her office, a narrow room with dark wood features and walls covered with posters for musical performances in New York City and Europe. "How can I help you?"

"Tawanda told me you know Elizaveta Kertész?"

"I do."

"How do you know her?"

"I'm her advisor, and I teach voice so she's taken all my vocal courses. She's a very talented musician. Can I ask, is she okay?"

"I'm sorry to have to tell you, but she was found dead early this morning."

She reared back in her chair, stricken, and touched a hand to her chest. Her nails were a deep purple. "What happened?"

"She appears to have been a victim of violence."

"Oh, how awful."

"I'm trying to get some background to see if we can account for the last few days. If there's someplace she might have gone to, or some people she might hang around with."

But she couldn't seem to get past the shock of the news. "This is really awful," she said.

Trombley waited.

"I don't even know what to say."

"When was the last time you saw her?"

"Last week. We have private instruction tutorials on Thursday mornings. Last Thursday was our last session." She paused at the implications of her words.

"How'd she seem?"

She pulled a face, looked around the room. "Same as always, I suppose. Bright. Enthusiastic. Eager to improve."

"Did she seem bothered by anything?"

She brought the back of her hand to her forehead in what seemed to Trombley to be an overly self-conscious dramatic gesture. Then she sighed.

"I should tell you," she said, "I find it useful to get very involved in my students' lives. Sometimes their problems can be overwhelming, but for that reason, and because they're all developing artists, they need more support and engagement than students in other disciplines. So I practice what we call 'intrusive advising.' But Elizaveta, she was more resistant to my intrusions. More private. It seemed like she set more boundaries than my other students. When we'd meet we'd talk about deepening the warmth and agility of her mezzo-soprano, and as I say she was incredibly dedicated to her craft so she took all my comments to heart. But she kept her personal life private. So if anything was bothering her, I just couldn't say."

"Understood. Is there anybody you can think of who knew her well?"

She thought for a few moments, then said, "She hangs with a group of music students, but I can't imagine any of them would be mixed up in her death. They're all serious musicians. None of them would lead her astray, if that's what happened."

"Could you give me their names?"

"Of course." She wrote down a list of seven names and handed it to Trombley. "These are the ones she's closest with. Tawanda can get you their contact information."

"Anyone else you can think of who I should speak with?"

She thought some more, said, "No. Sorry. I think her life outside the classroom was well hidden from us all."

"If you think of anything else, please give me a call?"

He left his card with her and stopped by Tawanda Pippen's office to get the numbers and addresses for the students. They were all over the metropolitan area . . . in several locations in Detroit, in Hazel Park, and in West Bloomfield.

Before leaving the building he walked upstairs to the Theatre Department and made a circuit of the halls. Except for names and faces that he didn't recognize, it was all just as he remembered, as if little had changed since the day he left the program.

He returned to the Shanahan comfortable in the life decisions he had made.

He began his calls starting with the women.

Two didn't answer so he left messages. Two he spoke with; they claimed not to know very much about Elizaveta, and didn't even seem upset to learn she was dead.

He got through to two of the three men. The first hadn't seen her for over a week, and the second couldn't add anything to what Trombley already knew. He left a message for the third man to call him as soon as possible.

So much for Cherie Schraeder's insights into Elizaveta Kertész. And so much for the richness of Elizaveta's social support system. She didn't seem to have any close friends in her program, and no one knew that much about her. She didn't hang out with the other students, didn't date any of them, didn't even see them much off-campus.

He was fleshing out his brief notes from the interviews when one of the women students called him back.

As it turned out, Deborah Turner said she was Elizaveta's closest friend in their program.

Finally, he thought. Someone who knows that poor young woman. And cares she's been killed—Deborah sobbed for a full minute when Trombley told her as he waited on the other end of the line.

When she could speak, they talked for almost an hour. Deborah said even though they were friendly, Elizaveta was closed-mouth about her background but as they got to know one another she often talked about her philosophy of life.

"She was convinced chance plays a monumental role in our lives," Deborah said. "She used to say, for all our planning and hoping it was dumb luck that was behind most of what happened to us . . . dumb luck and misunderstandings. It was just chance we were born where and when we were, just chance that brought some people into our lives and kept others out . . . She used to say her entire life was a series of million-to-one shots."

The young woman paused. "She sings—sang—like an angel. But there was always this, like, deep sadness in her heart. And now you tell me what happened to her, it's almost like she's been waiting for this all along. Almost like she was expecting it."

Maybe she was, Trombley thought. "Deborah, can you think of anyone who would want to hurt her?"

She thought for a few moments. "First thing pops into my mind: her ex-husband. If you're thinking about any kind of foul play, I'd say he should be at the top of your list."

21

"I just got an earful about Elizaveta's ex," Trombley said.

"What'd you hear?"

Trombley sat in the guest chair in Preuss's office. "This is all from her friend at school, who I just spoke with. Her ex's name is Scott Furlong. He left her for another woman, and for a while afterwards she didn't hear from him and he ignored their daughter. But he's become a nuisance in Elizaveta's life again."

"In what way?"

"He broke up with the woman he left her for. He seems to be a controlling kind of guy, a real thug. I ran him through the system. He's well-known to the various PDs around southeastern Michigan. He's a battler and a drinker, with multiple arrests for assault—mostly bar fights, none filed by Elizaveta—and DUIs. Matter of fact, his license is under suspension for DUI. According to Elizaveta's friend, he seems to have this notion she's been seeing someone and he's been coming around acting all jealous. Says he wants her back."

Preuss considered that. "Her landlady said she's never seen him. Daughter didn't mention him."

"Well, according to the friend, Elizaveta said he's been making a nuisance of himself, coming around in a jealous rage."

"Is she seeing somebody?"

"Not that anybody knows about. But her ex seemed convinced of it. And the thing is, Elizaveta told her friend he used to beat her when they were married, and he's threatened to kill both her and her imaginary boyfriend on several occasions."

"I'd say that makes him number one on the hit parade."

"I thought so too. Thought you might like to talk with him."

Preuss thought about how to tell Trombley he was no longer on the investigation . . . but the appearance of the ex made him feel too close to finding the young singer's killer. Was he willing to pass on this chance to close the case?

"Martin? You coming?"

"Sure," Preuss said. "Let's find him."

Furlong's home was a tiny bungalow on Karam Court in Warren. There was no answer to Preuss's knocking, either at his house or the neighboring homes on the street. Trombley went around the back but Furlong's little place was buttoned up tight.

Sitting in Preuss's Explorer Trombley got hold of Furlong's probation officer, who told them he was current in his visits and had a job at Chrysler's nearby Warren Stamping Plan.

At the plant's Human Resources Department they learned he was a large press operator, and when they tracked him to his work site Furlong's supervisor told them he had not been to work for two days.

"No notice or nothing," the supervisor said. "Just hasn't shown."

Preuss said, "How much leniency do these guys get? Seems like somebody doesn't show without notice, that's it, they'd be history."

"Ordinarily that'd be true," the supervisor said. "But, well, in his case I'm cutting Scottie some slack."

"Why?"

"All his troubles."

"What would those be?"

"He told me his ex-wife got sent to prison so he has full custody of his daughter."

"Prison, huh."

"Yeah."

Preuss and Trombley shared a look. "Wonder how many ex-wives he has," Trombley said.

Preuss said to the supervisor, "You don't know her name, by any chance, this ex-wife?"

"No. But I remember him telling me his daughter's name is Rachael."

"Rachael," Preuss said.

"Talks about her all the time. I like it when a fella steps up like that. Shows a lot of character."

"I don't know how to break this to you," Preuss said, "but Furlong hasn't seen his daughter in years. And his ex-wife's never been in prison. In fact she just showed up dead. He played you, pal."

They left the supervisor standing open-mouthed and stopped at the Tim Horton's on Van Dyke in Warren to regroup over coffee.

"That was cruel," Trombley said.

"He'll survive. Meantime, this guy seems to have anger issues, he's been missing for three days, and now his ex turns up dead."

"Want me to keep after him? Or do you want to?"

Preuss didn't reply. It was one thing to sink his own career. To jeopardize Trombley's was something else.

"Better coordinate with Bellamy."

"Why would I do that?"

"He's working the case. By himself. I was warned off it."

"By who?"

"Bellamy."

"Since when is he warning you off cases?"

"Since Russo's pulling his strings."

"So being taken off the case, that comes from Russo?"

"Horse's mouth."

"That explains why Bellamy told me to look into Elizaveta's background. I was wondering why it came from him and not you." He thought for a few moments, then said, "I'm speechless."

Preuss was about to tell him what Russo said earlier, but waved it off. "Business as usual with that guy," he said instead.

"So this thing today, looking for Furlong . . . ?"

"The momentary thrill of the chase. Couldn't resist it."

Trombley shook his head. "I'll tell you, man, I don't know if I want to work for a department treats its best investigator like this."

"It's the same everywhere, Reg. Look what happened to those two cops in Detroit, the ones investigating Kwame. They got shitcanned for doing their jobs. You talk to enough cops, you find out everybody knows somebody who got screwed in departmental politics. And not just cops, either."

He took a sip of coffee.

"Look," Preuss said, "forget about Russo for a second. What do we have? This young woman, a music student, everybody thinks she's quiet, conscientious, talented, does everything right, loves her daughter. Now her crazy ex-husband shows up in her life again, threatening her over a relationship he's convinced she's having that nobody else knows about."

"And this guy stalks her until he can't control himself any longer, and he ambushes her while she's out driving one of the residents in the home where she works. And then dumps the boy off at a church where he thinks he'll be found, dumps the body not far from there, and takes a powder himself."

They thought about that.

"Too many pieces don't fit," Preuss said. "We still need to find the minibus and those two duking it out in the parking lot. How do they fit in?"

"Now the jealous husband scenario isn't so simple."

"Maybe one of the guys in the surveillance video was Furlong. Maybe the guy driving the paint van. Or the guy in the hoodie. We never saw their faces."

"If that's so," Trombley said, "what's the connection with the paint company?"

"That's the $64 question."

"They don't do any work for the auto industry, do they? It's a stretch, but there might be a connection with Furlong's job in the factory."

"No," Preuss said, "they seem to be just residential and commercial. The one thing that seems clear is Zach's an innocent bystander of whatever went on."

"Who would want to steal a handicapped bus like that? It's not like it's inconspicuous."

"It could bring in a lot of money with the right buyer. Or could be sold for parts. Nothing's popped on the hot sheets?"

"Nope. So what's next?"

"If this were my case, I'd say look for the ex-husband," Preuss said. "Talk to Bellamy, let him know what you found and suggest that."

"Leaving out your participation, I assume."

"That would be wise. Meantime I'll concentrate on finding the minibus, which is what I'm 'allowed' to do. I'm certain the cases'll come together at some point."

It was after seven by the time they got back to the Shanahan. Trombley clocked out and Preuss sat in his office and watched the church surveillance video three more times.

He froze it at various points, concentrating on the lettering on the van. It was not, he realized, the same as the lettering on the other AAAdvantage vans he had seen that day. The same information was there—the company name and phone number—but something was different.

In fact, several things were different. For one, the lettering font was different from the font on the other vans. The letters on those were sans serif while the letters on the white van in the surveillance video showed the traces of serifs. Even though the video quality was not sharp, now that he was looking for them he could see the little tabs at the base of the letters.

The letters in the name of the company also seemed more faded on this van than on the other three. That suggested the lettering on this white van was older.

As he sat staring at the screen another possibility occurred to him. Some streaks were more faded than other parts of the lettering, as though an effort had been made to remove words, then abandoned . . . Like somebody tried to remove the lettering and found it was too much trouble so he gave up and decided to live with it.

He called the paint company number but got the jarring voice of Dolores on the recording. He called the cell number Campanella had given him but got his recorded message, mawkish nonsense about how important the call was and wishing the caller a blessed day. Preuss asked Campanella to call him back as soon as possible and disconnected.

He made a search of stolen vehicles that had been reported going back six months but found nothing matching the white van in the video.

He was just about to leave for the night when his cell rang.

22

"Detective Preuss," Rosa Martinez said, "I found something you might be interested in. I know it's late but maybe you can swing by and pick it up?"

"Sure."

"Great. I'm not sure it'll help you find who killed Elizaveta but it'll give you a better sense of her."

He said he'd be there in a half hour and they disconnected. He tossed the phone onto the desk. He was exhausted. It felt like a week since he delivered his bad news and received, for his pains, a delicious Mexican pastry. But more than that, he had felt taken care of in a way he had not for—how long? Years? There had been a sweetness in sitting back and being served despite the terrible news he had brought.

In the solitude through which he passed most of his days, he had forgotten how good that was.

He roused himself and set off for her house in southwest Detroit.

She answered the doorbell right away, as though she had been waiting for him.

"How's Rachael?"

"Sleeping now," she said. "But very sad. As you'd expect. Come in."

She stood aside and Preuss entered her home. It was warm after the warm day and fragrant with odors from a dish Preuss didn't recognize. He remembered he hadn't eaten since morning and was famished.

As if reading his thoughts, she patted his shoulder and said, "Come into the kitchen. You look like you could use a meal."

He followed her slender back into the kitchen where there was a pot on the stove. It was the source of the luscious smell.

"Do you like paella?"

She lifted the lid and showed him a pan of saffron-hued rice mixed with mussels and clams (their shells open like hungry mouths), shrimp, diced green and red peppers, and disks of chorizo. The pan made his empty stomach do flips.

"Sit," she said. "It's still hot."

"I wouldn't want to put you out. Especially since you already fed me once today."

"No trouble."

Without speaking he watched her stir and spoon out a plateful of the savory stew and place the steaming plate in front of him. "What to drink?"

"Nothing, thanks." He took in a forkful of the paella. "Oh man. This is delicious."

"Eat up. Lots more where that came from."

"I am capable of taking care of myself, despite what it looks like. I get so involved in the cases there's no time to sit down with a good meal."

"No explanation necessary. Food is always a source of comfort."

As he ate she retrieved an envelope from the counter and placed it in front of him. In it was the jewel case of a CD.

"I found this after you left this morning. It's a recording of a vocal recital Elizaveta gave at the DIA last year."

He removed the disk from its case. A printed label read, "Spring Concert, Detroit Institute of Arts, April 12, 2009."

"She had such a spectacular voice," Rosa said. "I wanted you to hear it. As I said, it probably won't help you find who did that horrible thing to her but you'll hear how talented she was. And what a loss to the world this is."

"I'll listen with interest."

"I called her sister this morning, after you left. She's coming up tomorrow to take Rachael back to Ohio."

"How do you feel about that?"

"I'll be sorry to see her go, of course. But she needs to be with her family now."

"I'm sure Elizaveta would appreciate what you're doing for her."

"We have to, don't we? We have to take care of each other. Or we die."

We die anyway, he thought. Being taken care of is gravy.

He ate another few forkfuls.

"Like it?" she asked.

"Very much."

"Let me know when you're ready for more."

He was about to tell her how he lived alone and didn't often make this kind of elaborate meal for himself when he heard the front door open and heavy footsteps plodded through the house to the kitchen.

A man came into the room with a long bottle in a brown paper bag. When he saw Preuss sitting there he stopped dead. He was stocky with a high forehead and wavy grey hair hanging to his shoulders from his balding dome. He had a full grey beard and mustache.

He looked from Preuss to Rosa, smiling. "Hello," he said.

Preuss felt as though he had been caught at something.

He lowered his forkful of rice and clam and wiped his mouth with his napkin. He rose in his seat.

"Hernan," Rosa said, "this is Detective Preuss. I told you about him. He's working on Elizaveta's murder."

To Preuss she said, "This is Hernan Tamayo. My partner."

The man set the paper bag on the kitchen table and held a hand out to Preuss. They shook and Tamayo said, "Pleasure to meet you."

"Likewise."

"Oh, wasn't that a terrible thing about that poor girl? Rosa told me what happened."

"It was."

"I hope you catch the bastard."

"We're doing our best."

"Detective Preuss came to pick up Elizaveta's CD and I asked him to stay for a bite."

"Wonderful," Tamayo said. "You'll stay and have a drink with us, too?" To Rosa he said, "They were out of the Rioja but I got us a nice Tempranillo."

He pulled the bag away from the bottle of wine, which he showed to Rosa. He went to the counter for a corkscrew and Rosa said, "Detective, will you join us?"

"No," Preuss said. "But thanks."

He watched the two together at the counter, Hernan opening the wine and Rosa putting cheese and fruit on a plate. He envied their comfortable domesticity, and felt even more like an interloper than usual. He stood, said, "Time for me to go."

"Are you sure?" she asked. "There's lots more paella."

"No thanks. I appreciate your hospitality. This was lovely."

He needed his Toby fix.

He thought he would just stop in and give his sleeping son a kiss goodnight, but Toby was still up though it was almost eleven. He was lying in bed, eyes wide open, curled on his right side. The music his aides put on for him had ended. Preuss leaned over the bed and planted a wet one on the side of his face. Toby picked his head up and gave him a serious and thoughtful look that redeemed the day.

"How come you're still up?"

Toby hummed.

"Waiting for me to kiss you goodnight?"

A twitchy little smile.

"I brought something to listen to."

He took Elizaveta's CD out of its case and placed it in the tray of Toby's CD player. He sat in the chair beside Toby's bed and held his son's tight crooked hand while they listened to Elizaveta's vocal concert.

Rosa Martinez was right, she had an extraordinary talent. Accompanied by a piano, she sang classical and pop songs as well as a few show tunes. She had a honeyed, compelling voice that was almost otherworldly in its emotionality. He closed his eyes and lost himself in the music.

One song, an aria from the Rossini opera *Semiramide,* was so lovely it brought up the hairs on the back of his neck. Her cover of Leonard Cohen's "Hallelujah" made him forget the other three hundred versions.

He opened his eyes and saw Toby listening too, his wonderful brown eyes wide open and staring up at his father. Sometimes it seemed as if Toby could see more than people thought he could. Sometimes, like now, he seemed to be able to look right into your soul.

As the CD played, Preuss thought about the promise that had died with this young woman's death, and as he did he began to reflect on his own past. He remembered the life he had imagined for himself when he was a teenager. He never once thought about being a policeman. When he was younger he wanted to be a musician.

He began playing guitar when he was fourteen and knew at once he had found his instrument. In high school he was part of a series of bands that formed and dissolved with outlandish names: the Lumbering Lumberjacks of Death, the Rolodex of the Damned, Radiation Mutant Babies. He didn't care for the music of the '80s that was popular then but he loved the music of the '60s and '70s. Eric Clapton and some of the older bluesmen like Brownie McGhee and Sonny Terry, those were his inspirations and idols. He practiced for hours and saw his future self not as a rock star but as a gigging musician.

Then he met Jeanette and everything changed. They went together during their sophomore year at Michigan State University where his parents taught. When she got pregnant with Jason and refused to consider abortion, he began his junior year as a married man and knew he had to get serious about supporting a family. Her father was Nick Russo, at that time a sergeant with the Ferndale Police Department, and he convinced Preuss that the life of a policeman was both a value to society and, at times, exciting enough to satisfy a young man's urge for adventure.

And in general Preuss found the work worthwhile. He avoided both extremes of becoming too cynical and too careless, did well, and got on . . . until Jeanette died, and Russo turned against him with such a vengeance.

Listening to Elizaveta (now singing Irving Berlin's "What'll I Do"; she had an amazing range) he thought about his own early promise and how he had if not squandered it then failed to steward it.

He looked at Toby, who by this time had fallen asleep. Russo took his anger at Preuss out on Toby, refusing to have anything to do with the boy. Luckily for Toby, Russo's ex-wife adored her grandson and made her home in Traverse City wheelchair accessible to accommodate Toby's monthly visits.

If his life had followed a different course, if he and Jeanette had never married or if they split up after Jason was born (he had pondered both at different times), there would have been no Toby. And Preuss knew in his heart no different kind of life would be worth giving up Toby. The sight of his son—so beautiful, so peaceful, so vulnerable—reminded Preuss how the boy brought out aspects of his character he never could have predicted or understood but which constituted his best self.

When Elizaveta sang the last song ("Here, There, and Everywhere") and the final applause died away, he popped the CD from the player. In the silence he heard Toby's gentle purring. It extinguished the anguish and regret that gnawed in his chest and filled him with gratitude for the way everything in his life, every good decision and every bad one, every success and every failure, had conspired to bring him here, to the peaceful sleeping figure in this room.

23

The man on the other end of the phone said, "He wants to talk to you." His voice low, calm and serious as always, even mechanical. "Soon."

"What about?"

"How about you call him and find out?"

"Why you gotta give me such a hard time about everything?"

"I'm not getting the feeling you're taking this seriously, that's all."

"Jesus, I'll call him, all right?" Elton Deetz said.

He rolled his eyes and held his hand up and made a yack-ety-yack gesture with his thumb and the tips of his fingers for the benefit of the man behind the bar at the Shamrock Pub on Dequindre in Madison Heights. The bartender's mouth curled in a humorless grin and he ambled to the other end of the bar.

"Now," the other man said, and disconnected.

Deetz snapped the cell phone closed. It was 11:30 but the place was still packed with the Thursday night crowd, working class guys trying to get a break from their terrible lives.

Deetz took a long drink from his bottle of Bud and belched. The sound system cranked up with some Aerosmith and he start-ed to sway his shoulders to it, feeling the music, feeling good, glad he wasn't one of the losers that populated this dive.

He drained the Bud and went outside.

He was a tall man with a perpetual sneer on his face, as though the world had said something bad about his mother and he was contemplating giving it a beating. He had thin blond hair worn long and combed all the way back and he had a sparse goatee. He wore a black Harley tee shirt with tight Levis.

He strolled down the sidewalk to get away from the noise from the pub. Got his errand boy to call. What's going on now, he wondered.

His back to the street, he ducked into a doorway and took a small vial from his pocket. He opened the vial, sprinkled some powder on the side of his hand between his thumb and forefinger, and snorted it up one nostril. He shook his head from the rush and punched in the number on his cell.

"Hey," he said when he got through. "It's me."

"There's trouble."

"What kind?"

"About the other night. Word's getting around mighty fast."

"What do you mean?"

"I mean the wrong people know about it."

"Already? How is that possible?"

"I don't know, Elton. You got any ideas?"

"How should I know? What, you think I'm spreading the word myself?"

"You better find out who is. And then you better do something about it. There's some open mouths that need to be closed. Fast."

"Yeah yeah, no worries. I'll take care of it," Deetz said, not quite sure how but not wanting to come across as clueless.

"One more thing. Those parts you ordered? They're ready for pickup."

Deetz disconnected and opened his vial of powder again and tapped some on the side of his hand and sniffed it up the other nostril.

He stood there, letting the juice spread throughout his body, warming it up and cooling it down at the same time.

He had a thought.

He made another call. The line rang until a voice told him the Verizon customer wasn't available.

He'd told the kid to stay near the phone.

He thought about what he was going to do now with something like pleasure.

On the way back into the Shamrock one of his regulars at the bar loomed in front of him, an ugly hulking man Deetz had done business with many times. Even in the dark Deetz could see his eyes were red-rimmed and there was the sharp smell of need coming off him.

"Hey brother," Deetz said. "Same as always?"

He drove his midnight black Camaro down Woodward to State Fair, after the overpass from Ferndale at Eight Mile. He parked in front of a dilapidated two-story home where the windows were painted over with black paint and the weeds grew leggy and thick on the lawn.

A raggedy-ass old white guy with a pony tale and heavy stubble stood smoking on the porch with a young black guy in a do-rag. When the old guy saw the Camaro he flung his cigarette into the bushes and strolled down to the street and leaned his head into the car, the black guy close behind him.

Deetz said, "'Sup, Worm? Everything cool?"

"Busy night. Glad to see you, though."

"Bet you are."

Worm held out his hand behind him and the black guy gave him a small greasy paper sack. Worm passed it through the car's open window to Deetz. "Present for you," Worm said.

Deetz reached over and took the sack, then handed Worm the blue and grey Detroit Lions travel bag beside him on the passenger seat. Worm handed it to the black guy, who took it up the front walk into the house.

"Time for a beer?" Worm asked.

"Not tonight. One more stop to make."

Deetz grabbed a handful of tie-dyed tee shirt and pulled the kid behind a dumpster at the side of the party store on Fourteen Mile in Clawson and threw him against the brick wall.

"Hey!" the kid said. "Watch my arm!"

"Or what?" Deetz cuffed him on the head. "Huh? Or what?"

The kid put his good arm up to defend himself but Deetz slapped it away and punched the kid in the face. His nose erupted in blood.

"What's that for?"

"Don't you ever change your clothes?"

"That's why you hit me?"

Deetz slapped him hard and turned him around and threw him face-first against the wall.

"Whyn't you answer my calls?"

"What calls?"

"I been trying to get you."

"My phone's out of minutes. Whaddaya want?"

Deetz leaned close to him, his big forearm pressing the back of the kid's neck.

"We got trouble, man," he whispered in the kid's ear. "Our little dance the other night? Turns out somebody was watching."

The kid turned his head and looked at Deetz with wide eyes. "Not possible."

"After you left I went back for a minute to get rid of the guy in the wheelchair. Know what I saw? A woman in the park watching us."

"Can't be."

Deetz pressed the kid's head into the bricks.

"She looked homeless. Must have seen the whole thing."

"So? Even if she was there, what could she see?"

"What she saw or didn't see, you got to take care of her."

"Why me?"

"This is your mess. Or did you forget that part?"

Deetz spun him around.

"You want to get through this in one piece, you'll find her and make sure she keeps her mouth shut. Forever. Understand?"

"Yeah."

"Don't make me tell you again."

"It's cool, dude, it's cool."

Deetz was about to turn away but slapped the kid's face hard and pulled at the cast on his arm for good measure, which brought a yelp of pain. As if that unlocked something inside him, he shoved the kid backwards against the wall again and grabbed a handful of the skanky shirt. He pulled the kid forward and stuck his foot out so the kid went facedown into the concrete of the alley.

Then Deetz gave him a pounding neither would forget.

Friday, June 11, 2010

24

In the morning Preuss found an envelope on his desk chair at the Shanahan with Reg Trombley's name printed in careful block letters. The return address was Robinson Photo Studios.

What was inside the envelope cheered him up a little: enhanced photos from the church security video. They weren't crystal clear but they were sharper than the original video. They still didn't show the face of the guy in the hoodie but they showed an image of Tie-Dyed that would allow for a reasonable comparison with the actual guy when they found him.

And they showed the numbers on the license plate of the AAAdvantage Painting van.

He ran the plate in the DMV system. William Simpson popped as the van's owner.

It was a name he had run into not long ago.

He pulled out the sheet with AAAdvantage employees and ran his finger down the list. There was a Billy Simpson with an address in Madison Heights matching the DMV record.

Gotcha.

On his way out to the parking lot he bumped into Tanya Corcoran.

"Just the man I want to see," she said. "You got a call from somebody who says he needs to get in touch. Says it's urgent." She held out a slip of paper with a name and phone number. "Said his name is Emmanuel Greene."

Preuss took the paper and ran the name through his mental index but couldn't place it. "He tell you what it's about?"

"No. Just that you're going to want to talk with him."

"Right, because he needs to know how I'm fixed for life insurance."

"Martin, I'm just the messenger, okay?"

He handed her back the slip. "I'm on my way out. Can you leave this on my desk? I'll look at it when I get back."

"Hank also gave you the CDRs for the Kertész woman. I'll leave those, too."

He parked in front of the paint company on Wyoming in Royal Oak Township. The side office was locked and empty. He walked straight through to the back where three men were loading the green van with tarps and paints and painting supplies. The broken down white van was still parked where it had been on his last visit.

"Help you?" one of the men said. He was wearing a coverall spattered with paint.

"I'm looking for Billy Simpson. He around today?"

"You mean Homer?" The other men guffawed.

"I thought his name is Billy."

"We call him Homer. For Homer Simpson. Those two, same smarts."

"Homer Simpleton," one of the men said. The others laughed.

Preuss said, "Where I can find him?"

"He didn't come in today. I were you, I'd check his house. He's probably under the covers, sleeping one off."

Preuss stood on the front stoop of the ranch house on Dorchester Street in Madison Heights and thought, Doesn't anyone work anymore? First Elizaveta's ex-husband who's a suspect in her murder (if not the prime suspect so far), and now this dude. No wonder nothing ever gets done right . . . nobody's ever on the job to do it.

The white Econoline from the surveillance video was parked in the driveway. Same plates, same lettering on the side, same ladder rig.

Preuss rang the doorbell and after a few minutes the inside front door swung open. Standing in the front entranceway was a heavy-set, lumpish man, early thirties, deep reddish tan on a blocky face and blond hair chopped into a brush cut.

"William Simpson?"

The man nodded and Preuss introduced himself and asked if he could come down to the Ferndale Police station.

"What for?"

"I want to ask you some questions about a case I'm working on."

The man kept looking at Preuss. He had a dim cast to his eyes that made Preuss wonder if he was retarded and that's what prompted the ridicule from his co-workers.

"Won't take long," Preuss said. "I'll have you back by noon."

"I guess. Can I text my sister so she'll know where I am? She always wants to know where I am."

"Go ahead."

Billy Simpson dug his phone out of his pants and stepped out onto the front stoop, closing the door behind him, and tapped in a message with thumbs on huge hands.

"You said Ferndale, right?"

25

The big interview room was taken so they had to sit in the smaller one. It was no bigger than a closet, just a tiny eight-by-six room with three walls made of concrete blocks and a window fronting the hallway. There were a table and three molded chairs, two on one side of the table and one on the other. It was a good room to impose maximum claustrophobia on an interview subject, but Preuss hated the close contact the room demanded even though that forced intimacy often worked to his advantage.

He put Simpson on the side of the table facing the concrete block wall.

"Billy," Preuss said, "as I was saying, I'm hoping you can clear up some questions for us."

"Sure." Simpson sat slumped, slack-jawed in his chair with his hands clasped between his legs.

"You work at AAAdvantage Painting?"

"Uh-huh."

"What do you do there?"

"I'm a house painter."

"Why aren't you working today?"

He gave Preuss a foolish grin. "I had a little too much to drink last night and couldn't get up in time. I'm okay now."

"You're feeling well enough to talk with me?"

"Uh-huh."

"Before we get started, I want you to understand a couple of things. The first is, you're not in custody. That means you can leave at any time. Do you understand that?"

"I guess."

"The second is, this is just a conversation between us, not an interrogation. If the discussion starts to veer into an area that may touch on your involvement in a crime, we'll stop and I'll inform you of your right to remain silent. Do you understand?"

Billy shrugged, said, "I guess."

"Good. Now, that Econoline parked in your driveway, is that yours?"

"Yeah."

"Where'd you get it?"

"I bought it."

"When?"

"Couple years ago."

"Who from?"

"Guy I work for."

"Al Campanella?"

"Yeah."

"Why does it still say the name of the company on it? It's not still used in company business, is it?"

"No. I tried to scrub off the lettering but it was too hard so I just left it all on. I figure I'll paint over it one of these days."

"Anybody else drive it besides you?"

"Nope."

"Your sister never drives it? Or anybody at work?"

"No. I wouldn't let those guys drive it."

"They give you a hard time, don't they?"

"Sometimes."

"Last Monday, did you drive it to work?"

"Sure."

"What about after work? Did you take it anywhere at night on Monday?"

"If I went anywhere, I guess I was driving it."

"I'm asking, did you go anywhere?"

"I don't remember."

On the table between them Preuss laid out copies of the photos of the van from the church security camera.

"Is that your van?"

Simpson took a close look at the photos. "Looks like it."

"Looks like it to me, too. These are pictures from the parking lot of the Ferndale Cornerstone Community United Lutheran Church from last Monday night. Do you remember being there?"

Preuss could see the wheels turning with difficulty as Billy Simpson tried to figure out what was going on here, and what would be the smart way to play this. It didn't look like he had much smart in him.

Preuss caught himself. Now he was thinking like the men Billy worked with.

He said, "There's a close-up of the license plate. It's registered to you, Billy."

Simpson was silent.

"In these photos you can't see who was behind the wheel. But it was you, wasn't it?"

Simpson looked at the photos again, as if there could be some doubt.

"Billy?"

"I'm not sure."

"Come on. You just told me you never let anybody else drive it."

"Yeah."

"So this is you, isn't it?"

"That was me."

"What were you doing there?"

Preuss waited while the wheels turned some more.

Finally Simpson said, "I gave somebody a ride."

"Who?"

"This guy I know."

"What's his name?"

Simpson screwed up his face as though trying to think hard. "Not sure I remember."

"You don't remember your buddy's name?"

"I didn't say he was my buddy, I just said it was a guy I know."

Preuss dealt another photo in front of him. He pointed to the man in the hoodie. "This guy?"

Another long pause.

"What's this guy's name, Billy?"

"I don't want to get anybody in any trouble."

"I know. But this guy, Billy? I need his name."

Now Simpson began to squirm in his chair.

Preuss leaned forward as if he were going to tell him something confidential.

"Because see in this other picture? There was another vehicle, a minibus. Inside there was a young guy in a wheelchair. Did you know that?"

Billy shook his head.

"Didn't think so. Somebody took him off this minibus and left him in the middle of this parking lot after you drove away. And then stole the bus. Can you imagine how scared this kid was, left in the parking lot by himself? At night? A guy with handicaps, in a wheelchair?"

Simpson swallowed hard.

"Can you imagine that, Billy?"

"Yes."

"And there was a woman driving that bus before this guy"— Preuss tapped the face of the young man in the tie-dyed tee shirt—"stole it. But you know what? She's dead, Billy. Somebody killed her."

"She's dead?"

Preuss nodded. "And she left behind a little eleven-year-old girl who doesn't have a mother anymore. Can you imagine how she feels right now?"

Simpson didn't answer and Preuss said, "I want to find out who did this."

"It wasn't me."

"But I think one of these guys did, and you need to tell me everything you know about them. Because you want to see justice done, don't you, Billy? For that little girl who lost her mother?"

Before Simpson could answer, there was a knock at the glass wall of the interview room. Paul Horvath stood in the hall.

Preuss waved him inside and Horvath said, "Detective, can I speak with you?"

"Wait right there, Billy," Preuss said. He followed Horvath out into the hall.

"You have to stop," Horvath said.

"Why?"

"Mr. Simpson's sister's in Reception and she's hopping mad. She doesn't want you talking to him."

"I'm making progress here. This guy's almost ready to give me a name."

"Doesn't matter. You have to let him go."

Preuss went out to the reception area in the front of the station, where a woman who looked to be a little older than Billy Simpson was pacing. Where he was heavy, she was round and more voluptuous, though they were both from the same gene pool.

"I'm Detective Preuss."

"Do you have my brother back there?" She was fuming.

"Is your brother Billy Simpson?"

"Yes. You shouldn't be talking to him without a lawyer. Did you read him his rights?"

"I'm sorry, who am I speaking with?"

"Don't you worry about who I am. You let my brother go."

"Your brother isn't suspected of anything. He's not being detained. He's helping me with one of my cases."

"That's bullshit, excuse my French. You can see he's slow and you're taking advantage of him just by him being here. I want you to let him go right now."

She was right, of course, he was taking advantage of Billy. And he didn't have enough to hold him for suspicion of murder. Even if he charged Simpson, any arraignment judge would bounce the case.

"He's not being held for anything. He's giving me information."

"You bring him out here right now so I can take him home. And if you don't, I'm getting a lawyer."

"He's an adult, he can speak with us if he wants to. I made sure he understands he's free to go."

She flashed a sheet of paper in front of him. "This says I'm his legal guardian. And I say he comes out. Now."

Preuss returned to his office and closed the door. He was shut out from Elizaveta's killing, and now he was shut out from making headway in the minibus disappearance. Oh for two.

He sat at his desk and stared at the clutter of papers and files. Why even bother continuing to do this? he thought. Why not ditch this job and these people and the gross, abject stupidity and meanness that filled his days? Could he say he was making a difference anymore?

His desk phone rang. He stared at it, incensed that even this was interrupting his forward motion today. He couldn't even sit there and think dismal thoughts.

He picked the receiver up and barked into it. "What!"

After a few moments of silence, the voice on the other end said, "Detective Preuss?"

"Yes?" Softer this time. "Who am I speaking with?"

"This is Emmanuel Greene. I'm a friend of Max Halperin. I think he mentioned me to you?"

"Mr. Greene, I don't have time to speak with you right now."

"Detective, I really think we should talk."

26

One of the running gags throughout *A Hard Day's Night* is the big deal everybody makes about Paul McCartney's grandfather being a clean old man. That was the first thing that popped into Martin Preuss's head when he met Emmanuel Greene . . . such a clean old man. Tall, straight, slender, he was turned out in a fitted navy blue suit, with slicked-back steel grey hair and keen searching eyes behind round silver metal frames.

And Preuss thought he couldn't be a day under eighty.

Emmanuel Greene was already waiting for him at the Starbucks on Main Street in Royal Oak, sitting in a booth at the rear of the shop with one leg crossed elegantly over the other.

They shook hands and Greene held up a container of coffee. "I took the liberty. I didn't put anything in it so you can add what you want. It's their basic too-expensive coffee. Fixings are over there." He pointed to the counter with metal containers of milk and cream and sweeteners.

"I take it black."

"You may regret that," Greene said. "I can't abide their coffee without adulterating it with as much cream and sugar as I can stand."

"So why are we meeting here?"

"Convenience. It's midway between my office and your station. And this time of day it's quiet and I thought you could get here without a problem."

"I did."

Preuss took a sip of coffee, which was strong and bitter. Greene watched him for his reaction.

"Was I right?" the older man said.

Preuss shrugged. "I've had worse."

"I'm a coffee snob, I admit it. I roast my own beans and there's nothing quite like the smell and taste of fresh roasted coffee. Anyway, where we meet is immaterial. The important thing is we speak."

"You're the friend Max told me about."

"I am. I've known him for years. He told me about that poor young woman, Elizaveta Kertész." He pronounced it the way Halperin had, CARE-tase.

Preuss held his hand up. "Mr. Greene, before you—"

"Manny, please."

"Before we go any further, I should tell you Elizaveta's death is not my case anymore. If you have information about it, you should be getting in touch with Detective Hank Bellamy. I'll give you his number."

"You're the one I want."

"Why?"

"Max said you were a good man. That means a lot, coming from Max."

"I've known him a grand total of five minutes," Preuss said. "He stepped in at the last second to help me with an interview."

"They must have been a good five minutes, because you impressed him. Max is a hard man to impress."

Greene withdrew a business card from his jacket pocket and handed it to Preuss. "That's me."

The card read *Greene Investigation Services*. Underneath those words was a Michigan PI license number.

Preuss put the card on the table between them and looked at Greene.

"I'm eighty-three," Greene said. "In case you were wondering."

"I was. Don't take this the wrong way, but most of the PIs I know retire long before they get to be your age."

Greene smiled. "I came to it late. I work as an investigator for one personal injury attorney. Low risk, high reward. I leave the derring-do to the youngsters."

"What's your interest in Elizaveta?"

"Like you, I want to know who killed her."

"Did you know her?"

"I did. She was extraordinary. It's a cliché to say someone is 'full of life,' but in her case it was true. Just being around her made you feel good about being alive."

"What do you know about how she died?"

"Nothing about who killed her. But when Max told me she was dead, I thought she might have been killed because of what she was involved in."

"If you have a theory of the crime, I'm listening."

"I don't know if I'd dignify it by calling it a 'theory.' If you'll indulge me, I'll tell you a story. And at the end of it if you're not interested, there's no harm done and you got an expensive cup of bad coffee out of the deal."

"You have my attention, Manny."

"Then my story starts with an accidental encounter," Greene began.

"Five years ago, a group of friends took a woman out to dinner for her ninetieth birthday. The woman's name was Netty Cohen. A remarkable woman. There are two important things to know about her. The first is, she's a Holocaust survivor. She was eating dinner with her friends, and all of a sudden she started screaming her head off. Nobody could figure out what the matter was at first—her friends thought she might be having a stroke—but once they got her calmed down she told them she thought she'd just seen a man she recognized from the concentration camp she was in during the Second World War. One of the guards from that camp, a particularly brutal individual named Bogdan Kovalenko.

"He was in a wheelchair but she recognized him. There are some nightmares you never forget, no matter how hard you try."

Greene took a sip of his coffee, made a face, and pushed it away.

"When she got home that night, Netty called me, and this is the second important thing about her. She's the widow of one of my cousins, the one who got me into doing the work that led me to get my PI license. He was an attorney, you see, and I started out doing occasional process serving for him to help him out. I got into more and more investigative situations until he suggested I'd be more useful if I were a licensed private investigator. Prior to that I ran a men's hat store downtown. Maybe you've heard of it—Manny the Hatter, in the Fox Theatre Building?"

"In fact I have," Preuss said. "Years ago there used to be a magic store in that spot, right on Woodward Avenue. My older boy was interested in magic when he was little and I used to take him down there to buy tricks."

Until he grew up and made himself disappear, Preuss thought.

Greene said, "I took the shop over when the magician died and I turned it into a hattery. I started small, then took over the entire ground floor. We even opened a shop in Oak Park before I turned it all over to my son. Not the kind of preparation you'd expect for a PI, but there you have it.

"When Netty talked to me, I believed her. She asked me to find out if this man was the guard she remembered, and if so she wanted to see justice done. So I found a researcher in the History Department at Wayne State who specialized in World War II atrocities."

Preuss's cell phone rang, but he silenced it. "Sorry," he said.

"As luck would have it," the older man went on, "this woman was making plans for a trip to Russia to do research in Soviet-era archives that had been opened to the West. She was interested in my story, and she made a point of looking for Kovalenko. She found someone by that name who'd served as a guard at some of the worst concentration camps in occupied Poland. Among the documents she found was Kovalenko's identity certificate showing his place and date of birth. And she discovered he had indeed settled in America. When she returned to Detroit, she let me know what she found.

"What do you think so far?"

"So far it's fascinating. But I'm waiting for the connection to Elizaveta Kertész."

"Patience, Martin. This is all prelude."

27

Sheila Hawkins hung her head over the plastic bucket and combed her hair down one side in a long straight fall.

She ran the comb through her mane several times, starting from the nape of her neck and drawing it straight over her head and down the right side of her hair. The comb was missing several teeth and she liked the way it separated her tresses into uneven furrows. It felt like she was in a cavern beside a waterfall, shut away but at the same time open to the afternoon air.

The comb wrung tepid water into the bucket. When she had gotten it from the drinking fountain at the baseball field on the other side of the park from where she sat, the water was hot from being in the fountain in the sun. The bucket was a battered five-gallon orange container from Home Depot that she found after a picnic one day in the spring. The picnickers—members of a family reunion, from all appearances—had left it behind among a sea of garbage overflowing the trash containers.

The water dripped from her hair into the bucket as she squatted beside it. Sometimes the roar of I-75 near the park reminded her of the ocean. She remembered the sound of the ocean from when she was a girl in California where she lived with her parents before they split up. That was a long time ago, before her family cut all connections with her and left her on her own, at the mercy of her terrible memories—the ones from Afghanistan, from the scars inside and out from all the the men who beat her, from the beautiful little son she loved with all her heart but who was taken away in the arms of the state workers who paid no attention to her pleas . . .

A spasm of anger shot through her, as it always did when she thought about her past and all its bad luck and heartache. She stopped combing and squeezed her eyes shut. "Stop," she hissed to the trees and grass. "Stop!"

After she left the army she was institutionalized when she was found wandering the streets in Henderson, Nevada. The shrinks tried to teach her to handle her anger by reestablishing control over it.

When she calmed herself she resumed combing her hair with slow and methodical strokes as though putting herself into a trance. She loved how it felt.

The drops falling from her hair sounded like water dripping in a cave. Plink, plunk. There was even a tiny echo inside the bucket and a little atoll of soap bubble floating on the surface of the water.

She drew the comb through her hair a few more times, then placed the comb on the grass beside the bucket and with both hands wrung out the long strands. When it was wet, her hair was almost three feet long. When it was dry it was fluffy and curly, her proudest possession.

She wrung as much water out as she could and waggled her head and then flicked it all back in a solid wet mass and let it slap, sodden and cold, against her back. It felt so good it made her laugh out loud.

She gave a sigh of contentment. The feel of her hair. The warm breeze. A full stomach from the food pantry. These were small mercies. Of such was her life filled, and they were enough. Many people didn't even have these, she knew.

See, she told herself. They add up. Stay positive, the shrinks at the Seven Hills Behavioral Institute taught her. Tell yourself life was good and it would be.

Martin Road Park was her home during the warm weather. That police detective was trying to do the right thing by finding her a place to stay. She was willing to think the best of his efforts. (Stay positive.) But she couldn't stand to be cooped up with four walls and a ceiling and a door shutting her in from the world, all just so she could receive mail, which she didn't want to get anyway. She only agreed to stay because he promised to take her to see Tom, and when he went back on his word she left to return to the park. Her home.

Today, as most days, there were no people at the park. Sometimes at night people came, families and young kids playing baseball on teams. If people came, she tried to keep out of sight. The contacts she had with people were usually unpleasant. The young men who came at night taunted her with verbal insults, and when the boys had been drinking the exchanges turned violent. A few times the attacks became sexual until she pulled the knife she kept in a sheath tied to her leg and the young bastards ran for it.

The police confiscated her knife and never gave it back so the sheath was empty.

But tonight, with no one here, she thought she wouldn't need it. She was happy. She would be happier if Tom could be here. She told the police detective she called him Tom because he looked like Tom Hanks, but really that was the name of the son who was taken from her. Tom's father was a platoon leader she met incountry just before her tour ended. He looked her up when he returned stateside and it wasn't until she was pregnant that he told her he was already married.

Then after her little boy was born, the rat bastard had her declared unfit and took custody of her beautiful son.

Now she wondered how both her Toms were, and her heart flared in fury against the policeman for telling her he would take her to see her new Tom and then breaking his promise.

Another man who betrayed her. Anyone who believed men and their lies was a fool, she thought.

Her anger wound tighter and tighter until she felt like her chest was caught in a vise. She held her fists up to the side of her head and hissed, "Stop! Stop!"

In a few minutes this episode passed. She turned the orange bucket upside down and dumped the water out and the bucket became a seat. She settled herself on it and closed her eyes, basking in the smells and feel of the day. She imagined both Toms were with her, the one she found and the one she gave birth to as he would be today. She pretended they were all chatting about the loveliness of the day.

Stay positive. Life is good.

She did not hear the man sneaking up on her. She opened her eyes in time to see a flash of dull white as he pulled a pillowcase over her head. She grabbed for her knife but it was gone.

She struggled against him and almost got herself free but he pounded all the air out of her body and then wailed on her head with something hard through the fabric of the pillowcase until she lost the strength to fight.

He dragged her over the grass and wrestled her into the trunk of a car. The light of day filtering through the cotton around her head disappeared as he slammed the trunk closed and she was trapped in the airless enclosed space as the car sped away from Martin Road Park.

28

"Elizaveta emigrated from Hungary," Emmanuel Greene said.

"She lost all of her family during the war, except for her father, whose name was Baruch. Along with 12,000 other Jews, Baruch and his parents and brothers were sent to the Trawniki camp, a slave labor camp in occupied Poland. Baruch alone survived, which was a miracle in itself since virtually all the other prisoners there were exterminated. After the war, he tried to put his life back together in Hungary. He married and started a family. In the eighties Hungary was hard hit by the global recession, and Baruch moved his family to America and settled in Cincinnati, where there were relatives who escaped from Europe before the war. According to Elizaveta he never spoke a word about his time in the camp until right before he died. He told her about his experiences, including those with the violent psychopath Bogdan Kovalenko.

"After her father died, what he told her weighed on her mind so much she decided to go to Washington D.C. to do research in the Holocaust Memorial Museum's collection on war criminals. She wanted to find out what happened to Bogdan Kovalenko."

"And she saw the work your researcher did?"

"No, this was before Professor Steinhart published her research. Elizaveta did it all on her own. She discovered Kovalenko had indeed come to America and was thought to be living in the Detroit area. But she couldn't find an address. There was no record of anyone with that name in the metropolitan Detroit region. If he adopted a new name, as many did, she didn't know what it was so she couldn't find him."

"So she did all this independently of you?"

"Yes. We hadn't met yet. She was so determined to find this man she moved up here with her husband and daughter. Though her life took several sharp turns once she got here, including a break-up with her husband."

"Who seems to have re-appeared in her life. Do you know anything about that?"

He shook his head. "She never talked about that part of her life. I intuited things weren't going well for her, but I didn't pry. She kept her private life private."

He sighed. "When she moved up here from Ohio, she visited the Holocaust Memorial Center in Farmington Hills. They have an extensive research collection related to the extermination of European Jewry. She didn't find anything new about Kovalenko, but the people there put her in touch with me because of my previous work with Kovalenko. For the past couple of years Elizaveta and I have been working together to find him. We assumed he adopted a different name but with the large number of Poles and Slavs in this part of Michigan it was like finding a needle in a haystack."

"What did she want to do once she found him?"

"I asked her. She wouldn't tell me."

"What's your sense?"

Greene drew a thumb across his throat. "Taking her revenge for a crime that still beggars understanding. That's the only thing that would explain her drive to seek him out."

"Were you close to finding him?"

Greene reached into a leather satchel by his feet and withdrew a manila file folder and opened it on the table.

"Meet John Kowalczyk," Greene said. "AKA Bogdan Kovalenko."

Preuss looked at a headshot of an unsmiling man in his 60s with a doughy bulldog's face, heavy around the jowls and with cold sleepy eyes. "Passport photo?"

"Yes."

Preuss skimmed the information in the attached dossier. He lived in Sterling Heights, and was retired from the Chrysler Assembly Plant. He had a wife, deceased, and a daughter.

"How did you get this?"

"What do they say in New York? I know a guy who knows a guy."

"How long have you had it?"

"I just got it from my source on Monday."

"This past Monday?"

"Yes."

"Did Elizaveta know?"

"Yes, but she didn't get it from me. My source told her before he told me."

"When was the last time you spoke with her?"

"It's been a few weeks. Before Memorial Day."

"I'd like the name of your source. It might be important for establishing the timeline of her last days."

"Sorry, that's not possible."

"Why not?"

"If you knew this individual, you'd know he wouldn't take to having his name mentioned. Especially to a policeman."

"This is a murder investigation. You have to cooperate. If it comes to it, I'll subpoena you."

Greene thought about that.

"How things work, Manny."

Greene said, "Let me talk with him first. He'll never speak to you unless I tell him you're okay."

"You need to do it fast."

"I'll call him as soon as I get back to my office."

"Have you spoken with Kovalenko?"

"I tried. I went to his house but his daughter slammed the door in my face. I was hoping if we went there together, she'd be more inclined to talk."

Now it was Preuss's turn to say, "Sorry, that's not possible."

Greene smiled. "Touché. If you speak with him, will you at least let me know what you find? I have as much interest in knowing what happened to that young woman as you do. More, maybe, since I knew her. Her death hit me hard. Such a lovely girl . . . so much to live for."

"I can do that," Preuss said. He took out his notebook and copied down Greene's information about Bogdan Kovalenko, then handed the file back to Greene. "Many thanks."

Preuss gave Greene one of his own business cards. "My cell number's on it. Call me as soon as you talk with your guy, all right?"

"I will."

The older man reached across the table and offered Preuss a hand. "Let's hope the two of us can get some justice for that poor young woman."

29

The call that came in while he was talking with Emmanuel Greene was from the secretary at the Ferndale Cornerstone Community United Lutheran Church. Sitting in the car after leaving Greene, Preuss called her back and she told him she had seen Sheila Hawkins at the food pantry that afternoon.

He drove to the church but Sheila wasn't inside. The food service was over and the Fellowship Hall was clean and empty. Outside he crossed the broad lawn of the park to where she had been making her camp. He saw an overturned orange Home Depot bucket and her belongings scattered over the ground.

With an electric pulse of fear coursing through him he recognized the comb with missing teeth and the bits and pieces of her life he had sorted through earlier . . . dolls and wrist watches and dog leashes spread around as if somebody had kicked her plastic bags and the contents spilled out.

He was certain she was in trouble. This was his fault, he knew. If he had remembered to take her to see Zach Warranow as he promised, she would have stayed at the motel room the shelter arranged for her and she never would have gone back to the park.

Steady, he told himself. You don't know that. She might have left the motel anyway. She was a woman who had problems. If she could think the way you do she wouldn't be living on the street, so don't beat yourself up about this.

Yeah right. Make excuses for yourself all you want, Preuss told himself. This one's on you.

He returned to the Shanahan and put out a BOLO on the missing woman. In his office he sat with his head in his hands and forced himself to think.

There could be any number of explanations for where she might have gone . . . she could have run off and decided to bunk in another park. Something or somebody might have scared her away and she left without her stuff, maybe planning to return but maybe just leaving everything behind to start over. Kids might have rummaged through her belongings . . . the homeless earned little respect.

Those were possible, but not likely. As with most people who had no shelter, her stuff was important to her, regardless of how insignificant it might seem to others. She wouldn't have just left it all behind.

She might have been picked up by one of the other police agencies, maybe the Hazel Park police since Martin Road Park was near the border of Ferndale and Hazel Park.

By far the worst alternative, and to Preuss's mind the most inescapable, was that somebody from the surveillance video saw her watching them and snatched her to keep her quiet. If that happened, and the same people were the ones who killed Elizaveta Kertész, then Sheila Hawkins was in a world of trouble.

"Martin?"

Reg Trombley standing in the doorway.

"Looking shaky there, my brother," Trombley said. "Everything okay?"

Preuss shook his head. "Sheila Hawkins dropped out of sight."

"That's not good."

"One of many things going wrong right now. On the bright side, I found the unknown driver from the church."

Preuss told him about his interrupted interview with Billy Simpson.

"So he put himself at the scene that night," Preuss said. "We'll have to get him back in here with a lawyer, but at least we know he was driving the second van. Even though we couldn't see his face so his lawyer won't even break a sweat getting any case against him thrown out. What's happening with you?"

"Got news about the ex-husband. A buddy of mine in the Macomb County Sheriff's Office told me Scott Furlong just surfaced in the Macomb County Jail in Mt. Clemens. He was in a fight last night and he's awaiting arraignment for assault."

"Great news. When can you talk with him?"

"Well, here's the thing. I just bumped into Bellamy."

"And you told him about it."

"He asked me, Martin. I had to tell him. He wants to interview Furlong himself. Says it's his case."

"Yeah."

"Sorry."

"No, don't apologize. Let me know what Bellamy finds, okay?"

"Soon as I know."

Preuss told Trombley about his meeting with Emmanuel Greene.

"Wait'll you hear what he told me."

Afterwards Preuss and Trombley debated whether Preuss should follow the leads Greene had given him. With his usual impetuosity, Trombley was all for Preuss going for it. Yet the Kertész case wasn't Preuss's, and he had been warned not to pursue it.

And Preuss knew that going off half-cocked on his own could destroy whatever case they could build against the young singer's killer.

"But Martin," Trombley said, "you know in your heart they're connected, right?"

"It's impossible to think they're not."

"Okay then. If you follow this, you might find what happened to the minibus she was driving. And that *is* what you're charged with."

When their conversation ended Trombley got up to leave, then paused at the doorway to Preuss's office.

"Did you hear Gail Crimmonds passed the sergeant's exam?"

"No. But that's terrific."

"Great future ahead of her."

"At least somebody has one."

Preuss spent the rest of the afternoon on a new case, interviewing a clerk at one of the retail shops on Nine Mile accused of ringing up partial sales and pocketing the difference. Then he walked down to Christine's, a storefront restaurant serving Eastern European cuisine in the strip mall at the corner of Nine and Hilton. He ordered beef stroganoff and potato pancakes, thinking the talk with Emmanuel Greene might have put him in the mood for this food.

Walking back to the Shanahan, he thought about Trombley's argument. The younger detective was right, and under normal circumstances it would be natural to pursue Kovalenko. But that assumed the squad was working together, which wasn't happening here. Russo kept throwing obstacles in his path to isolate Preuss and move him out of the department.

He considered accepting the futility of struggling against it. Instead he would find alternative routes to get where he needed to go. As Toby taught him, there were always ways to work within the restrictions of situations. His son went with the flow of his own capabilities and lived a quality life that he loved.

Preuss could do the same. If he could just figure out how.

When he got back to the station he picked up Elizaveta's Call Detail Records that Tanya had given him earlier. He couldn't resist looking through them.

Bellamy had already worked his way through the numbers so the copy was annotated with his spidery handwriting marking the names associated with the numbers and in most cases the relationship to Elizaveta.

Preuss had to admit this was thorough work . . . Bellamy could be good police when he put his mind to it. Preuss had no such hopes for Bellamy's administrative chops if he should get the job of chief of detectives.

Two numbers had no annotations. He called one number that had several incoming and outgoing calls, the last for twelve minutes on the Monday before Elizaveta disappeared. It rang eight times and went to a recording that said the recipient had not set up call messaging and disconnected with an abrupt "Goodbye!"

The other number came through at 3:27 on the Monday Elizaveta disappeared and lasted for six minutes. When he called that number he heard the characteristic series of rapid beeps of an exchange that was no longer in service. He guessed the phone was a burner.

He tossed the sheath of papers on his desk. Not my case, he thought.

Not my circus, not my monkeys.

His cell phone rang.

Emmanuel Greene.

"Got a pencil? I have the name and number of my source for information about Kovalenko. He's waiting for your call."

Preuss thanked him and disconnected. The number was identical to the first number he had just tried. So Elizaveta had been in touch with whoever owned this number.

He decided it would be both foolish and bad police work to ignore this.

He punched in the number again. The call was answered this time though no one said anything until Preuss said, "Hello?"

When there was still no sound from the other end, Preuss said, "I'm a friend of Manny Greene's. He said you're expecting me."

There were a few seconds of silence and then a ragged male voice said, "'Bout damn time."

Saturday, June 12, 2010

30

Preuss woke before the birds again. He showered and shaved and stood at the counter in his kitchen brewing coffee and gazing out the window into the back yard. It was too early to go to Toby's so he took a cup of coffee out to the deck.

He stretched out on the lounge chair. Though it wasn't yet light out, the day was already warm. He closed his eyes.

He must have dozed off. He jumped awake at the sound of his phone.

His head cleared when he saw who it was, and he smiled. "Hello, stranger."

"Is this the soon-to-be chief of detectives?" Janey Cahill said.

"Wrong number. You want Henry Bellamy."

"For real? Where are you getting that from?"

"Just a feeling. Nothing'll be announced till after Russo's appointment. Look, I'm in too good a mood to go into it right now. I'll tell you later. Where are you?"

"Home. We rolled in late last night."

"I thought you were gone till tomorrow."

"That was the original plan. Tommy got a call about a job that starts today so we came home early."

Her husband Tommy was a union carpenter who often had to travel out of town to find work because there hadn't been much for him around the area during the past few years. After the financial crash of 2008, construction work disappeared and hadn't rebounded yet.

"It's not bad," Cahill said. "I can't take too much time off with the family anyway. I start to get palpitations."

"Relaxing does that to me, too. Why I do so little of it. How was Myrtle Beach?"

"Hot as hell. Kids loved it, though. Where are you?"

"Home." He looked at the time on his phone. "In a little while I'm heading over to Toby's."

"Got plans for the day?"

"I was thinking about going to the zoo."

"Want company?"

"Sure."

"Great. I'll bring the boys. We'll make a day of it."

Toby was still sleeping when Preuss began to shave him. His seizure medication gave Toby a heavier beard than he should have for his age though his skin was still tender.

Preuss moved the disposable razor down one side of Toby's face with the grain of his beard, then drew it up against the grain. The boy began to squirm. He had trouble making the transition from sleep to waking and now he started snuffling and snorting and gasping and shrugging his narrow shoulders as he made the long trek up to wakefulness.

A quick seizure grabbed hold of him and his muscles locked and his mouth formed a tight grimace as though he were struggling hard against what gripped him. Preuss stopped shaving and wrapped his son in a hug. The only thing to do was comfort him till the seizure passed.

Toby whimpered and then went limp and smiled. That was the end of it. Preuss said, "Did that hit the funny button?"

Awake now, Toby tolerated his father touching his face. Preuss gazed down at this son and marveled—yet again—at how Toby handled his physical and mental limitations with such grace and courage. He loved his life. He enjoyed every second.

By the time Preuss finished the shave, the aide came around to get Toby dressed and ready for their day.

There was a long wait at the Big Boy on John R in Madison Heights, their usual Saturday morning stop, so he circled back to Nello's on Woodward Avenue in Royal Oak.

Preuss pushed Toby in his wheelchair up close to a table by the plate glass window overlooking traffic. They had been here before so the server recognized them and gave Toby an elaborate greeting that brought a squeal of joy from him.

Toby had finished his morning feeding in his g-tube before they left his house. Preuss didn't have much of an appetite but he tried to get as much of the bacon and eggs down as he could.

He struggled to the end of it and the busboy swept the plate away and the server came back to refill his coffee. Just what he needed, more caffeine.

Preuss sat back in his chair and laid out the events of the Kertész case, including all the political infighting, since the last time they talked about it. As usual, Toby listened intently, watching his father out of the corner of his beautiful almond-shaped brown eyes. He held his favorite set of red rings, which he would bang down on the tray of his wheelchair as though to punctuate something his father had said.

He told Toby about his conversation with Emmanuel Greene, and explained what happened when he spoke with Billy Simpson. When he told Toby about the concentration camps, Toby said, "Oooohhhhh," and when he mentioned Kovalenko's involvement Toby said, "Um." It was as appropriate a pronouncement as was possible to have. Though it was hard to tell what Toby really understood, he seemed to have a gift for sensing the emotional climate of situations and responding appropriately.

At times he could even echo what was said to him, as when his father told him he loved him and Toby responded with what sounded like "I love you, Dad."

"The other problem is," Preuss continued, "that woman who doesn't have a place to live is missing. I'm afraid something's happened to her."

"Num," Toby said.

"You think she's okay? Do you know where I can find her?"

Toby raised his shoulders up toward his ears.

"Yeah," said Preuss, "neither do I."

He took another sip of coffee. Toby seemed to be considering it all too. Then he burst out with a chirp of laughter.

Preuss reached a hand across the table to cup Toby's face in his palm. The boy copped a nose rub against the fleshy part of Preuss's thumb. Preuss never would have believed his heart could hold as much love as it did for this child. He loved his older son, but he had to admit Jason's constant testing and rejection of him tried Preuss's feelings for the boy—sometimes past the breaking point.

But there was no limit to the love Toby kindled. And returned.

The day turned out to be scorching hot, but in the middle of the afternoon a breeze picked up that gave some relief. The Detroit Zoo on Ten Mile at Woodward in Royal Oak was mobbed.

Preuss was happier than he thought he would be when he saw Janey Cahill marching her two boys toward the gift shop by the entrance where they had agreed to meet. Small and tightly wound, her wild ungovernable hair peeking out in electric blonde curls from her Tiger's baseball cap, she flashed a broad smile when she caught sight of him standing with Toby. They hugged and he realized he had missed her. She hugged Toby and Preuss hugged her two sons, who squirmed in discomfort at all these shows of affection.

Walking around the grounds of the zoo, he and Cahill chatted nonstop about her vacation, his cases, his increasing isolation within the Detective Bureau, the imminent departure of Chief William Warnock, the all-but-certain investiture of Nick Russo as the next chief, and the calamitous prospect of Hank Bellamy becoming the next chief of detectives.

Their chatter was interrupted by her shouted warnings to her children who were frisky as the otters in the otter house. At two o'clock they sat together in the cafeteria while he gave Toby his afternoon meds, squirting the syringes into his g-tube port, then following it with a rinse. Preuss hooked up Toby's afternoon feed.

Cahill stroked Toby's shoulder. "How are you doing, sweetheart?"

Limp and wiped out from the heat, Toby gave her a wan grin.

"You're such a flirt."

She bent to kiss the top of Toby's head. She patted Preuss's arm. "How are you holding up?"

"Hanging in there. You?"

"Been better."

"What's going on?"

"Tommy and I are splitting up."

"No."

"We've been tiptoeing around this for a long time. As you may or may not know."

"It's been clear things weren't going well. I figured you'd tell me about it when you were ready."

"At first I thought we should stay together 'for the sake of the children.' But then I realized it's more stressful for them if they have to live with all the tension in the house. So we decided we're going to do this civilly. We're going to split custody."

He said nothing.

"That's the long-term plan," she said. "Of course now we can't afford two living situations so he's gonna stay with a buddy. He's gone most of the time anyway. We thought about him moving into the basement but that sort of defeats the purpose of splitting up."

"Nice way to end your vacation. Tell the kids yet?"

"Yeah."

"How'd they take it?"

"Almost all their friends have parents who're divorced so it's like they've been the odd ones. And I have to think they were expecting it."

Neither spoke for a few moments, till she said, "Is it even possible to split up with someone who's never there?"

When he didn't reply she said, "Anyway I just wanted to let you know."

"Thanks."

They shared a long look that flickered through a range of unspoken possibilities. They worked together often and at times over the past few years Preuss felt like they were edging toward something more. But one or the other always took a step back because they were colleagues and Preuss knew and liked her husband. Now at least one of those impediments was about to disappear.

The look they shared ended when her two boys came running up demanding money for an ice cream bar.

They decided to have lunch and afterwards, with Toby rejuvenated, they saw every exhibit in the sprawling zoo, from the damp fishy penguinarium to the lions, the butterfly house (butterflies flocked to Toby with his bright red tee shirt), the giraffes and camels and huge submerged hippo.

Her boys liked the Arctic Ring of Life best. There a polar bear rested his enormous butt on the clear glass tunnel that curved through the underwater marine exhibit.

In late afternoon the Cahill boys whined about wanting to go around again but their mother said she was too tired and Preuss promised they could do this again soon.

On parting he and Cahill hugged again, and again Preuss realized how much he had missed her, and wondered what her new status would mean for them. One of her kids stepped in between them, perhaps too uncertain about what their parents' separation meant for the family, and they all said goodbye. Except for Toby, who had fallen asleep, drained as he was by the heat and activity of the day.

Preuss didn't feel like taking him back to the group home yet, so they drove to his house in the neighborhood below Nine Mile Road in Ferndale called the Dales. Preuss had built a ramp up to the deck behind the house, so he rolled Toby up to it and they sat protected from the late afternoon sun by the shadows of the towering oak trees in the backyard. He put a Jorma Kaukonen CD on and when it was over they both dozed.

Preuss popped awake to hear Toby whimpering. He was in the throes of another seizure, his body stiff and his arms and legs outstretched and his face twisted in a rictus of a grin even though what was happening to him was not at all humorous. Heat and humidity made his seizures worse. Preuss wrapped his arms around him and said, "Come back. Come back, Toby."

This was a long one and Toby didn't smile when the seizure passed. Instead it left him disoriented.

Preuss went into the house to collect a bath towel, an extra diaper, and a package of wipes, then lifted Toby from the wheelchair onto the towel spread over the chaise on the deck and changed the boy's diaper, which he had soiled during the seizure.

"Feel better?" he asked.

Toby was still too wiped to respond so Preuss lifted him back in the wheelchair and sat holding his hand for a while longer. When Toby was back to himself and began to hum Preuss wheeled him down the ramp and they took a walk around the neighborhood. It was still warm and humid and the weather combined with the aftermath of the seizure made Toby drowsy again though he didn't fall asleep.

Preuss pushed the wheelchair up Allen Road to Nine Mile, and turned left toward Woodward. Traffic on the main road was getting heavy as the day eased into night and what seemed like every twenty-something in southeastern Michigan poured into Ferndale. Every year saw more bars opening in the downtown and while it was good for the city, it annoyed older residents. He had heard more than one lament the way Ferndale was turning into Royal Oak—like Ferndale a once sleepy suburb but now a hopping destination.

Back home, Preuss sat with Toby on the back deck for another hour, enjoying being outside and together. Watching his son, Preuss had a sudden thought: if he retired, he might be able to take Toby back here. If he had all day to spend with his son, would he move Toby from where he lived now?

Rather than mention it, he decided to file it away as one of the possibilities a retirement might allow.

He roused himself and pushed Toby back down the ramp to the Explorer in the driveway. He lifted Toby into the rear seat, then folded up the wheelchair and stowed it in the rear of the SUV and took his son back to his group home.

31

"Baby, aren't there any other detectives in that department?" Sandy Trombley said. "Why do you always have to be the one working the weekend?"

Trombley wished his wife could understand without his having to explain it again that he was doing it, one, because the work needed to be done and they were short-handed, and two, because he was the youngest detective on the squad and needed to prove himself so he could advance. He knew she was complaining for the best of reasons—she wanted him to spend more time with her and the girls—but still. He wished she understood how much this job meant to him.

Or any job meant to any man, for that matter. A woman had so many more options for how to live and be happy, Trombley always thought, but Trombley's father had drilled into him that a man was what he did for a living. Trombley knew in his heart this was wrong, but he also knew he believed it anyway. Everything he had seen and heard growing up reinforced it.

But more than that, Trombley loved being a detective. He loved telling people he was one, and even more than that he loved the work. He loved the social impact of the job, he loved the problem-solving and creativity it demanded, loved the crazy cops-and-robbers adventures, he even loved the soul-numbing boredom of parts of it. He never regretted the switch from acting.

He promised Sandy he would spend two hours and then he would take the family out to the beach at Kensington. It was a sunny day with a forecast in the 90s so this plan appeased his wife even though Trombley could tell she didn't believe he would work for two hours.

Truth to tell, he wasn't sure he believed it either.

In his cubicle in the Detective's Bureau, he reviewed his notes on the Kertész case. The killing was Hank Bellamy's investigation, but the bosses gave Trombley their blessing to work his part of it because he had caught the original report of the minibus being stolen.

Besides, everybody knew the cases were connected, and letting Trombley work the Kertész murder was yet another slap in the face to Martin Preuss.

That was one thing he didn't love about the job . . . the politics. Preuss was the best detective he had met, better even in his way than Tony Tullio, and Trombley couldn't stand the way Russo treated him. As the squad's junior detective he wasn't in any position to protest, or do anything other than the best job he knew how to do in the hope that someday he would be in a position to say something. As his father—himself a detective in the Detroit Police Department—had often said, there were times when the best you could do was the best you could do.

He opened the computer file and read through Preuss's notes.

Preuss had identified at least one of the men from the church's surveillance video, the driver of the white van. But who was driving the minibus, and who was the guy who got out of the white van?

Preuss said his interview with Billy Simpson was interrupted by his sister, Simpson's legal guardian. Why did he need a legal guardian? He knew Preuss had a tendency to be abrasive and impatient when he was too focused on a problem . . . would a kinder, gentler approach make a difference to Simpson or his sister?

Preuss's file noted Billy's address in Madison Heights, but no phone number was listed. He hauled out the Oakland County phone book but there was no listing for Billy or William Simpson. Nor could he find a listing for a cell phone. If there was a phone number it must have been in his sister's name, and there was no indication in the file what that was.

He cleared the top of his desk, as he always did before he left for the day, and headed out to make one stop before taking his family to the beach.

The address for Billy Simpson was in a street of modest ranch homes in Madison Heights, one of the largest suburbs of Oakland County, bigger than Ferndale in population and area. Trombley rang the doorbell and knocked several times and waited but there was no response.

He looked up and down the street. There was some late Saturday morning activity, lawns cut, dogs walked. In fact, a dog walker, an old white dude, had stopped in front of the house and was giving Trombley the hairy eyeball right this minute.

"Can I help you?" the man said, it seemed to Trombley with an edge of aggression. Trombley was reminded that Madison Heights was overwhelmingly white, which made his presence an anomaly. He was in his usual Saturday clothes, a green Wayne State University tee shirt, Levis, and New Balance running shoes.

As always, he got immediately pissy in the face of the kind of attitude the old guy was copping. He came down off the porch and walked right up into the man's face and showed him his FPD shield.

"There a problem?" Trombley said.

"Oh, sorry," the man said. He backed right off. "Didn't know you were police."

Damn straight, Trombley thought.

The dog, a fluffy white mutt with rheumy eyes who was as old in dog years as the old guy was, growled.

"Better control your animal," Trombley said.

The dog began to bark and the man made a show of trying to leash it in. Like Trombley couldn't drop kick it into the road if he wanted to. He toyed with the idea of asking for the mutt's license and vaccination papers.

"You see strangers on the street, you don't know what to think," the man said.

"Uh-huh."

Trombley glared at him, daring him to say more, until the man pulled his dog away and continued down the sidewalk.

"Hey," Trombley said. "Wait up."

The man stopped and turned.

"You know the guy who lives there?" Trombley indicated the Simpson house behind him.

"I've seen him around." Now suspicious again.

"Seen him today?"

"No. But this is the first time I've been out all day. I don't keep tabs on my neighbors."

No, Trombley thought, just black folks who come around.

"Okay then," he said. Trombley dismissed him with a nod.

The man continued on his way and Trombley gave the house one more look-over and then returned to his Taurus.

What *am* I doing spending my Saturday in Madison Heights, he asked himself.

Sandy was right. Spending time with his wife and girls was much more important than this.

* * *

Elton Deetz peeked out the front window and saw the old guy was still walking his dog. The mutt was taking a crap on somebody's lawn.

He eased out the front door and fast-walked over to them.

"Hey," he called, and the man turned.

"I saw you talking to that fella with a sun tan came up to my door. He say what he wanted?"

"Asked if I knew you."

"What for?"

The old guy shrugged. "Didn't say. Said he was a cop."

"A cop?"

"Showed me his badge. I think he said he was from Ferndale but he flashed it so fast I can't be sure."

"What'd you tell him?"

"The truth. I hadn't seen you."

Deetz nodded and went back inside his house.

He made straight for the cupboard in the kitchen and searched behind a stack of dishes for a pill container. He withdrew it and shook four little tan tablets into his palm and washed them down with the can of Bud open on the counter.

He leaned against the counter and waited for the Adderall to kick in.

How could the police have zeroed in on him so fast? This must be what that phone call the other night was about . . . word was getting around to the wrong people.

He walked around the house. His mouth was going dry so he sipped his beer. He crushed the empty can and threw it into the sink and called the kid.

"You take care of that thing I asked you?"

"Yeah," the kid said. Deetz could hear him get on his guard. "Right after we talked."

"You're sure you took care of it?"

"Dude, you told me to and I did."

"So there's no way that bitch could have gone to the cops?"

"Where I got her, they'll never find her."

"And what about you? You been talking to anybody you shouldn't?"

"Don't even worry about that, man. I ain't been outta the house for days."

"You haven't been talking to any cops?"

"Come on, man. No way."

"All right," Deetz said, and disconnected. He walked around the house, trying to puzzle this through. Even if she talked, there wasn't any way that woman would know to send the cops to his house. She couldn't know his name or where he lived.

He wasn't sure about that kid, though. It was possible he had said something, though again how would he know where Deetz lived? Had somebody seen his car? He tried to remember if he had taken his car anywhere it might have been seen.

He had a bad feeling about that kid. He was too jumpy . . . if the police questioned him, Deetz was certain he'd fold and give him up. All the cops needed was a name and they'd do the rest.

But the kid didn't know his real name. Still, it was too much of a risk having him roaming the streets. Something needed to be done about that boy.

32

Sheila Hawkins came back to consciousness with the world graduating into color. She was on her back, staring into a round light fixture that resembled a face, with two dots for eyes, an ornamental filial for a nose, and another dot for a tiny mouth. Like some character from the comics but her brain was too fuzzy to remember who it was.

She tried to pick her head up but a stab of pain brought a white light to her eyes and her side was killing her. The last thing she remembered was the world going dark when something was swept over her head and then someone pounced on her and rained punches over her entire body.

She moved her head in increments through the pain to see where she was. On a bed, in a small room, bare walls, a single dresser. This was not the motel room they found for her . . . it was someplace else, a dark room . . . nighttime. A shade was drawn over a window. No curtains. Watermarks on the ceiling, cracks in the plaster walls.

She raised a hand to explore her head and discovered painful bruises all over. Her cheeks were swollen, her lips puffy. Somebody did a job on her.

She tried again to lift her head but was overcome by dizziness. She opened her mouth but her tongue felt too large and dry to make any noise. This wasn't from a beating, this was from drugs, she knew. Somebody must have been pouring drugs into her.

She did an inventory of her body—limbs, feet, fingers—and felt a telltale sharp ache between her toes . . . somebody was injecting her there with a substance that was slowing her down, fogging her up, keeping her docile.

How long had she been like this? Where was she?

After what seemed like hours she gathered herself to try sitting up. She edged her feet over the side of the bed and her body twisted into a sitting position. She was in terrible physical pain but otherwise the world seemed to exist at one remove from her. But she couldn't stay in bed any longer. She needed to find out where she was. And get away.

She got her feet to the ground and sat upright. There were no sheets or blankets on the bed, just the ticking of the bare mattress.

She pushed herself to a standing position and wobbled but remained on her feet. She tried a step but nausea overtook her and she stayed where she was and fought it back.

She listened hard for a clue that would let her know where she was, but all she could hear was a ringing in her ears. No other sounds penetrated.

Including the sound of the door behind her opening, or the steps slipping over the hardwood floor.

She felt a touch on her arm. Despite the pain she sprang away from it.

Nausea again overtook her and she couldn't keep her feet under her and fell against a wall away from the figure—a man— who stood before her. She leaned forward and vomited. The retching set off pain throughout her body.

When it was over she collapsed on the floor beside the foul puddle she had made.

"That's gross," the man said. "Now I'm going to have to clean that up."

She noticed he was carrying a syringe. She tried to shrink from him but there was no room to escape.

"Easy," he said. "I'm not going to hurt you."

"Who are you?" Her voice a croak.

"I guess that's the twenty-four dollar question, isn't it?"

"What?"

"Do you know me?"

She focused on him now that he was so close. Long lank hair, scraggly beard, pointed nose.

"No."

"Never seen me before?"

"No idea who you are."

"Good answer."

The man reached out to stroke her face and without thinking she knocked his hand away.

He responded with a quick hard slap.

She put her hands up to fend off any more blows but he knocked them away and grabbed her by the hair and pulled her head back. It felt as though he would pull all her beautiful hair out by the roots.

"I'm trying to be nice to you and you're not making it easy."

She squirmed to escape his grasp but didn't have the strength. He grabbed her arm and she felt a prick on the inside of her elbow. He banged her head against the wall and after a brief explosion of pain the hurt receded and she slipped back into blessed, comforting darkness.

33

"Neighborhood's so trendy you can't even score a drink without running into these young Americans thinking they're having the genuine urban experience."

Ernest McShane hawked and spat on the sidewalk as he led Preuss away from the Mercury Bar on Michigan Avenue in downtown Detroit. He was right, there was a lot of activity on this warm summer Saturday night in Corktown. McShane bulled his way through clots of young professionals toward the downtown center, throwing his comments back over his shoulder to where Preuss was following.

"Time was," McShane said, "the yups were too afraid of the city to come down here. Not any more. Can't turn around without hitting a lawyer from Bloomfield Hills in a Red Wings jersey thinking his shit smells like roses and hey, ain't this a happenin' town."

McShane's voice was hoarse and harsh and no one would ever mistake him for the yuppies he griped about. He wore a dirty polo shirt that had once been blue and a pair of khakis soiled and frayed at the cuffs. He looked to be in his sixties and his hair was long and grey and tied in a pony tail though his Van Dyke was neatly trimmed.

"Where are we going?" Preuss asked.

"Someplace you can get a decent drink."

They turned left on Trumbull at the vast dark empty lot that used to be Tiger Stadium before it was torn down, and kept walking over the Fisher Freeway and into the neighborhood. Three blocks in he turned into the parking lot of the Truck Drivers Local 299 union hall and banged on a door at the rear of the brick building.

The door opened and a nasty-looking man peered out. He nodded to McShane and gave Preuss a hard look, but he stepped aside for them to enter. McShane led the way down a long winding hallway to a conference room that had a wet bar. There were maybe a dozen big men sitting at round tables drinking and murmuring together. Several raised a glass to McShane while ignoring Preuss.

"Not a legal drinking establishment," McShane said. "But you drink with the salt of the earth and you don't have to elbow a young American on the make out of the way to get to the bar. What'll you have?"

"Seltzer with lemon."

McShane looked at him.

"Sober seven years."

McShane sighed, said, "Jaysus, one of those," and ordered a pitcher of Bud for himself and a seltzer and lemon for Preuss.

"Let's go upstairs," McShane said. He handed Preuss his drink and carried the pitcher and an empty glass up a stairway to a dark office on the second floor. The floor was covered with a short-pile beige carpet and the walls were plasterboard painted swimming pool aqua. The room was empty except for three chairs, a desk, and a sleek brown sofa.

McShane kicked the door closed and spread out his drinking supplies on the desk. He crossed to the window and peeked around the drawn vertical blinds. Satisfying himself no one had followed them or was watching the building, he turned on a gooseneck lamp on the desk after first examining the switch and metal shade and the plug.

"You wouldn't believe what modern listening technology can do," McShane rasped. "That's the problem with hanging out in a union hall. Government's got its knives out for the unions so you can't be too careful."

McShane stood before Preuss and said, "Now you. Spread 'em."

Preuss lifted his arms and McShane patted him down, front and back, top and bottom.

"Where's your weapon?" McShane asked.

"Don't carry one."

"You don't carry one! That's a first. Never heard of a policeman without a weapon. Thought all you guys were militarized up the wahzoo these days."

"Not me."

"Why the hell not? It's a dangerous world out there. Even in Ferndale."

"I'd prefer not to participate in the violence of the world any more than necessary."

"Sometimes you have to participate. The world won't let you be a conscientious objector, you know."

"Sometimes carrying a gun makes you feel more powerful than you really are."

McShane snorted. "Greene said you were different."

He pulled Preuss's wallet and badge from his pockets and examined them. He tossed them on the table and pulled Preuss's iPhone from his pocket and removed it from its case and turned it off. With a tool from his pants pocket he withdrew the Sim card and tossed it on the table.

"You'll get it all back after we're done. Sit."

McShane sat on one of the chairs at the desk and Preuss sat at another. Manny Greene said this guy was ex-FBI but didn't mention the paranoia he was showing now.

Preuss said, "Why all the precautions?"

"If you knew what I know about what the government's up to, you'd do the same, believe me. How do you know Manny Greene?"

Preuss explained what he had been working on during the past week. When he said Elizaveta was dead, McShane went quiet.

"How?"

"Killed. Strangled."

McShane let out a deep sigh and and got up and walked to the window.

"Know who did it?"

"Not yet."

McShane peeked outside the shade but didn't seem to be looking for anything in particular. It was just something he did to keep his surprise and grief under control.

"I take it you knew her," Preuss said.

"Met her once. We talked on the phone a few times. Seemed like a sweet kid."

"That's what people tell me."

"You didn't know her yourself?"

"No."

"Too bad. I liked her."

McShane let the shade fall back into place and leaned a shoulder against the wall beside the window. "What do you want to know?" His voice was flat now, the paranoid inflections dulled by Preuss's news.

"When was the last time you heard from her?"

"Couple weeks ago." He examined the pattern of the dark wood paneling. "She called me. Said she wanted to know if I'd found anything about that Nazi she and Greene were after. I told her what I had."

"Which was what?"

"His new name and where he was living."

"How did you get that? Manny Greene's been looking for him for years."

"So have I," McShane said. "Since I left the Bureau, I've been making a study of these animals. You wouldn't believe how many ex-Nazis are in this country. It's taken me a while to work through all the sources and bypass all the obstacles the government's put in my way, but I'm doing it. Slowly but surely. This Kovalenko? The Justice Department's known about him since the 1950s. The 50s, can you fucking believe it? But operating under the direct orders of J. Edgar Hoover, the Bureau refused to act on the information."

"Why not?"

"Hoover was such a crazy anti-Red he assumed everything we got about former Nazis was disinformation supplied by the Soviets. So he chose to ignore it all. Thought in the great Armageddon to come, there'd be the Soviets on one side and us and Jesus on the other. Thought the Germans would be valuable allies against the Reds when the time came. So Kovalenko's file was protected ever since his involvement in the Second World War became known. But I found a way to get through."

"How?"

"Can't tell you. Let's just say I still have contacts in the Bureau who feel the same way I do about bringing these criminals to justice. It was a matter of peeling back the layers and finding where the guilt was hidden."

"So Hoover squashed the information and the feds were powerless."

"Right."

"What about the Israelis? Wouldn't they do something if they knew?"

"You might think so," McShane said, "but you'd be wrong. Israel's never sought extradition of former Nazis in America, and hasn't prosecuted any Nazis since the Eichmann trials in the six-ties. They didn't want to dilute the impact of that, which was a major coup for their security services. Today even if they were going to put a suspected Nazi on trial, it wouldn't be a small fish like Kovalenko, no matter how heinous his crimes were. And this guy was one of the worst."

"Manny said."

"Kovalenko was one of the group known as the 'Trawniki men.' They were civilians conscripted by the Nazis to help imple-ment the Final Solution. In addition to working at Trawniki, they served at most of the other concentration camps in Poland and took part in a great many atrocities, including putting down the Warsaw Ghetto uprising. They were ignorant, ferocious peasants, and they were manipulated by political and historical forces they didn't have the ability to understand.

"Kovalenko's brutality was legendary, even at a time when the rules of decent society had broken down. They called him the Butcher of Trawniki. He cut the breasts off women, he castrated men, he beat prisoners to death with a whip and his own hands, he hanged little girls in front of their parents, he set dogs onto prisoners to tear them to pieces. He locked Jews in their barracks filled with hay doused in gasoline and set fire to them while he danced around the flames singing. He forced prisoners, adults and children, to beg for their lives before slaughtering them while he laughed and laughed. There didn't seem to be any limit to his depravity."

"How do you know this?"

"Some of it's public record. Some of it's in files that my sources in the Bureau have access to. And some of it, like the Kovalenko material, was locked away in places that took years to open. Elizaveta said she was going to pass on to Greene the infor-mation I got. But this week he called and asked me for it. Turns out she never shared it with him."

"Why not?"

"Can't say for sure. I wouldn't be surprised if she had something in mind for when she found him she didn't want Manny to be part of. Or even know about."

"Some kind of elaborate revenge scheme."

"Yeah. Wouldn't peg her for the avenging angel type. But she asked me if I could get ahold of a gun for her, so I assumed she had something bad in mind for him."

"Did you get her one?"

"No. I asked her what she wanted it for and she said it was for a friend, but I figured it was for her. Unlike you, I'm not philosophically opposed to weapons, I just don't want them in the hands of amateurs."

This was new, Preuss thought. He hadn't found a weapon when he walked through her apartment. Had she gotten one somewhere else? And if she did, what happened to it? Did it disappear in the minibus hijacking?

"Whatever she had in mind," Preuss said, "she was trying to protect Manny by keeping him out of it."

"Sounds like it cost her her life."

McShane blew a rush of air through his teeth and said, "I was afraid of this, you know."

"Of what?"

"Somebody would come after her."

"Why? You think there's a connection between Kovalenko and her death?"

"How can there not be? Way I see it, she was killed for one of two reasons. First, this was perpetrated by agents working for the large group of former Nazis who live in the United States to get her out of the way so they could continue their work."

"Which is what?"

"To bring all the ultra-right-wing wackjobs together in a wave of extremism that would overwhelm what's left of the democratic institutions of the United States. Or else she was killed by agents of the United States government itself."

"Why would the government kill a poor music student?"

"Why does the government kill anyone?" McShane said. "Because she knew too much, man. She was a danger to the imperial corporate forces that run this country and she had to be eliminated."

"But—"

"There aren't any buts, Preuss." He was starting to raise his voice. "I've seen it before. The rapacious oligarchical elites and their dishonest corporate stooges who perpetrate the crimes of global capitalism think they're unstoppable. You get in their way, they roll right over you."

He was beginning to spin out of control. Preuss said, "McShane, sit down and we'll—"

"This isn't any time to sit down, this is the time to stand up. Like Elizaveta did. She disrupted their plans, this 'poor music student,' as you call her. If she'd been allowed to pull at the thread of this single governmental coverup then the entire fabric of the crimes of global capitalism would start to unravel. Our corporate overlords couldn't allow that."

Against his better judgment, Preuss said, "What evidence—"

"Evidence! Pull your head out of your ass, man, this isn't some petty crime you need to investigate. This is a scourge on the planet and these people must be eradicated. And nobody else can do it but us. If the people don't dismantle their machinery and obstruct their plans, they're going to crush us in their quest for domination.

"The Dark Ages of global capitalist fascism is coming, Preuss. And if we don't stop it we're going to be doomed. *Doomed!*"

Sunday, June 13, 2010

34

Preuss made himself scrambled eggs with cheese and onions and took his plate and coffee into the morning sunshine of his deck. The reedy voice of Neil Young on *Harvest Moon* came from the speakers in the living room.

He gobbled his breakfast and set the empty plate on the side table next to his chair and sipped his coffee. The day was already warm, with a humid heaviness that felt Floridian.

In the quiet of the Sunday morning he thought about his talk with Ernest McShane the night before. So Elizaveta Kertész had the information about Kovalenko without letting Emmanuel Greene know. It helped to fill in her last days, and gave him a better sense of the woman.

Even though this wasn't his case, something about it resisted his efforts to walk away—beyond his refusal to be warned away from it. Much of it had to do with the way she was acting on her own, which resonated with him. He felt a kinship with her even though he had never met her.

He went back into the house and returned to the deck with a copy of the the paper he had pulled from a newspaper box on Trumbull after he left the union hall. It was the *Metro Voice*, one of the area's alternative newspapers. On the cover was a photo of the incinerator off I-94 in downtown Detroit, the largest waste-burning facility in the country, and a headline that screamed, "Detroit's Cancer Factory." The byline was Shelley Larkin.

He glimpsed it on the way back to his Explorer last night and walked by it, then went back to retrieve it. Shelley Larkin was a young writer who did free-lance work for the *Voice*. Though she was a good fifteen years younger than he was, they had tiptoed around a relationship ever since they met while he was working the Madison Kaufman case two years before and she was doing a story on . . . what was it? He couldn't remember since the story never appeared and their own drama had occupied him. Something to do with how the culture treated young women . . . thus exploiting poor Madison at the same time as she wanted to use Madison as an example of that exploitation. Which of course would advance her own career.

Even though they never had more than the possibility of a relationship, it took him a long time to get over her. She was the first woman he had let himself fall for since his wife died, and the fact that she kept sending him double and triple messages in her texts and phone calls made it hard to move on. He would go months without hearing from her, then she would text him that she was thinking of him and when he would text back she would disappear again. Finally he stopped responding to her at all.

Now he stared at the tabloid. The cover showed the stack of the incinerator belching smoke. There had been a storm of protest while it was being built, and multiple complaints of the vile smells and other hazards that came from it once it went into operation. He presumed the article would chart those, and, judging by the headline, the article would amass all the damning evidence for the incinerator as a health hazard.

He last saw her when she bumped into him while he was playing with the Flynns at a bar in downtown Ferndale.

Do I want to read this, he asked himself.

Last night he was interested enough in it to retrieve it from the newspaper box. But now?

Another dilemma: to do or not do. He seemed to be running into lots of these.

But this decision was the easiest of all.

He tucked the *Voice* under his arm and took his cup and plate into the kitchen. He tossed the paper into the trash bin under the sink. Goodbye to you, he thought. Finally, after long last, he felt ready to move on from whatever might have happened between them.

He loaded up the dishwasher with the dishes from the past few days. Then he went into work.

There he saw Reg Trombley had been in the day before and added his notes to the case file for the minibus.

He checked his phone messages and found a call from Emmanuel Greene from the day before. He decided to give Greene a try and the older man picked up after two rings.

"Martin. Working Sunday? No rest for the wicked." He chuckled. "Did you talk with McShane?"

"Last night. You didn't tell me he's batshit crazy. I would have brought my aluminum foil hat."

Greene laughed. "Did he talk about how the terrorist threat will provide cover for the crimes of global capitalist fascism?"

"He started to. I left before he got fully cranked up."

"Still, he's a good man to know. He loves his country. He sees through a lot of the lies we get told and he has an amazing network of contacts. I heard he was cashiered from the Bureau in some internecine squabble about ten or fifteen years ago but still knows who the players are and where to get information."

"He looked devastated when I told him about Elizaveta."

"It's hard to be otherwise, Martin, if you ever knew her. Sorry you never got the chance."

"Me too." Though I feel like I do know her, Preuss thought. She's speaking to him through the others who knew her.

Preuss told him what he had learned before McShane's rant.

"So by a week ago last Monday Elizaveta had the information about Kovalenko," Greene said. "And didn't share it with me. Oh, Liz. That little act of selfishness might have cost you your life."

"She could have thought she was protecting you. It's possible she didn't want to involve you in whatever she had planned for Kovalenko. If that's the case, she wasn't being selfish at all. She was trying to save you, maybe from whatever unpleasantness wound up taking her own life."

"Whatever vengeance she had planned for Kovalenko, I'd be in the clear."

"Yes."

"Well," said Greene, "that sounds like her, too."

After disconnecting, Preuss straightened all the files on his desk, aligning their edges. If you can't be good, he thought, be neat.

The ship's helm clock that his older son Jason had given him was ten minutes behind so he adjusted the time, and wondered again where in the cosmos Jason was and how he was doing. The last he had heard, several months ago by now, Jason was being held on a charge of vagrancy in Needles, California. The young man himself never contacted Preuss anymore to ask for money, but Preuss had been able to trace his movements through a network of police contacts he developed as Jason traveled across—and spent jail time in—the American west.

As far from Ferndale as his son could get, Preuss thought.

He had almost given up hope his son would ever forgive him for what happened to their family. Like Russo, Jason blamed Preuss for Jeanette's fatal encounter with a drunk driver. It was after one of their worst fights. If he hadn't been drinking that night, she might still be alive.

There wasn't anything he could do about it now. Jason would come around or he wouldn't. Russo never would, he was certain.

In the meantime Toby needed his father, and Preuss would always be there for his sweet, loving, vulnerable, innocent younger son. If he had a shot at redemption, it was through Toby.

He stood up with the intention of leaving to spend the rest of the day with his son, then his cell phone rang.

Janey Cahill.

He sat back down.

"Hey."

"Hey," she said. "How'd your night go yesterday?"

"Good. After we left the zoo I took Toby back to my house and we chilled. Doesn't get better than that."

He was going to tell her about his meeting with McShane but she said, "We had a great time at the zoo. The boys can't stop talking about the polar bear."

"They like big butts."

"And they cannot lie."

"Toby had a good time, too, despite the heat. It really does him in."

"It was good to see you."

"Ditto," he said. "I'm glad you're doing well."

"Yeah. This is gonna be best for all of us."

"Janie, whatever I can do, just let me know, okay? I've been through this and I know it's hard to do alone."

"Thanks, Martin."

"It's not an idle offer."

"I know. I appreciate it." Then she said, "You're a good friend," as a kind of afterthought. It occurred to him this might be another instance of their coming to the brink of something until one of them, unable to overcome conflicted feelings, made a strategic retreat.

But then why would she call him?

They both let the moment stretch. He wondered if she wanted to get together later on, but didn't know how to ask.

He no sooner formed the intention to ask her than she said, "Well, I just wanted to say thanks for yesterday. I'll see you tomorrow." And disconnected.

He sat for a few minutes more. The call unsettled him. He felt like calling her back and asking her if something was going to happen between them or not.

Instead, unwilling to leave the station, he wandered down to the canteen to get another cup of coffee. He saw Gail Crimmonds sitting in a booth at the rear of the room and remembered what Trombley had said about her.

He went over to her and said, "Gail, I heard about your promotion. Congratulations."

"Thank you, sir."

"Every once in a while something good does happen."

She acknowledged the praise with a dip of her head.

"Look," he said, "if you have some time, I have a project for you."

"Sure. I'll make time."

He told her about his Fred Samuelson case.

She said, "The skell who ambushed the woman in her apartment?"

"He's the one. He sustained some serious injuries. Can you call around to the hospitals in the area one more time? I'd like to grab him."

"Of course," she said. "I'll get on it right now."

He thanked her and spent the rest of the day with Toby.

35

When Deetz woke up just before noon he saw the text Louise left on his phone.

At Joanne's. Home later.

He called her. "Hey babe. Seen your brother?"

"I told him to go to the store and get some milk."

"Yeah? Which store?"

"He likes to go to the Meijer's up on Thirteen."

"He went all the way up to Meijer's to get a gallon of milk?"

"He likes it there. He likes to walk around, check things out. Why?"

Deetz said, "Nothing. I owe him some money. I wanted to pay him back."

"Are you hitting him up for money again?"

"Nothing like that, babe. No worries."

"He's probably not there anymore anyway. This was a couple hours ago. He said he was going in to work."

"On Sunday?"

"They got crews working seven days a week this time of year."

"All right. Maybe I'll talk to him when he gets home."

"Whatever."

He disconnected. He walked around the house, thinking, and wound up down in the basement rec room that Louise fixed up for her brother. He pawed through the underpants and socks in his dresser drawers, then sorted through the mess of change and papers on the nightstand beside Billy's bed.

At the bottom of a pile of gas and fast food receipts Deetz found a business card. The name on it was Lieutenant Martin Preuss, Detective Bureau, Ferndale Police Department. There was an office number and a cell number.

Deetz pocketed the card and drove into Royal Oak Township.

He parked down the block on Wyoming and walked around the back of the paint company building, where he found Billy Simpson's white van among the pickups that belonged to the other workers. Through the open garage door at the back of the warehouse he spotted Billy working with another man in the mixing room, preparing paint colors and filling up five-gallon containers. Ray Bouchard stood watching them.

Deetz ducked back out of sight. Wouldn't be cool to be caught here. He would have to wait for Billy to leave at the end of the day. He went back to his Camaro and gulped down a few Lexies to help him wait.

By the time Billy clocked out at three, Deetz's ears were ringing and his heart was pounding but he felt like he could do anything.

Billy trudged to his van. Deetz was waiting behind it.

"Billy."

Simpson stopped dead, said, "Hey. What are you doing here?"

"We need to talk."

"Why don't we just talk at home?"

"No, man, let's go someplace else. Leave your ride here and hop in."

With Billy beside him, Deetz drove down to Northend, a street of light industrial businesses in Royal Oak Township. All were closed. He took a right on Meyers and made a left into the driveway of a plumbing supply company and parked.

They walked around the back of the plumbing supply, which was surrounded on all sides by a hurricane fence topped with razor wire.

"Hey Elton, what are we doing here?"

"Follow me, Bill."

Deetz led Billy around the back of the plumbing supply company and held up an edge of the fence so they could both slip underneath. When they got to a spot behind the building that was shielded from the street and the other buildings, Deetz stopped and lit a cigarette. He offered one to Billy and lit it for him.

"Louise doesn't like it when I smoke," Billy said.

"She ain't gonna know, is she?"

"I'm not going to tell her," Billy said with a loopy grin.

"All that matters, dude."

They stood smoking in silence. "Man," Billy said, "what's in this cigarette? Kinda bitter. Making me feel kinda dizzy . . ."

"You don't wanna know. Just enjoy it."

Deetz sucked his smoke down to the filter and tossed it in the gravel. "So we had a visitor at the house yesterday."

"Yeah? Who?"

"Some cop."

Billy took another drag on his cigarette. "What he want?"

"I didn't talk with him. Louise was out so I let him stand there and ring the bell. I had to guess, I'd say he was looking for me."

"Why?"

"Well, see, that's what I wanted to talk to you about, Billy. Why would a cop from Ferndale be looking for me?"

Billy smoked without speaking for a few seconds, then said, "How do you know he was?"

"He was what? A cop?"

233

"No, looking for you."

"Who else would he be looking for? You?"

"Why would a cop be looking for me?"

"I don't know, Billy, that's sort of what I want to find out."

Deetz lit another cigarette. He held up the pack. "Another one?"

"No thanks, still working on the first one."

"So did you talk to them, the cops?"

"Me?"

"'*Me?*'" Deetz mocked the other man. "Yeah, you. You talked to them, didn't you?"

Billy looked down, and then up at Deetz. That's it, Deetz thought. If I had any doubts, that big dumb cow-eyed look just took care of them.

"Did you talk to the cops? Don't lie to me, Billy."

"Once. I talked to them once. But I didn't tell 'em nothing," he added, "I swear to God."

"Then how did they know to come to the house?"

"I dunno, Elton. I got no explanation."

"Well, see, I got one. Wanna hear it? My explanation is, you told them what you and me did the other night and you gave them my name, and now they're looking to jam me up for it."

"Why would I do that?"

Deetz sighed. "I know it was you."

"Oh, no, Elton, I wouldn't do that. Uh-uh. Wasn't me. They asked me, I won't lie, they asked me for your name but I never gave it to them."

"Yeah, you did. Don't lie to me!"

"I'm not!"

Deetz rushed at Billy and drove him backwards into the wall behind him with his hands around his throat. Then he popped Billy in the face. The punch snapped his head back and bounced it off the wall.

"Elton," Billy cried, "I didn't say nothing! Please, I didn't—"

Deetz took a roundhouse swing at him and knocked Billy to the ground. His fury was out of control now. He kicked Billy in the pit of his stomach and looked around for something to hit him with that would cause more damage than his fists or his feet. He saw a metal bar over by a pile of construction materials and he ran to it and brought it back to where Billy was lying. Deetz hit him with it again and again, on Billy's head and shoulders and arms and body. Billy cried with every blow until he couldn't protect himself any more and lay still while Deetz continued to pound him.

Deetz paused, huffing. He spat the cigarette out of his mouth and coughed. "I knew it was a mistake getting you involved," he huffed. "But you got to pay, you mo-mo. You got to pay."

He took another swing at the motionless body and carried the bar with him back to his car. He took one last look at where Billy lay whimpering, and then drove away.

Later, at home, when Billy didn't come back, Louise asked him if he ever met up with her brother.

"No," Deetz said. "Matter of fact, I haven't seen him all day."

"You didn't go looking for him?"

"Nah. I figured I'd see him when he got home."

What was that expression his mother used to say?

As if butter wouldn't melt in his mouth.

*   *   *

The Tabernacle of Praise was a small brick church on Northend in Royal Oak Township. Sunday services were famous throughout the township for their length and fervor. Once the pastor got warmed up he could go on for hours, sermonizing and singing with a deep bass voice that was a source of much (some of his parishioners would say too much) pride for him. And when the gospel choir was in full throat it wasn't unusual for churchgoers to spend most of Sunday in the throes of religious rapture.

It was hard to keep the children quiet for so long, especially the boys, who had a hard time sitting still under any circumstances. So when the service ended on this particular Sunday one boy, Cletus Petty, couldn't restrain himself any longer and exploded out of the chapel ahead of his grandmother and three older sisters. His grandmoms tarried to tell Pastor Kenyata Cobb how much she enjoyed the sermon, while Cletus's three sisters went to the Fellowship Hall to start warming up the food they had prepared the day before—chicken and potato salad and lasagna and round buttery rolls.

Cletus had another reason for wanting to bust out of there. Four of the boys who lived in the building next to his in the Royal Oak Township Housing Authority had threatened to kick his ass after services today. The twelve-year-old Cletus was bookish and shy, and the other boys took his reticence as superiority. Calling him Urkel and teasing him for talking white weren't enough . . . they needed to punish him too.

So before the last notes of the choir's final song had faded Cletus sped up the center aisle and out the door.

He ran down Northend. His Language Arts teacher had given him a book of poetry by a man named Langston Hughes. He had brought it to church and was anxious to find someplace safe to sit and read. The night before he had read one poem about a mother who talks to her child about how hard life had been for her but how she kept going anyway, and it had sounded so much like what his grandmoms always said that she could have written the poem herself. He couldn't wait to read the others.

He looked behind him as he raced down Northend to make sure the boys weren't following him. He ducked down Meyers Road with the intention of walking up to the Oak Park Alternative Education Center, where he could lie out on the grass and read in peace and imagine what his future would be like. He was sure he would be safe walking this way, since the roofers' union building he passed was closed, as were the textile factory, the lighting supply company, the truck parts store, and all the rest of the businesses.

After the thunderous voice of the pastor and the tumultuous responses of the congregation, the silence of the street was a pleasure. He pulled the book of poems out of his back pocket and as he walked down the deserted street he opened to a page at random and read a poem about deferred dreams.

The poet could have written this poem for me, he thought. He felt as if the poet had looked right into his most secret heart and written about what he saw there.

He was so moved by the poem that he stood still and read it again, this time out loud.

He wanted to be a writer when he grew up, and now that he had read Langston Hughes he thought he would like to be a poet. In the silence that rang when he had spoken the final words of the poem about deferred dreams he imagined he had written such a poem and it spoke to everyone who heard it the same way it spoke to him. He imagined the people who heard the poem responded to it with as much emotion as he had. He imagined his poem touched people so much it made them cry.

He paused when he thought he really did hear someone crying.

As he listened, he realized he was hearing something. It must be a cat, he decided. But the more he listened the more it sounded human, and in terrible, terrible pain.

He held his head up and tried to follow the sound as if it were a smell. He walked a little further down the street until he came to the plumbing supply company, and he thought that's where the sound was coming from.

He walked around the back, to a secluded little courtyard where he had on occasion in the past sat and read or written in his journal or just looked at the sky when the building was closed and there was no one to bother him.

He heard a commotion, the thumping and slapping of fists on human flesh and another sound, something hard hitting bone again and again. And the involuntary grunts and cries coming from someone being beaten.

He hung back until he didn't hear anything else except a man's heavy breathing. Then he saw a man—a white man—walking to a black car and tossing what looked like an iron bar into the back seat. He slid behind the wheel and pulled out of the parking lot in a plume of dust.

When he was certain the man was gone, Cletus edged around the corner to see what was left behind. There, in the weeds, he saw another white man lying on his back and making a sound that was a cross between a cat's meow and a baby's cry. There was blood on his head and blood on the the stones and the weeds and the scrap wooden boards beneath him.

Cletus stood transfixed by the man's pain. He had seen people beaten around the projects many times, had been beaten himself, but never before had he been able to study the effects of violence up close like this, without worrying about being seen. The man's agony horrified him, but there was something magnetic too that drew him in and wouldn't let go.

He crept closer and knelt near the man and took it all in . . . the swelling of the man's face, the rips in his skin and clothes, the blood oozing all around him . . . whoever had done this had brought a terrible power down on this poor man. The proximity to the violence made Cletus's heart beat faster and, he had to admit, thrilled him.

But in the end it made Cletus sick to his stomach. He was disgusted with himself for giving in to the fascination of what one person could do to another.

He ran back to the church to let someone know.

Monday, June 14, 2010

36

"Missed another memo?" Tanya Corcoran asked.

"I know it's against your nature, but try not to get snide, okay? I can't 'miss' a memo unless it's sent to me."

"Russo's meeting everybody in the Chief's conference room."

"Why aren't you there?"

"Just for the grown-ups."

When he reached the conference room all the detectives along with Paul Horvath were seated around the table. They must not have started the meeting yet because Nick Russo was going on about Obamacare, which the House had passed the month before.

"My doc says it's going to be a catastrophe for the health care system in this country. It'll never recover." The others were listening without taking part in the rant.

When he saw Preuss he stopped, said, "Nice of you to join us."

"Nice of you to let me know it was happening."

"My mistake."

Preuss took a seat next to Janey Cahill and Russo called the meeting to order by rapping his knuckles on the table. He said something about how good it was to be back. Preuss just heard "blah blah blah" because he was too angry to bother listening.

Russo asked them to go around the room and update him on their cases. He filled both sides of a yellow legal-sized paper with his notes of their answers to his questions in his cramped scrawl. The ballpoint looked like a toy in his big fist.

Bellamy said he had found the road-rage driver who had beaten Joe Delancey. The man couldn't tell them for sure if Elizaveta's body was in the weeds when he beat Delancey senseless because it was dark but he may have seen a bundle in the ditch that he thought was trash.

Bellamy made it seem like he'd single-handedly tracked down Elizaveta's ex-husband and was going to visit him in the Macomb County Jail later that day. Preuss and Trombley shared a look and both gave an imperceptible shake of their heads.

When it was his turn, Preuss was careful to limit his description of his work. He talked about progress on the Helen Vlastos attack, the spate of stolen motorcycles from the cycle shop on the east side of Woodward, the old man who was mugged for his wallet while walking his dog on Ardmore, the clerk who was embezzling from her store, the latest on the father-and-son team of villains he caught, and progress on the missing minibus.

Russo continued writing on his pad long after Preuss finished his report. Perhaps he's making out his shopping list for dinner, Preuss thought. Russo's attempt to get up his sleeve was almost comical.

Done at last, Russo drew his brawny shoulders up around his ears and made a show of stretching his bull neck. Then, without a comment or question for Preuss, he said, "Janey, your turn. What do you have?"

"A stack of files on my desk." She had brought the folders into the meeting and slapped a hand on them. "I haven't had a chance to look through them all yet. I'll get started this morning."

"Good deal," Russo said. "Welcome back. We missed you."

"Thanks."

"Before we break, I have one piece of news. You might have heard rumors I'm interested in Chief Warnock's job. Well, the rumors are true. I've put in my application to the City Council and I would be honored to serve as your new chief."

There was no response around the table. Everybody already expected this.

"When the Council meets this week, recruitment of the next chief'll be on their agenda. If I make it past the first round, there'll be a series of interviews with the finalists. I've heard they want to make the decision so the transition from Chief Warnock will be smooth.

"If I'm appointed, there'll be an opening for head of this Bureau. As far as I'm concerned, that job is going to be very competitive. If anybody here is thinking of going after it, know there are a lot of good people in the pool."

He looked around the table, ending by locking eyes with Preuss. In other words, Preuss thought, it's never going to be you regardless what your buddy Bill Warnock says.

Preuss returned his stare, then decided this telepathic pissing contest was fruitless and looked away. But not before turning up his mouth in a brittle grin.

With no prospects for promotion and no support for his current work, Preuss wondered why he shouldn't do what he knew was the right thing. To hell with the rest of it.

So after the meeting broke up, without telling anybody he set out for the address Emmanuel Greene had given him for Bogdan Kovalenko. It was a street in Sterling Heights, a large suburban Detroit city of endless winding subdivisions with a large Polish population in Macomb County. A higher percentage of the population in Sterling Heights was Polish than in Hamtramck, even though most people thought Hamtramck was still predominately Polish.

Kovalenko's address was one of many one-story homes on Mt. Cisco Drive, not far from Chrysler's Sterling Heights Assembly Plant where the man had worked, according to Ernest McShane's information. There were twin peaked roofs over the home and attached two-car garage with beige brick all around, well-manicured lawn, and two high mullioned windows on either side of a sculpted tree giving the impression of a cartoon face. The differences between it and every other house on the block were subtle variations in the plantings in the front gardens near the house.

The doorbell unleashed a furious barking from somewhere inside. When there was no answer, and the barking continued, he knocked and after another minute the door swung open and a hatchet-faced woman looked back at him. She wore a blue medical scrub top over mannish khaki slacks. Her silver hair was cut short and parted on the right side of her head.

Behind her the dog was beside itself with barking. She kicked at the animal and the pooch scrambled away. She turned to face Preuss again. If he had been smaller she might have aimed a kick at him, too.

He held up his badge and identified himself. "Is there a John Kowalczyk living here?"

Her stern eyes never left his.

"Ma'am? Did you hear me? I'm looking for John Kowalczyk."

"*Nie rozumiem co mówisz*," she said, and slammed the door in his face.

He remembered Manny Greene saying he got the same treatment. He pounded on the door with his fist, which amped up the dog's level of fury.

In another few moments the door was opened again, this time by a woman who was short and very heavy. She had lank brown hair framing a round face with a pug nose.

"Yes?" Harried, as though the interruption was the last straw in a terrible day.

Preuss held his badge up. "Detective Martin Preuss, Ferndale Police. I'm looking for John Kowalczyk."

"What do you want with him?"

"Does he live here?"

"Yes. He's my father."

"And who am I speaking with?"

"Oksana Baranski. Can you tell me what this is about?"

"I'd like to talk to your father about a case I'm investigating."

"My father can't help you. Sorry."

She began to close the door and he held out a hand to stop it.

"Please take your hand away. I'll call the police. I'm sure you don't have jurisdiction in Sterling Heights."

"This is a murder investigation. I need to ask your father a few questions. The sooner you cooperate, the sooner I'll be out of your hair. If you don't let me in, I'll subpoena your father and take this to a whole other level. Do you want that, ma'am?"

"I'm certain my father has no involvement in any possible crime."

"I'll decide that for myself."

She thought about that for a moment and let up pressure on the door. Behind her, Preuss saw a younger woman looming at the end of the hallway leading into the house. She was short and heavy, like Oksana Baranski, but wore long bleached blonde hair and a black sweater over a black and white geometric dress. She looked very unhappy.

"My father is a sick man," Baranski said. "He's had a stroke and has advanced Alzheimer's. He won't be able to answer any of your questions. He won't even be able to understand you."

"I'd like to speak with him, please."

"He's in the backyard. Go through the garage and I'll meet you around back."

The garage door opened, revealing a spotless well-ordered area lacking in any garden tools, A door at the rear opened onto a patio with a table under an umbrella and four aluminum chairs. The backyard was as well-manicured as the front yard though devoid of flowers or adornment. The lawn ran back to a shed in front of a chain link fence on all three sides.

In one of the chairs at the table was the woman who had closed the door in his face, sitting beside an old man in a wheelchair. He looked to be in his nineties, with wispy white hair and a network of deep wrinkles over his blank face. He wore a polo shirt under a wide bib stained with his meal. His knobby hands and stick-thin arms were covered with purple and black bruises.

The man was an older version of the face in the passport photo that Emmanuel Greene showed Preuss. He sat sunken in his wheelchair like a pile of old clothes. What was most striking was his passivity . . . he could have been an infant sitting with his mouth open waiting to be fed a hot dog cut into little bites. The woman beside him shoveled a forkful of hot dog into his mouth and he chewed with his mouth open. A gruel of half-chewed food and saliva oozed down his chin and onto his bib.

Oksana Baranski slid open a door at the rear of the house and trudged over to the old man in the wheelchair. She stood beside him and laid a hand on his shoulder.

"This is who you're looking for," she said to Preuss. "Are you satisfied?"

Preuss came closer, smelled the rank odors of urine and feces and stale old-man sweat. He said, "Are you John Kowalczyk?"

The old man ignored Preuss until his daughter gave his shoulder a small shake. He looked up at her without interest or recognition, then turned back to the woman feeding him.

"Sir," Preuss said, "are you John Kowalczyk?"

This time the man looked at Preuss, but there was nothing in his eye . . . no spark of intelligence, or interest, or connection.

He was a shell of an old man who was not able to respond to or even process what Preuss was saying. He turned with his mouth open to the woman who was feeding him. She offered him another forkful of hot dog and he continued chewing.

Oksana Baranski said, "He doesn't even recognize me. He doesn't know where he is or what's going on around him."

Preuss leaned close to the old man.

"Mr. Kowalczyk, my name is Martin Preuss. I'm a policeman."

The man known as John Kowalczyk ignored him. All he cared about was the hot dog coming his way.

"You won't get anything from him," the man's daughter said. "You're wasting your time."

"Mr. Kowalczyk, do you recognize the name Bogdan Kovalenko? Weren't you once known as Bogdan Kovalenko?"

Preuss watched the old man's eyes for a flicker of recognition but they were empty of any comprehension.

"Do you know a woman by the name of Elizaveta Kertész?"

Nothing. It was true, the old man was gone. Whatever he had been when he was younger, there was nothing left now. He turned toward his minder and opened his mouth like a baby bird waiting to be fed.

So this was the worst of the fearsome Trawniki Men who spread such terror during the Second World War, Preuss thought. Who still haunted the nightmares of those who had the misfortune to cross his path sixty years before. What was left of the brutality and violence of his younger days was this empty husk, fed, cared for, and protected by the people around him in this suburban Detroit neighborhood, the barbarous guilt of his younger days hidden within the innocent trappings of ordinary American life on an ordinary sunny day in June.

The Butcher of Trawnicki could be any old man waiting for the end of his days after a life filled with generosity and grace.

Preuss gave up and went back out through the garage door to the front yard.

Baranski followed him. "You can see what kind of shape he's in," she said. "There's nothing he can help you with. I'll ask you not to bother us again."

"Mrs. Baranski, was your father once known by the name Bogdan Kovalenko?"

She said, "I've never heard that name before," but the spark of recognition missing in her father's eyes was present in hers.

She knows, Preuss thought. She knows all about her father.

"What about Elizaveta Kertész?"

"What about her?"

"Has she been in touch with you?"

"Someone by that name has been harassing us, but no, I've never met her. Look, my father is an old man who lived a decent life in spite of what some people might say, and now he can't do anyone any harm. Let him live out his remaining days in peace and quiet. And leave my family alone."

"Did your father ever talk about his life in Europe?"

"My father is a devoted family man who loves his adopted country. Please, please leave us alone."

He said, "Some people are convinced your father was a guard in Nazi concentration camps during the Second World War."

She raised her hands to her head as if to block his words from her ears. "I can't help what people believe. I know the truth."

I'll just bet you do, Preuss thought.

He handed her a business card. "If you change your mind and decide to talk with me, would you give me a call?"

"That's not going to happen," she said, but she took the card and turned back into the house.

He took the Woodward exit off 696 and drove down to the Wendy's south of Nine Mile. He ordered a hamburger and fries with iced tea from the drive-through and returned to the Shanahan.

While he ate he typed up his notes from his visit to Sterling Heights. Kovalenko's daughter was right, the old man was far gone in his disease. He hated to rule anything out at this point in an investigation with as many moving parts as this one, but he didn't think Kovalenko himself would be a factor here.

As he thought about it he remembered there was a Mafia boss in New York City who foiled prosecution for years by pretending to be crazy. Preuss used to see photos and videos of him walking around the streets of Little Italy muttering nonsense in a bathrobe. His ruse didn't work when his associates turned against him and testified to his fitness to run the crime empire and he was convicted.

He couldn't see that happening here. He saved his notes to a separate file and called Emmanuel Greene.

"I was just thinking about you," Greene said. "Did you see Kovalenko?"

"I went to talk with him this morning."

"Any success?"

"No. He seems useless as a source of information. Unless he's a phenomenal actor, he's too far gone in Alzheimer's. He doesn't know where or who he is."

"Too bad."

"I also spoke with his daughter. She wasn't much more help than her father was. Just asked for us to leave him alone in his last days."

"Do you think he's as bad as that?"

"I suppose a medical examination might prove he isn't faking it. But we'd need more compelling evidence before a judge would order it, and right now there isn't anything to suggest he's anything other than what he seems."

"Well, you tried. Though I'm not sure this is the end of it."

"What does that mean?"

"I might have another trick or two up my sleeve."

"Manny, don't do anything crazy, all right?"

"I told you, I leave the derring-do to you kids."

They disconnected and Preuss crumpled up half of his hamburger in the wrapper and threw it away along with the fries and tea, which was supposed to be unsweetened but they gave him sweet tea by mistake. He was about to get a coffee from the machine in Tanya's office when his cell phone rang.

He didn't recognize the number but took the call.

"Detective Preuss?"

A male voice. A cop. He recognized the tone.

"Speaking."

"This is Sheriff's Deputy Brian Dougherty. I'm calling at the request of Inspector Emma Blalock."

At the sound of her name his heart sank. He had not seen or heard from her since the previous spring but knew she had been promoted to director of her unit when her former boss, Jim Cass, died before Christmas last year.

"Inspector Blalock asked me to let you know the Ford minibus you've been looking for, Michigan license Hotel Delta Six Three Niner Five? It's turned up."

"Where?"

"In Pontiac, sir. The driver's in custody. Inspector Blalock wanted me to tell you to expect her in Ferndale within the hour."

37

The sally port door in the rear of the Eugene Shanahan Law Enforcement Complex began its slow upward rattle.

Preuss stood watching it from behind the two locked doors between the station and the garage. Beside him the day shift duty officer, whose name was Keegan, gave a monumental yawn. "Sorry," Keegan said. "This is the second half of a double. My ass is dragging."

"We've all been there," Preuss said. "But you're not much good to anybody if you can't keep your eyes open."

"No sir."

A black SUV pulled into the garage. Preuss made out two Oakland County Sheriff's deputies sitting in the front seat and a third person in the back seat, sitting forward with his wrists hand-cuffed behind him.

The sally port door closed and was secured and the two deputies stepped out of the car. He didn't recognize the driver, but saw the woman in the passenger seat was not a deputy but Inspector Emma Blalock of the Oakland County Sheriff's Office Special Investigations Unit.

When they secured their weapons in the lockers, the deputy opened the back door of the SUV and helped the prisoner out. He was a short sinewy man with a headful of thinning mouse-colored hair and boney shoulders in a tank top and scuffed Levis. Ropey arms were handcuffed behind him. The word "Lost" was tattooed vertically on the back of his left upper arm in Old English script and "Soul" tattooed on the back of the right arm.

Keegan unlocked the door to the garage and stepped aside as the Sheriff's deputy led Lost Soul into the building. "Left," Keegan said, and unlocked the larger of two interview rooms for them.

Preuss hung back. "Hello," he said to Emma Blalock.

"Hello." She held out a hand and he shook it.

Nobody picking up the frostiness of her greeting would suspect she had majorly pursued him for a relationship six months before, and he had as majorly tried to evade her. It caused problems between Preuss and Trombley because she was still married (information she neglected to share with Preuss) and Trombley was good friends with her husband. Trombley thought, wrongly, Preuss was chasing her. The tension between the two had eased and they were close again.

"Sorry to hear about Jim Cass," Preuss said.

"Thanks."

"What happened? I heard he died but didn't get any details."

"Massive heart attack in his office the week before Christmas. He hung on for a couple days before he gave out."

"Family?"

"Three kids scattered around the country. He'd been divorced for years."

"Too bad."

"Yeah."

"Thanks for bringing this guy down here."

"I could have processed him up in Pontiac but I figured you'd want to talk with him as soon as possible."

"I do. I appreciate it."

"Whatever."

She brushed by him in the hall and headed toward the interview room. "You're going to love this," she threw back over her shoulder.

The deputy unlocked the cuffs from Lost Soul and he took a seat at the table. Keegan led the deputy down the hall. Preuss stepped into the interview room and took the seat next to Emma Blalock, across the table from the prisoner.

"Here we have James Tomasulo," Emma said. "James, this is Detective Preuss of the Ferndale Police Department."

Tomasulo looked at Preuss with cloudy, heavy-lidded eyes.

"Detective Preuss is investigating the disappearance of the vehicle we found you with."

Tomasulo turned his vacant eyes on Emma.

"James was arrested by the Oakland County Sheriff's Office at 8:13 this morning," Emma Blalock said. "He was found in possession of the group home minibus listed as the missing vehicle in the BOLO the Ferndale Police Department put out last Monday. He has not satisfactorily explained how he came into possession of said vehicle. He's waived his right to an attorney."

"Do you still waive that right, James?" Preuss asked.

"I told this lady," Tomasulo said, "I don't need an attorney because I ain't done nothing wrong. And I have explained how I got that vehicle. You just don't believe me."

"It's Inspector Blalock," Preuss said. "Not 'this lady.'"

Tomasulo gave a quick shrug of his boney shoulders. "Don't change nothing."

Preuss said, "What are you doing with the minibus, James?"

Tomasulo grinned, showing a mouth full of empty spaces where teeth used to be. "I found it."

"Where?"

"Up to Pontiac there, where I stay."

"He claims," Emma Blalock said, "he was walking down the street and there it was. Keys in it and everything. Parked by the side of the road."

Preuss said, "Lucky guy."

Tomasulo said, "What I been saying."

"When was this?"

"Wednesday night. Nine o'clock maybe," he added when he saw Preuss was about to ask for more specifics.

"Where were you?"

"The street I stay on."

"Which is what?"

"Floradale Road."

"So you're walking down Floradale Road at nine on Wednesday night and you find a minibus customized to transport handicapped people with the keys in the ignition, and you decide it's going to be yours. That's your story?"

"God's truth."

"Uh-huh. Anybody inside?"

"Nope."

"And you didn't think to call the police?"

"Why would I do that? Soon as I saw it was abandoned—"

"How did you know it was abandoned?"

"It was parked next to a row of vacant lots. And I watched it for a while to make sure nobody was coming back for it. Nobody in my neighborhood leaves a vehicle like that unattended for long. So like I say, when I saw it was abandoned, I figured it became mine. Possession being nine-tenths of the law."

"You know that's not literally true, James, right?" Emma Blalock said. "There's no actual principle of law stating that. What it means is, you have the responsibility to prove you're the legitimate owner of something."

"That's just your opinion," Tomasulo said.

She rolled her eyes and Preuss said, "What did you do once you found it?"

"I got in and drove my new van around for a while."

Preuss turned to Emma. "How'd you find him?"

"James stopped at a bar in Pontiac for an eye-opener this morning. A deputy who was cruising the area noticed the minibus parked in the lot and discovered there was a BOLO out on it. He called for backup and when James exited the bar and entered the vehicle he was apprehended."

"And they shouldn't have arrested me, neither."

"Because you're innocent," Preuss said.

"That's right. I wasn't doing nothing wrong."

"Well," Preuss said, "see, that's where you're wrong. You were in possession of stolen property."

"Got nothing to do with me. I didn't steal it."

"Doesn't matter," Preuss said. "Remember what Inspector Blalock said about proving legitimate ownership? We're a hundred percent certain—that's ten-tenths—you're not the legitimate owner of that vehicle."

He turned to Emma Blalock. "What's he have in the way of priors?"

"Convictions for receiving stolen property, possession of Class B narcotics, several arrests for possession with intent to distribute, and assault with intent."

"Quite a history there, James."

Tomasulo allowed himself what he might have thought was a sly smile. The missing teeth in his mouth made the grin macabre. "I've made a few mistakes in my life. I admit it."

"Inspector," Preuss said to Emma Blalock, "may I speak with you outside?"

"What are you going to do with this guy?"

"Take him back to Pontiac to get him arraigned for possession of stolen property," Emma said.

"I don't see him as a car thief. Seems more your basic low-level dealer."

"He is. Very low. He's been on and off our radar over the years. There's an outstanding warrant on him for intent to distribute so we'll hold him on that for now, along with a Section 535. I'm also having a forensic workup on the bus as we speak."

"Let me know what you find?"

"Sure."

Back inside the interview room, Preuss said, "James, Inspector Blalock and I both think your story's lame. But neither one of us clocks you as a car thief. But here's the really bad news. The woman who was driving that minibus when it was stolen turned up dead. So we have a case of carjacking and murder in connection with the vehicle you were found with. Now James, who do you think we're going to go after for all that?"

"Wait, somebody died?"

"What happened to that sunny little smile there, James?" Emma Blalock said. "Things not so funny anymore?"

"I don't know nothing about nobody dying."

"You're looking at life in prison," Preuss said. "Is telling us your ridiculous little story worth spending the rest of your life in prison?"

Tomasulo looked from Preuss to Emma Blalock and then back to Preuss.

"I think it's time for me to see a lawyer."

38

James Tomasulo's attorney was a short woman named Alice Kennedy. She had dark hair held back from a long face with a barrette.

"James," Preuss said, "are you ready to talk with us?"

Alice Kennedy nodded to Tomasulo and he said, "Yeah."

"How about you start from the beginning and tell us how you came into possession of this bus? And save your story about finding it because that insults our intelligence."

"I didn't find it," Tomasulo said.

"Good start," Emma Blalock said. "How'd you get it?"

"Somebody gave it to me."

Preuss and Emma shared a look.

"No," Tomasulo said, "it's true."

"Somebody gave you a $60,000 wheelchair transport," Preuss said.

"That's the truth, my hand to the good lord."

"Who was it?"

"I don't know his name."

"That's all," Preuss said. He started to gather up his papers. "Let's go," he said to Emma Blalock.

"No, wait," Tomasulo said, "what I mean is, I don't know his real name. I just know him as Rickie."

"Rickie."

"Yeah."

"And how do you know Rickie?"

"Jimmy, don't say anything else," Alice Kennedy said.

"What's in it for me if I cooperate?" Tomasulo asked.

"A better question is," Preuss said, "what are the consequences if you don't?"

His lawyer pulled him into a short conference with her hand in front of their faces.

"Detective," Alice Kennedy said when they sat back, "my client is cooperating with you in good faith on what he knows about the disappearance of the vehicle in question. I advise him not to proceed unless you give him immunity from any crimes he should mention pursuant to his helping you."

"We're not interested in jamming him up for anything else right now. We just want to know what he can tell us about the missing minibus."

"So you agree to recommend immunity for what he might tell you about any criminal acts or conspiracies he might be involved in?"

"Fine," Preuss said. "We'll make our recommendation but the final disposition isn't up to us. It's the ADA you have to negotiate with."

"But you'll stipulate as to the recommendation."

"Yes. So what's the answer, James?" Preuss said. "How do you know Rickie?"

Alice Kennedy nodded to Tomasulo and he said, "I've done business with the guy."

"What kind of business?"

"I get rid of things for him."

"What kind of things?"

"Things he don't want no more. Cars, guns, items he might come across one way or another and don't want to keep."

"You do that for other people, too?"

"Sure. People give me things, I got other people who take them off my hands. I get a commission."

"So you're a fence?"

"I wouldn't put it that way. I like to think of myself as a middleman."

"Rickie gave you the minibus to get rid of?"

"Yeah."

"How were you supposed to do that?"

"Sell it off and give him what I made, minus ten percent I get to keep. I was gonna make arrangements with a chop shop to sell off the pieces."

"So why haven't you done it yet?"

He raised a boney shoulder. "Kinda liked riding around in it."

"When were you planning to get rid of it?"

"As luck would have it, I had it all set up for later today."

"Bad timing."

"You said it."

"This Rickie, when did he give it to you?" Emma Blalock said.

"Tuesday night."

"Walk us through what happened," Preuss said.

"So Rickie calls me up and tells me he's got a job for me. I meet him Tuesday night. And the plan, the plan is for me to make the vehicle disappear so it wouldn't be a problem."

"Are those his words? 'So it wouldn't be a problem'?"

"His exact words. So it wouldn't be a problem."

"But he didn't say what kind of problem."

"No. And I didn't ask."

Preuss sat considering the man across the table.

"What's Rickie's last name?"

"Dunno. I just know him as Rickie."

"Where can we find him?"

"No idea. When people need me, they get in touch."

"You have his number?"

"Not any more. He changes burners all the time. Never has the same number twice."

"Are you willing to come back to Pontiac and sit with an artist?" Emma Blalock asked.

"What about my client's plea deal?" Alice Kennedy said. "We're not going anywhere without some assurances."

"Before you take him back for arraignment," Preuss said to Emma, "let's get Carnahan over here for a talk."

Late in the afternoon, after Emma took Tomasulo back to the Oakland County Jail at the county campus in Pontiac, Preuss filled his Tim Horton's coffee mug at Tanya Corcoran's machine and was sitting in his office when his cell phone rang.

Janie Cahill.

"Martin," she said, "where are you?"

"The station. The minibus turned up. We may have a lead on the second guy in the surveillance video. A guy named Rickie."

"Rickie? Not much to work with."

"No," he said, "but Emma Blalock's got her forensic team on it. We might learn something from that."

"Wait. Emma?"

He explained about Lost Soul.

"How was she?"

"Cold as ice. Janie, don't start, okay? She was your idea, not mine."

"I know. I wasn't going to say anything."

"What's up?"

"After I left report-out this morning I started working through my case files. The most recent one was a report about a

kid from the Township who found a guy beat half to death yesterday. I'm over here with the boy and his grandmother now."

"How's he doing?"

"He's a little shaken up but he's gonna be okay. But the name
of the vic rang a bell because I just heard you talking about him
this morning. William Simpson."

"My van guy? Billy Simpson?"

"The same."

"Where is he now?"

"At Providence. Martin, they're saying he might not make
it."

39

"What are you doing here?"

Billy's sister was standing outside the Providence Hospital surgical stepdown ICU waiting room. She was leaning against the wall to Billy's room with tears running down her cheeks.

Preuss said, "I came as soon as I heard. What happened?"

"My brother just died, that's what happened. Look, I don't want you here."

"But what—"

"Just leave!"

Rather than stand there and engage with her anger and grief, Preuss said, "I'm sorry for your loss," and went off to find a nurse who could tell him what the situation was.

He found the charge nurse for the unit.

"What can you tell me about this?"

"He was in surgery all night," the woman said. "He had major head trauma and broken arms, legs, and ribs. Plus organ damage to his spleen and liver. Somebody did a number on this poor guy. Nobody thought he'd live out the day."

The loudspeaker announced, "Code Blue, Surgical ICU, bed 12.

The nurse said, "Sorry, gotta run," and dashed away to another patient's room where a medical team was already converging with a crash cart.

Cletus Petty lived with his grandmother, three sisters, and his older sister's toddler in one of the duplexes that were part of the Royal Oak Township Public Housing Authority. The home he lived in was one of a row of one-story brick buildings along Wyoming Avenue on the same block as the AAAdvantage Paint Company.

The boy was a skinny, handsome kid with dark skin the color of expresso beans. Sitting on the sofa beside his grandmother, an imposing woman in a floral housedress with heavy, swollen ankles and a constant cigarette in one hand, the boy repeated his story for Martin Preuss, who sat beside Janey Cahill on a love seat in the living room. The place reeked of cigarette smoke.

When he was finished, Preuss said, "Would you recognize this man again, Cletus? The one who beat the guy you found?"

"I think so," Cletus said. "When he was beating this other man, I couldn't see his face. But then he turned around to go and I got a good look at him."

"Was there anything you remember about him?"

"He was white."

"Okay. Anything else you remember about his appearance?"

The boy shook his head.

"Did he have a beard or mustache?"

"No."

"What was his hair like? Long? Short?"

"Real long."

"What color was it?"

"Sort of light brown, I think."

"Do you remember how he was dressed?"

Cletus looked thoughtful, then said, "No. I was just, you know, so shocked at what he was doing."

"Sure," Preuss said. "And then you went to tell your grand-mother what you saw?"

The boy nodded.

"That was very brave."

Cletus ducked his head at the praise.

His grandmother put a hand on his head. "My grandbaby won't get in no trouble now, will he?"

"No ma'am," said Preuss. "He's doing a good thing here."

Outside Cahill lit her own cigarette and sucked smoke deep into her lungs.

"Man," she said, "I was dying in there, watching her light up one after the other."

"You could have just taken a deep breath. I hope Cletus spends a lot of time outdoors."

"Did that help, talking to him?"

"It'd be more helpful if we could show him some photos once we get a line on somebody. I'm thinking this has something to do with Billy Simpson's part in the theft of the minibus."

"Why?"

"To shut him up, maybe. I talked to him about it last week and he admitted he was there on the night it was stolen."

"So somebody knows he talked to us and got antsy about what he might have said."

"It's a good possibility. The troopers caught the case so I'll need to work through them."

He looked down the block to the corner with the paint company. "Think I'll make a stop down there first."

"What's on your mind, detective?" Alberto Campanella said.

"Billy Simpson. One of your employees, and also your nephew?"

That smile again, even more vulpine if possible. "I like to keep everything on a professional level at work so I ask him not to call me Uncle Al. But he is my dear nephew. Do you want to talk to him? Dolores, is he in today?"

"No, Mr. Campanella." Dolores was still glued to her chair in the AAAdvantage Paint Company office. She was scraping the last bit of yogurt from a container.

"I'm not looking for him," Preuss said. "I'm sorry to have to let you know this, but Billy died earlier today of injuries he sustained in a beating yesterday."

"Oh my lord!" Dolores said.

Campanella swallowed, looked ashen, couldn't speak.

"He was found three blocks from here," Preuss said. "Do you know anything about that?"

"Oh no," Campanella said. "Oh no. He's my late sister's boy," he said, as if that explained something.

"When was the last time you saw him?"

"I was in on Saturday and I saw him here then. But I left mid-morning and didn't come back till after everyone was already gone and he wasn't here." Campanella turned toward Dolores. "Was he in yesterday?"

She rifled through the time cards on her desk. "He worked yesterday. He put in his full hours. But he didn't show up this morning. And didn't call in . . ." She stopped as she realized why.

"Oh dear god," Campanella said.

"Do you know anyone who might have it in for him? One of the workers here, maybe?"

"No. Everybody loved him. He was such a sweet guy. He'd give you the shirt off his back."

"Apparently some of the other men teased him because of his disabilities. Could one of them have done this?"

"I can't imagine that."

"I spoke with him last week. Do you know who might be aware of that?"

Campanella shook his head. "I have no idea."

Preuss regarded him. "Because it happened so close to this business and there may be a connection, the investigators will have to speak with everyone who works here. Especially the men I spoke with when I came looking for him."

"Wait, isn't it your case?"

"The State Police patrol Royal Oak Township so it's theirs. But there might be a connection with the case I'm working on, the missing minibus I talked to you about last week."

"You think Billy's involved with that?"

"I'm certain he was."

* * *

Campanella sat back in his chair and gazed up at the dingy ceiling stained with years of leakage through the roof.

This was bad.

And he had no confidence it would get better anytime soon.

He sat like that for another half hour, thinking his way through the alternatives.

Then he stood and went to the door of his office and looked around the warehouse. Most of the men were already gone for the day.

He returned to his desk and said, "Dolores, it's almost quitting time. Why don't you take off for the night?"

"Are you sure?"

"Absolutely. Enjoy your evening. I'll see you in the morning."

Dolores made some grumbling noises about wanting to work her full time but he shooed her out. She pulled her purse from the bottom drawer of her desk and heaved herself to her feet.

"Wait," he said. He reached into his pocket and pulled out a handful of dollars. "Before you come in tomorrow, how about you stop at the Tim Horton's on Woodward and bring in some Timbits."

"You're not supposed to have those, Mr. Campanella."

"I know. Just this once. They won't kill me." He forced a smile.

She shrugged and started out the door.

"Oh, and Dolores, one more thing."

She stopped and looked back with suspicion, as if he were going to change his mind.

"Have you seen Ray anywhere? I need to speak with him."

40

On the way back to the station Trombley called.

"Just wanted you to know, it's not the ex-husband," Trombley said. "Bellamy talked with him today. Turns out he was in the hospital last week when Elizaveta was killed. Sunday of that week he went on a bender during the day and got in another bar fight. St. John Macomb-Oakland held him for observation for a few days."

"The hospital verified it?"

"Yup. Cross him off the list. And Martin, we never had this conversation."

Gail Crimmonds was waiting for him outside his office. She was a tall woman, formidably bulked up with her Kevlar under her uniform shirt.

"Detective," she said, "glad I caught you. I thought you might be gone for the day."

"Still here," he said. "Come on in."

She followed him into his office and stood beside his desk.

"Want to have a seat?"

"No sir. That Fred Samuelson you talked to me about? I found him."

"Already?"

"Yes sir. I did what you said and called the hospitals. I got lucky at Detroit Receiving. Turns out he'd gone to ground in Detroit and collapsed from his wounds and the ambulance brought him there."

"So you went down to get him?"

"I got there just as he was being released. Good timing."

"Very impressive, Sergeant Crimmonds."

"Doing my job, sir."

Her formality made Preuss smile. "If you want to advance in this department, Gail, you need to understand one very important thing: I'm not the one you have to brownnose."

She laughed (except it wasn't a joke) and led him to the large interview room where she had put Samuelson. The man Preuss saw through the clear glass walls didn't look like he could cause the kind of havoc he was accused of. He was small and thin, almost child-like in his stature.

Preuss said, "Do you want to sit in on the interview?"

"I'd love to, sir."

Preuss made Fred Samuelson sit there while he read through the report, turning each page with deliberation. This was unnecessary since he had written it himself and knew what was there but he wanted to get up the little man's sleeve. Crimmonds sat beside him, taking it all in.

When he was finished he closed the folder and looked at Samuelson. He was a homely, dog-faced young man in his late twenties with thick black stubble, large ears, and a long skinny pencil neck.

"Fred," Preuss said. "You've been informed of your rights and you've waived legal counsel, is that correct?"

"Yes."

"How are you feeling?"

"Like crap." Not defiant but not repentant either.

Preuss indicated the bandages on his arms and face and the knot on his forehead. "Those look painful."

"They are."

"How'd you get them?"

"I was mugged. Besides these there's a huge knife wound in my side. It took twelve stitches to close up! Plus I got a couple broken ribs."

"Sounds bad."

"It is. I don't even know why *I'm* here. I'm the victim."

Preuss's phone buzzed with an incoming call but he hit Ignore.

He said, "Do you know who did these things, Fred?"

"No. I was minding my own business and these creeps jumped me."

"That's terrible."

"Yeah, tell me about it."

"Where'd it happen?"

"Outside my house."

"Anybody see it?"

"Guess not."

"Did you file a police report?"

"No."

"Why not?"

He shrugged. "They were long gone by the time I got to a phone."

"How many were there?"

"Three."

Preuss opened the file again and read some more. "Says here you live in Royal Oak."

"That's right."

"Thirteen Mile and Coolidge."

"Yes."

"Right down the street from Beaumont Hospital. You could walk there, it's so close."

"So?"

"So Sergeant Crimmonds here picked you up at Detroit Receiving. All the way downtown. What were you doing down there?"

"Oh, so now it's a crime where you go the hospital?"

"Don't get excited, Fred. It's just a question."

"I'm *not* getting excited."

"You're raising your voice."

Samuelson sat back and tried to calm himself.

"What I'm asking is, why did you go all the way downtown to get yourself looked at?"

"I was seeing a buddy lives down near Wayne."

"You have a knife wound that took twelve stitches, three broken ribs, and a host of other cuts and contusions, and you decide to go visiting?"

"I didn't realize I was hurt so bad."

"Ah."

Preuss read the file some more.

"Then there's the matter of the arrest warrant."

"What arrest warrant?"

Preuss looked at Crimmonds and she said, "Mr. Samuelson, I told you I was executing an arrest warrant."

"And I told you I didn't do anything."

Preuss sighed. "Fred, I've been a policeman for over twenty years. Do you have any idea how many times I've heard that phrase in my career?"

"No, and all due respect, I don't care. *I'm* the victim here."

"Do you know a woman named Helen Vlastos?"

"Never heard of her."

"She knows you."

Samuelson folded his arms and returned Preuss's steady gaze.

Preuss let out another sigh.

"See, Fred, I had a talk with Helen in her hospital room. And here's what she told me. She told me you were hiding in the closet in her apartment and you jumped out and attacked her with a knife. And you got those nasty wounds when her friends came to her rescue."

"That," said Samuelson, "is totally not what happened."

Preuss raised his hands. "Don't even bother, okay? It's been a long day and I don't have time for this. I have a statement from her and both men who were there at the time and they all identified you. In the morning she's going to come in and make the formal ID and then that's going to be the end of the story. We got you, Fred. Attempted murder, assault, breaking and entering. The trifecta."

There was nothing the other man could say to that.

Preuss leaned forward. "What I want to know is, why would you do such a thing?"

Samuelson shook his head. "You wouldn't understand."

"So help me out. Why did you do it?"

The eternal question, Preuss thought. Trying to figure out the reasoning behind behavior that sprung from cruelty, stupidity, irrationality . . . was there a more futile activity? And at the same time one that required, even demanded, a satisfying answer?

He remembered Tony Tullio, the detective who retired last year, saying you can't argue with crazy.

"She's done far worse to me."

"So you do know her."

"Yes, I know her."

"And she's done something worse to you than going after her with a knife?"

"Yes! Yes!"

"Easy there, Fred."

"Much worse! She's made my life a living hell! She sends me threatening emails, she calls my apartment at all hours of the day and night, she calls my employer and all my friends telling them how I screwed her out of money . . . I just wanted to reason with her and ask her to stop."

Preuss opened the file to the complaint. "'I'm gonna kill you, bitch,'" he read aloud. "'I'm gonna cut your heart out.' Sound like reasoned discourse to you, Fred?"

Samuelson sneered, a chilling sight even on his big-eared, clownish face. "Those are all lies. See, she's even lying to you."

"The complainant and two witnesses swore those are your exact words."

"Oh, I see what's going on here." Samuelson sat back in his chair and began tapping a fast tattoo with his foot. "She lies and they swear to it. And you believe them."

"Their complaint corresponds with the physical evidence at the scene."

Samuelson slammed his hands on the table and began to rise. "But they're lies! LIES!"

Crimmonds shot to her feet and pushed him back down.

"Calm down, Fred, or we'll handcuff you to the table."

Samuelson sat back in his chair. He continued to fume.

"I tried to reason with her but she laughed at me. She thought she was this queen who could treat me like dirt, make me feel like she was too good for me with her fancy clothes and all that junk jewelry she wears. I wanted to show her. I wanted to show her but good. She can't treat me that way!"

Preuss considered the rabid little mutt across the table from him, with his bandaged arm, stitches on his cheek, the awkward way he sat because of a few broken ribs and a gaping knife wound sitting in a police station facing years in prison. And lying to their faces.

A sudden exhaustion washed over him and his head began to pound. He propped his elbow on the table and rested his head in his hands and closed his eyes. How much more of this could he stand?

"Detective," Crimmonds said. "You okay?"

Preuss looked up to see her frowning concern.

After Billy Simpson died of a beating, this was more than he could take today.

"Would you process him? And call Helen Vlastos and ask her to come in for a formal ID in the morning?"

"Of course. You sure you're all right?"

"I'm okay. But I've had it."

He walked all around Martin Road Park but there was still no sign of Sheila Hawkins.

He picked up an order of General Tso from Hong Kong One on Nine Mile and took it to Toby's, where he ate it while they watched *Monty Python and the Holy Grail* on the television in Toby's room. He didn't think about anything except killer rabbits and black knights with no arms or legs until Toby fell asleep, and then he went home.

41

Sheila Hawkins opened her eyes and saw the man perched at the foot of her bed like a gremlin, arms around his knees drawn up close against his body. He was watching her. His head drooped but then he would shake it to clear it. Once her own brain fog eased she saw he was seriously messed up.

"You're back," the man said.

He grinned. "I gave you a little magic potion, help you sleep. Want some water?"

She nodded and he unfolded himself and disappeared from the room. She recognized his shirt, a tie-dyed tee shirt with swirls of purple and yellow and blue. She had seen that before . . . was it just yesterday? Or another time?

How long had she been here?

She moved her body. She was lying on a bed, though she wasn't restrained. She remembered being in terrible pain, but now the pain was little more than a memory in her bones and muscles.

And something else. She was naked.

How did she get here? She had a vague notion that this man was the one who had caused the pain in the first place . . . she remembered being beaten, but in her present foggy state she couldn't say if she was remembering an older beating from another time or if this man had been the one who hit her. She thought maybe it had been him.

The more she thought about it, the more certain she was that he had been the one hitting her.

She moved her hands around on the bed to find something to cover herself with but there was nothing. The mattress was bare. There were no sheets or blankets. Not even a pillow under her head.

The man came back into the room with an aluminum tumblerful of cold water. She guzzled it.

"Who are you?" she asked when her tongue came unstuck.

Instead of answering he took a spliff from his pants pocket and lit it with a kitchen match struck on his thumb. He inhaled and kept it in.

He held it out to her and she shook her head. He shrugged, let the smoke out in a rush.

"Why are you keeping me here?"

He shook his head, as though it were best not to know the answer to such questions.

"I don't want to stay. I want to leave."

"This is for your own protection. There are people out there want to hurt you."

"Who?"

"Can't tell you."

"I don't care. I don't want to stay here. And I want my clothes."

She started to bring herself to a sitting position. He was on her in a flash, pushing her down, saying, "You don't wanna do that."

"I don't wanna stay here."

"Forget it." He pinned her. She had no strength. "You're staying here."

"No," she said, louder this time. "I want to leave!"

"No!" As he held her down with one arm he fumbled on the nightstand next to the bed with his other hand. She realized there was a plaster cast on his arm and as if the mists cleared in her brain she recognized him, his shirt and his plaster cast. He was one of the men she saw in the parking lot of the church a week ago. And she began to struggle harder, revitalized by what she remembered.

He found what he was searching for on the nightstand and she felt a sharp poke on her shoulder, the pinch followed by darkness closing on in her.

"You know what they call this?" the man asked, his voice receding. "Rainbow. Because of all the pretty colors you see."

I don't see anything, Sheila thought. Except darkness.

Which embraced her, took her into itself as if it had been waiting for her for a long time.

Tuesday, June 15, 2010

42

The day began with a message from Emma Blalock waiting for him when he got in. *Please call. Urgent.*

"Martin," she said when he got her on the phone, "I feel like I owe you an apology. I came across a bit harsh yesterday."

"Don't worry about it."

"Well, I am. I never apologized for what happened between us. You know, before."

"There's nothing to apologize for, Emma. Forget it."

"No, I think there is. I regret waiting so long to say this. But I was so angry with you. I had a talk with Reggie and he told me I was the cause of some problems between the two of you."

"Reg and I worked it out. We're fine. You and I are fine. Everybody's fine."

"So we're good?"

"We're good."

"Okay then."

"Was that what you wanted?"

"No, that's not all. The preliminary report's back from the forensic analysis of the minibus."

"How'd you get it so fast?"

"My guys worked through the night. I can be remarkably persuasive."

Don't I know it, he thought.

"It's just a first pass at the findings, so it's sketchy. But I thought you'd want to start going through it."

"I do. Can you send it to me?"

"Doing it now."

He heard her clicking on her keyboard. "There's a ton of fingerprints, fibers, and traces of DNA. It'll take a while to sort out."

He said, "Most of that's from the house residents, I would guess." He thought of all the drool and other bodily fluids Toby's housemates produced. "Did your guys do any matches?"

More keyboard clicking. "Doesn't look like it. No. They haven't had time. I'll have them keep working."

"Okay. I'll comb through it, see if anything jumps out."

He opened his email and saw the message from her. "Got it. I'll be in touch."

"Thanks, Martin," she said, and disconnected.

He opened the file and sent it to print. When he retrieved it he skimmed through it, then read more carefully. Emma was right, there were dozens of samples of prints and fibers. None of the prints were labeled. Emma's team would run it all through the FBI's Integrated Automated Fingerprint Identification System.

No prints were found on the steering wheel, gear shift, and driver's side door handles. Someone had wiped them all clean. Most of the prints were from other areas . . . the dashboard, the inside walls, the tie-downs, and so on.

He thought back to the church's surveillance video, and the way Hoodie left Zach Warranow to fend for himself in the park. And he remembered standing with Toby while his housemates were being loaded onto their transport for the trip downtown to the Tigers game.

He paged through the report to see if any prints were picked up from the pad that controlled the wheelchair lift.

Yes. There was a perfect thumb print on the button that lowered the platform.

He called Emma back and explained what he needed. It was an hour before he heard from her.

"From the IAFIS data base there was a match made with the right thumbprint of an Elton Deetz. Is he one of the staff at the group home?"

"He is not," Preuss said.

But he was in that minibus.

Elton Deetz was Hoodie.

You must have forgotten to wipe off the control pad, Elton, he thought. He ran Deetz through the State Police Internet Criminal History Access Tool and found Deetz's criminal record (aggravated assault, A & B/simple assault, intent to distribute, attempted murder) as well as his last known address. A house in Eastpointe.

He drove east on 696 to the Ford Freeway, I-94, which he took south to the East Nine Mile exit. Eastpointe was a small community on the east side of the metropolitan area not far from Lake St. Clair. It used to be known as East Detroit but the residents changed the name by referendum to avoid being associated with Detroit. They hoped the "pointe" part of the name would instead remind people of the nearby, and much more upscale, Grosse Pointes.

Preuss's destination was a street called Cushing Avenue, south of East Nine Mile. It was another of the thousands of ranch homes scattered around the region.

An older man opened the door. He had several days' worth of grizzle on his face and his hair stuck out from the sides of his head like quills.

Preuss introduced himself and said, "I'm looking for Elton Deetz."

"Well," the man said, "you won't find him here."

"Did he live here?"

"Not really."

"What's that mean?"

"It means my wife's crazy cousin once let that nutcase use this address after his last stretch in Jackson Prison. She never asked me about letting him use it and I've been having conversations like this with people like you ever since."

"Who am I speaking with?"

"Walter Lubinski."

"Mr. Lubinski, I take it you know Deetz?"

"Oh yes."

"Do you know where I can find him?"

"I do. Shacked up with cousin Louise in the house she inherited from her mother. Wait here, I'll get the address for you."

He disappeared inside the house and five minutes later returned with a sheet of paper on which was scrawled the address of the house on Dorchester Avenue in Madison Heights where Billy Simpson had lived with his sister. Whose name was Louise.

"And if you can find another bed for him in Jackson," Lubinski said, "I wouldn't mind that either."

He sat in the Explorer and called Janie Cahill.

"I'm sending you a copy of a DMV photo of Elton Deetz. I'm certain he's the one we've been looking for in the minibus hijacking. I'm betting he's also responsible for Billy Simpson's death. How soon can you get to Cletus Petty's house and show him an array with that photo?"

"I'll put it together and head over there right now."

43

Louise Simpson tried to close the door in his face.

"Wait. Please."

"What are you, the angel of death?"

"We need to talk."

"I've had all the talks with you I'm ever going to have. And how do you know my name?"

"I was just speaking with Walter Lubinski."

"You spoke to cousin Walt? Why are you harassing me?" She leaned her weight against the door but he held it open with a straight arm. "Just go! I have a funeral to plan. Don't you people have any respect?"

"Listen to me. You need to hear this. I know who killed your brother."

That got her attention.

"It was somebody who wanted to keep him quiet about what he knows."

"Jesus, you can't protect us from the animals that prey on innocent people, so you make up these cockeyed conspiracy theories. My brother was the victim of a random mugging in that god-forsaken neighborhood where he works."

"No, that's not what happened. You don't know this, but when I spoke with him your brother admitted he was at a church in Ferndale last Monday night. That's when a minibus belonging to a group home for handicapped adults was stolen. The driver was a young woman who turned up dead two nights later."

"My brother wouldn't have anything to do with that. He just wouldn't. You must have forced him to say it."

"Your brother was too innocent to lie, Louise. You know that's true. And there's something else. I believe Elton is responsible for your brother's death."

She stared at him as if he were crazy. "*My* Elton?"

"I know this is a lot to take in. But there may be other lives in danger." He thought about Sheila Hawkins, who was still missing.

"That's not possible. Rickie wouldn't do anything like that."

"You called him Rickie?"

"He hates Elton. His middle name's Richard so he likes to be called Rickie."

Elton Deetz was Rickie . . . of course. It was all falling into place.

Preuss said, "Billy drove him to the church the night the wheelchair transport was stolen. We have Elton—Rickie—on a surveillance video driving the minibus away."

"No, that can't be. Billy was out, okay, I can see he doesn't have the sense to say no sometimes. But Rickie was working."

"At what?"

"He does construction. He told me he was out working late that night on a job."

"You know he's done prison time for selling drugs?"

"I know. But he swore to me he put all that behind him. I told him if he ever goes back to that life I'm history."

"He didn't go back because he never left it."

Preuss's phone chimed with a text. He looked at it and saw it was from Janey.

Cletus made a positive ID on Elton Deetz.

He held the phone up to show Louise. "A witness who saw Billy being beaten just made a positive ID," he said. "It was Rickie, Louise. There's no question about it."

Her face and neck glowed a deep red. As Preuss watched her, he saw the terrible knowledge form behind her eyes. She knew he was telling the truth.

She leaned against the doorframe as though all her energy, even her bones, had deserted her.

"Where is he, Louise?"

"I don't know."

"I don't believe you."

"It's true. He told me he was leaving for a few days on a trip to do some work out of town."

"Is there anybody who might know where he is?"

"I don't know. Please, I can't deal with this."

He handed her his card. "Here are all my numbers, including my cell. Call me as soon as you hear from him, okay? Do it for Billy."

At the mention of her brother she buried her head in her hands and sobbed.

In the Explorer on his way back to the Shanahan he called Emma Blalock and told her what he had learned about Elton Richard Deetz's connection with the murder of Billy Simpson. He left a message on her phone. The Simpson case belonged to the Oakland County Sheriff so she would pursue it.

On his desk at the station Tanya had left a phone message slip. Someone named Maria Baranski wanted him to call her ASAP.

He recognized the last name—that belonged to John Kowalczyk's daughter. But who was Maria?

He called and a woman's voice answered. "This is Detective Martin Preuss from the Ferndale Police Department. I have a message here to call Maria."

A long pause.

"This is Maria." Young, hesitant.

"How can I help you, Maria?"

"Mr. Greene said I should speak with you."

"Manny Greene?"

"Yes. I'm sitting here right next to him."

"What do you want to talk about?"

Another pause that was so long and silent Preuss thought the call had been disconnected. "Hello?" he said.

"Mr. Greene said you want to talk about my grandfather."

"Can I speak with Mr. Greene?"

The next voice was Greene's. "You're welcome."

"How'd you find her?"

"When I was at their house a couple days ago I saw her before they closed the door in my face. I had a hunch she had something to tell me. I waited till she left the house for work today and intercepted her."

"You're amazing."

"Not ready for the Old Folks' Home just yet."

44

The cell phone rang eight times and then stopped.

Elton Deetz lit a blunt. He took a deep toke and held the smoke in as long as he could, then let it dribble out of his mouth and up into his nose. When he was bored, as he was now, he liked to play a game with himself and try to guess who was calling. Nine times out of ten he guessed right.

This time he guessed Louise. She called a little while ago and left that snotty message for him and he hadn't bothered calling her back. If it was her again, he wasn't going to answer it this time either.

The phone rang again. He left it on the counter in the kitchen of the apartment on Second Avenue in Highland Park where he was staying. It was his buddy Larry's apartment but Larry was staying with his girlfriend in Southfield while Deetz needed the place for a while.

He drifted out to the kitchen and picked it up to see who was calling.

Not Louise. He toyed with the idea of not answering but decided that wouldn't be smart.

"What?" he said.

"He's not happy." That goddamn calm voice. That was probably the same voice he'd use if he called the fire department because his house was on fire.

"What are you talking about?"

"I'm talking about what you did."

"He told me to tie up loose ends. That's what I did."

"He didn't tell you to kill his nephew."

"Lookit, he didn't know how to keep his mouth shut. He turned me into the cops."

Now the voice on the other end of the line paused. "What do you mean, he turned you into the cops?"

"You didn't know that, did you? On Saturday a cop came to my house looking for me. How would they know about me unless he told them?"

"Did you talk to this cop? What was his name?"

"I didn't see him. One of the neighbors talked with him. And yo, tell him to chill, all right? There's no way they can tie either of us to this. I made sure of it."

"Where are you now?"

"Someplace safe. Don't worry about it."

"I'm not worried, Elton. You're the one who should be worried. Tell me where you are and I'll get somebody there to watch out for you."

"Forget it. "

"You sure about that?"

"Tell everybody to relax. This time tomorrow it's all going to be taken care of."

"What's going to happen tomorrow?"

"I'll have it all settled. There won't be nothing to worry about."

The calm voice said, "There better not be."

After they disconnected Deetz walked around the apartment, antsy, wanting to get out, wanting to do something.

He thought, Why put off till tomorrow what you can do today?

He stood on the stoop of the house on State Fair in Detroit and rang the bell until a tiny curtain swung away from an opening in the front door and an impassive black face under a shiny black do-rag peered out. Deetz's nerves were stretched and singing. He didn't know this guy. He was on instant alert.

"Who are you?"

"Never you mind who I am. What you want?"

"Send Worm out."

"Who want him?"

"Tell him Deetz."

The face behind the curtain grinned, showing a gold incisor. "Deetz."

"Problem?"

"Naw, Deetz. Huh-huh. Deetz. Yeah, no problem, Deetz."

"Just go get him."

Gold Tooth's loopy laughter turned to a sneer and he stuck a pistol out through the opening in the door.

Deetz stepped aside and pulled the hand holding the gun out and slammed the guy into the other side of the door. Gold Tooth squeezed off four harmless shots and Deetz twisted the guy's gun arm and he screamed.

He let the hand go and Gold Tooth dropped the gun and pulled his arm back inside. Deetz kicked the door open and pulled a Sig Sauer P220 from his pocket and smashed the guy in the face with it.

Gold Tooth fell back. Deetz was on him and shoved the gun into his mouth and the guy looked back at him with wide-eyed terror. Blood poured out from a cut on his cheek.

Deetz pulled the barrel from the guy's mouth and pistol-whipped him across the face. Two men appeared from inside the house and tried to pull Deetz away but Deetz shook them off and pounded Gold Tooth's head until the man was still.

Then Deetz let himself be pulled away and the others dragged Gold Tooth inside the house. Deetz returned the pistol to his pocket.

Worm stepped forward and urged Deetz out onto the front porch and closed the door behind them.

Deetz shook off Worm's hand and said, "Get off me. Who was that?"

"A new guy. Marcus. Hasn't learned the ropes yet. Doesn't know all the players."

"He'll know better'n to give me shit next time."

"I don't believe there'll be a next time, Rickie. I believe you've kilt Marcus."

"Then get rid of him."

They walked down to Deetz's Camaro. Worm got into the passenger seat and Deetz slid behind the wheel. Worm pulled a roll of money out of his pocket and handed it over to Deetz.

"From last night. Might improve your disposition."

Deetz peeled off a few of the sticky, wrinkled bills and handed them back to the older man. He pocketed the rest.

"How'd you like to earn a little extra? Ten minutes of your time. Fifteen max."

Worm said, "You know me, Rickie. Always open to offers."

* * *

"I hear things are not going well."

The old man cleared his throat, sounding like a car trying to start on a cold morning. "That your opinion, too?"

The younger man tried to keep his voice calm and mechanical as always even though he was roiling with anger and anxiety. "All due respect, sir, I think you should be worried, yes."

He paused and let that sink in. At the next table, a waiter lit a plate of saganaki and shouted "Opa!" as a long tongue of flame licked the ceiling of the Greektown restaurant.

"I'm already working on canceling one order," he continued.

The old man said, "Why?"

"The boss doesn't think the equipment is working properly."

The old man listened with his eyes half-closed, as though barely interested. "That so."

"Too many mistakes," the younger man said.

The old man's breath rattled in his chest. "I think maybe it's time to fire the boss, huh? What do you think?"

"I think things are getting out of hand."

The old man shrugged. "Recall both orders. When it's done, find a new place to store the merchandise."

"Yessir," the younger man said. "Consider it done."

"You're a good boy. You got a future ahead of you."

"Thank you, sir."

And right here's where it starts, the younger man thought.

45

Preuss turned into a strip mall half a mile up Van Dyke from Seventeen Mile Road. He parked in front of a Kerby's Koney Island and saw them inside in a booth at the rear of the restaurant, the old PI and the young woman with bleached blonde hair he had seen at the Kovalenko house.

He shook hands with Greene and extended his hand to the young woman. "Martin Preuss."

She took his hand and said, "Maria Baranski," without meeting his gaze.

"You're Oksana's daughter?"

She nodded. A young woman appeared beside the booth and set a glass of water in front of Preuss. "Can I get you anything?"

There was a sloppy plate with half a coney island and fries in front of Maria. Greene was drinking tea. "Just coffee."

When the waitress left Preuss said, "What do you have to tell me, Maria?"

"Mr. Greene said you want to know about my grandfather."

"I do."

"I saw you when you came to the house yesterday. You called him Bogdan Kovalenko."

"Have you heard that name before?"

"Mr. Greene said that was his name when he lived in Europe."

"Yes."

"I never heard it. At least until that girl started calling the house and asking for him."

"Did you ever talk to her?"

"Once I answered the phone when she called. She said he did some bad things back in Europe."

"He did some very bad things. Your grandfather was a guard in some of the concentration camps where thousands of people were killed during the Second World War. He made life even more miserable for the ones who were imprisoned."

She shook her head and dipped a French fry into a puddle of catsup on her plate. She sucked the catsup off the fry before eating it. She pulled a half dozen napkins from the holder to wipe her fingers and her mouth.

"It's hard to admit someone in your family did the kinds of things he did," Preuss said.

"You're positive it was him?"

"The people who know about him are, yes."

Greene said, "There's no question about it, Maria."

"He's always been so nice to me and my brother. When we were young he used to buy us things and take us to the circus and go on vacations out west with us . . . And look at him now, he's like a vegetable. But what he did in the war, that's why that girl wanted to get in touch with him?"

Preuss said, "Yes. Her name was Elizaveta Kertész."

"Was?"

"She was killed last week."

"And you think my grandpa had something to do with that?"

"It's clear he himself didn't. But there may be a connection we can't see yet. You said you spoke with her?"

"I asked my mother about it and she got real upset and said not to pay any attention to what the girl said about what Grandpa did. But then last week she turned up at the house wanting to see him."

"When?"

"Monday."

The day Elizaveta disappeared.

"What happened?"

"She got the door slammed in her face. Same as happened to you."

"Both of us," Greene said.

"Who did it?" Preuss said. "Your mother?"

"No, no, it was Danny."

"Who's that?"

"My brother. Everybody was out but him when she showed up. Besides Grandpa, of course, and Lyudmila. She's his aide. He never goes out of the house by himself. And Lyudmila never leaves his side."

"Your brother saw Elizaveta? And knew what she wanted?"

"She must have told him because he told us afterwards."

She chewed on another French fry, sucking the catsup off first.

"How did he know to turn her away?"

"I guess he heard us talking about her. He doesn't live with us, but he happened to be there. He's a real mess, my brother. Total loser, into drugs and everything. He came over to mooch some money, as usual, but I was in class and Ma was out shopping so he hung around till one of us got home. He came because he said he needed money to pay for his medical bills. He broke his arm a couple of weeks ago and expects us to pay for it."

Preuss said, "He broke his arm?"

"Yeah."

"How?"

"He wouldn't tell us."

"Where's it broken? His forearm?"

"How'd you know?"

"Does your brother ever wear a tie-dyed tee shirt?"

"Does he ever," Maria said. "He wears it till it's hella filthy."

46

It took a while for Louise Simpson to stop crying.

She sat with her hands clasped between her knees for a long time, feeling hopeless. Then she got up and went down to the basement where she had fixed up the room for her brother. When her mother died she had asked Louise to take care of Billy. More than that: she had commanded her to. It was the last thing her mother had ever said to her . . . not "Goodbye" or "I love you" or "Thank you for being my daughter." No, the last thing her mother had said to Louise was, "Take care of your brother. He'll always need you, no matter how old he gets."

And she had tried to do that, had watched him and saved him from more scrapes than she could count. But now he was dead.

The cop had told her Rickie had done it, and in her heart she believed that was true.

But she also knew who was ultimately responsible.

She was.

She wasn't the one who beat her poor brother to death. That was Rickie. But she had kept Rickie in her life, and therefore in her brother's life. She had many chances to give him the boot but she couldn't do it because she was convinced she loved him, and he loved her.

Or so he said.

Was it really that easy for him to lie to her? To look her in the eye and tell her whatever he thought she wanted to hear? He had sworn on his mother's life he put the drug business behind him. She met him through her job as administrative assistant at a Century 21 office in Royal Oak. One day she had to deliver some closing papers to a house that one of the agents was listing, and Rickie was there working with the company that was doing some repair work at the house. They started seeing each other and when she found out what his primary source of income was, she gave him an ultimatum . . . the drugs or her.

He told her he chose her, and she believed him. Because she wanted to believe he was changed, had made a new life for himself because of her. Cared for her more than he cared for his old ways.

Yeah, right. What a fool she was.

She thought back to their last conversation on Sunday. "Hey babe," he had said, "I'm going to have to go out of town for a couple days."

"Why?"

"Buddy wants me to go with him to cost out a job in Toledo."

"So why do you have to stay down there? It's only an hour away."

"He's paying the bills," he told her. "My job isn't to question what he wants me to do, okay? Buddy says go, I go. You wanted me to be legit," he added, just to give her an extra jab.

And she believed him.

Oh Billy, she told her brother. I'm so sorry. I've failed you. And I've let our mother down, too. You were both depending on me and I've failed you both.

She made his bed, which was as messy as he always left it, and sat for a while longer and cried because he would never need that bed again. Would never again leave it a tangle of sheets and blankets, or scatter his dirty clothes all over the floor.

She went back upstairs. On her phone there were three missed calls. The numbers were blocked but there was one message. Even before listening to it she knew who it was from.

"Louise. Do you know where he is? I need to see him. Call me when you get this. It's important." With a number. In that eerie voice of his, calm and level and pleasant but mechanical. She had never met the guy but his voice made her think of HAL the computer in that movie about the space odyssey. She imagined him as a big red eye.

She called Rickie's number, but it went right to voicemail. "Call me," she told the automatic answering message. "Soon as you get this."

And then, before disconnecting, she said, "How could you do it, you lying sack of shit."

She looked through the contact list in her phone, and tried Buddy Gustafson's number.

He picked up right away.

"Lou," he said, "how are you doing?"

"Hi Buddy. Do you know where Rickie is, by any chance?"

"No."

"He's not with you in Toledo?"

"Toledo?"

"He told me you were going down to Toledo for a couple days."

"Why on earth would I want to go to Toledo?"

"Where are you?"

"On a job in Southfield."

"That's what I thought. Thanks."

So Rickie lied to her, plus he told her a lie she could check out in about five minutes. How stupid did he think she was?

She called a few more numbers of men she knew were Rickie's friends. Nobody claimed to know where he was—though if Rickie would lie to her, why wouldn't they?

When she asked her question of the fourth guy she called, he said, "Um, Louise," and she knew she had him.

"I think you know where he is, Larry."

"Louise—"

"Don't bullshit me."

"You're putting me in an awkward position here, honey."

"I don't care. I need to know where he is."

Larry told her Rickie was staying in his apartment in Highland Park.

At first she was going to go down there herself and confront Rickie about what he had done. But just as she was walking out the door she stopped. What good would that do? Give him another chance to lie to her face again?

No, she silently told him, I'm finished. She went into the kitchen and retrieved the card that the detective from Ferndale had just left with her. She picked up the phone and was punching in his number when a call came through.

It was HAL's number, trying her again. She thought for a few moments, then hit the Accept button.

She recited the address Larry had given her and disconnected without another word. She didn't want to talk to him any more than necessary.

She went back downstairs to sit on her brother's bed and thought about the promise she made to her mother.

47

Preuss and Trombley walked up to the front door of the apartment building on Main Street in Clawson where Maria Baranski said her brother lived. Preuss turned to eyeball Manny Greene sitting in his Audi behind the Explorer and pointed a finger at him to remind him to stay where he was. Greene gave him a thumbs-up.

There was no lock on the outside door so they walked in. There was a bank of mailboxes to the right of the door. They were numbered but all the name slots were empty.

Preuss pulled out his cell to ask Greene to call Maria to find out the apartment number when he heard the gunshot.

It came from somewhere upstairs. He and Trombley shared a quick look and then both exploded up the stairs, Preuss in front and Trombley on his heels.

Before he got to the third floor Preuss heard a series of shots and leapt up the remaining stairs three at a time. More shots and a commotion came from 3B. The door to the apartment was closed and locked but Preuss threw his full weight against it and it burst open.

All the furniture in the living room was overturned and Preuss heard shouts coming from a back room. He ran through the living room and at the end of a hallway saw an older guy with a grey pony tail standing in the doorway to the back bedroom holding a pistol and firing while trying to dodge the lamps and table and drawers someone was throwing at him from behind a nightstand. The guy was a terrible shot because the bullets were slamming into the walls in the bedroom, showering the room with plaster dust.

"Police!" Preuss shouted. "Hold your fire!"

The man turned his weapon on Preuss.

Trombley yelled, "Martin, get down!"

But in that instant a man burst out of the bedroom pulling a woman by her hand. He knocked the gunman to the ground and pulled the woman around a corner into the kitchen. Preuss heard him fling the back door to the apartment open and race down the stairs.

The man escaping had a cast on his arm. Danny Baranski, Preuss realized, wearing the same tie-dyed tee shirt from the church video. The woman he was hauling behind him was Sheila Hawkins.

The gunman got to his feet and now fired at Trombley and Preuss. They scrambled out the front door of the apartment and hugged the wall away from the door.

Preuss pulled his phone out of his jacket pocket and punched in Manny Greene's number. When Greene connected he shouted, "Baranski and a hostage are coming out the back. Can you head them off?"

"On it," Greene said.

Trombley edged around the doorframe to fire his service weapon into the living room. But the gunman was not there.

Trombley edged around the doorframe with his gun up and entered the apartment.

Preuss followed Trombley into the apartment and searched through the rooms.

"Apartment's clear," Trombley said. "He must have gone down the back."

They barreled down the back stairs. When they reached the ground floor they found two doors. Preuss pointed at one and

Trombley went through it into a cellar. Preuss burst out the back door of the building into an alley.

There he saw the gunman lying on the ground with his hands raised behind his head. Standing over him, pointing a silver Smith & Wesson pistol at him, was Manny Greene.

"The others were already gone," Greene said. "I persuaded our friend here to stick around."

"You okay?" Preuss asked.

"Never better."

The gunman carried no identification though one pocket held five hundred dollars in a crumpled mass of grimy bills.

Preuss checked the man's other pockets and found bags of white powder with "Rainbow" stamped in red.

Heroin overdoses had been rising in Ferndale, as in many urban and suburban areas around the country. From the state of the man—not just the smell but his dirty cranberry-colored pants and running shoes with no tread or laces—Preuss guessed he was one of the group of men and woman who panhandled beneath the overpass at Woodward and Eight Mile, but who also were part of a crew that sold heroin and other drugs. The FPD had joined with the other local agencies and the state and feds in a narcotics crackdown that did little more than play whack-a-mole with guys like this.

"What's your name?" Preuss asked.

"Clarence Mueller," the gunman said. Now that the excitement was over he was sweating and breathing hard.

"Getting a little old for this life, Clarence," Preuss said.

"Tell me about it."

"Anything here going to stick me?" Preuss turned Clarence's pockets inside out and saw nothing else except tiny colored flakes that stuck to the inside of the lining.

Trombley came out to the alley. "Cellar's empty."

"No, they're long gone," Preuss said.

"The guy who fled, was that who you're looking for?"

"Yeah, Danny Baranski. And the woman was Sheila Hawkins."

Trombley squatted next to the man cuffed on the ground. "And who's Gabby Hayes?"

Preuss said, "That's Clarence."

"What's this all about, Clarence?" Trombley asked.

Clarence took a second and then, as if he had made a decision, said, "I got information. I wanna make a deal."

Preuss said, "Is that so?"

"Yeah. I'll tell you whatever you want to know. Okay? I wanna deal. I'm not going back inside. Not at my age."

"Maybe should have thought about that first," Trombley said.

Preuss said, "I can't promise anything, Clarence. You did some serious shit here."

"I'll take my chances."

"How about you start with who sent you?"

"Guy named Rickie."

"Rickie Deetz?"

"All's I know him by is just Rickie."

"He send you to kill these people or just scare the crap out of them?"

"No, I was supposed to do them in."

"What for?"

"No idea. I did what he paid me to do. Which wasn't to ask questions."

"Just following orders, right?"

"But hey, lookit, I can tell you things," Clarence said.

Preuss said, "Save it till you're under caution, Clarence."

They got him sitting up against the brick wall of the apartment building and Trombley called it in to the Clawson PD.

"What's your feeling about this?" Trombley said to Preuss.

"Deetz must think Baranski's a weak link in their chain. Just like Billy. Billy, Baranski, and Deetz, the three guys who jacked the minibus. And they must be involved with Elizaveta's murder, too."

"Deetz killed her and they're witnesses, so he's eliminating them?"

"Could be. We've thought all along Sheila was in danger because she saw what they did."

"Another possibility is, he sent Gabby Hayes over here to take out Sheila and Baranski got in the way."

"Or Gabby got the assignment screwed up. At least we know she's still alive," Preuss said. "Either way, we have to find her before Deetz does."

48

Deetz drove around and had a smoke. He told Worm he'd come back to pick him up in ten minutes, since he didn't think it would take long to put the kid on ice. There was a message on his phone from Louise and a couple from Larry but he couldn't be bothered listening to them now. He sort of had his hands full here.

When he rolled past the building where he'd dropped off Worm there was a Clawson PD police car in front. What the hell, Deetz thought. He drove past and made a u-turn down the street and pulled into the parking lot of a credit union and turned to watch what was going on.

It wasn't long before another car showed up, siren screaming, then another, cops pouring out and racing around the back of the building.

Worm, Worm, Worm . . . what have you done? I ask you to do a simple thing and look what this turned into. Because Deetz couldn't believe that all this commotion was for something other than the job he had asked Worm to take care of.

He couldn't imagine the kid was more dangerous than Worm. Maybe Worm was too old for this game. Or else he was dipping into the dope too often, skimming off the top a little more for himself than usual. And that dulled his reflexes so the kid got the jump on him.

Or maybe the kid was waiting for him all along in a para-noid state and got to him as soon as he opened the door to the kid's apartment.

No, the kid wasn't that smart. Or that good. Deetz went through it all to see if there was anything connecting Worm to him . . . he couldn't think of anything, except for the bills Deetz touched and handed back to Worm as payment for this simple task he so royally fucked up.

He watched for a few minutes more, then pulled away from the curb and drove around the area. No sign of Worm. Deetz would give him a few hours to make his way back to Woodward and Eight Mile and check in then to see if he was around.

This might still be salvageable, he told himself. Don't get jumpy.

Meantime he'd head back to his buddy's crib and lie low for a while. At least until Worm turned up. Then he'd see what was what and put this whole mess to rest.

49

"Shut up!"

Danny Baranski cracked Sheila on the side of her head with his fist. It made his arm throb but it closed her big mouth, and that was worth the ache. He needed to think and he couldn't do that with her constant nagging voice in his ear.

She slumped against the passenger side door. She wasn't out cold but he had stunned her. He needed to persuade her to stop yapping. He wanted some quiet to put this together.

So many questions . . . who were those guys? Who was the guy who opened up first, and then who were those other guys? Baranski had never seen any of them before. All he could think was that Rickie had sent the guy who looked homeless, but who the other two were he had no idea.

He thought one of them shouted something but his ears were ringing from all the shooting and he couldn't be sure what the guy said.

Maybe Rickie sent them to check up on the old guy, in case he screwed up.

Which he did, Baranski thought. Because I'm still alive.

But why was Rickie trying to kill him? He had done everything Rickie asked, he took care of the woman (well, as far as Rickie was concerned she was taken care of), he was keeping his head down and his mouth shut . . . But still all Rickie did was try to hurt him . . . first he broke his goddam arm, then he beat his ass for no reason, and now he sent somebody to kill him.

To kill him! What had he ever done to deserve that?

He sped south on Main Street to get away but his thoughts were so confused he couldn't even think where to go. He couldn't go to his mother's house, that was for sure. He couldn't think of anybody who would put him up for a while, not with this bitch tagging along. And he didn't have any intention of leaving her anyplace. She could identify him, and besides if Rickie ever found out she was still alive . . .

A cold fear gripped his insides. What if the guy who was shooting at them told Rickie the woman was still alive and they got away together?

Or what if those other two guys, whoever they were, got away and told Rickie?

Or what if somehow Rickie already knew the woman was still alive?

Yeah, he thought, that must be what happened. Somehow Rickie must have learned he hadn't killed her the way he told him to. And so he sent the senior citizen Terminator to finish her and make sure Baranski was also going to keep his mouth shut.

And then sent the other two to mop up. No muss, no fuss. No witnesses.

He began to see there was no way out for him. Rickie either already knew or was soon going to find out the woman wasn't dead. Baranski had already experienced Rickie's anger but this would push him over the edge.

The conclusion was inevitable: Danny Baranski was toast.

He had to get away. Leave the entire area behind, there were no two ways about it.

But how could he flee? He had no money, he had no drugs, he had no clothes or anything, he was hampered by this boat anchor bitch here, which was not turning out to be the best idea he ever had . . .

Okay, okay, he thought. He tried to get his galloping thoughts under control. First things first.

The very first thing he had to take care of was getting as far away from this place as he could. Then he'd be able to think better. He'd be so much calmer if he didn't have to keep looking over his shoulder to see who Rickie was going to send after him the next time.

Or maybe even Rickie himself would come.

But if he wanted to put some space between himself and everything else, he'd have to do it alone. He could travel so much faster. He could go anywhere and wouldn't raise suspicions by having a woman along who would be trying to escape every five minutes.

At first he thought he might be able to have some more fun with her, or at least come to an arrangement where they took care of each other for a while. But the way she was acting, he didn't think that was going to happen any time soon. All she did was piss and moan about wanting to go back to her park. She didn't appreciate anything he did for her.

Well, he thought, she wanted her park, he'd give it to her.

She could spend the rest of her short, happy life there.

Now he had a destination.

Like a drug, the decision calmed him. His thoughts weren't so scattered.

He was in control.

He stopped the car behind Martin Road Park. The woman was still slumped against the window on the passenger side.

The park was pitch black. The night was overcast and the only lights were from the houses facing the south end of the park. Perfect for what he needed to do.

He got out of the car with difficulty. Between all the excitement at the apartment and the crack he had given the woman upside the head, his arm was killing him. It hurt as bad as it first hurt when that psycho broke it. He had promised to pay what he owed, but Rickie wouldn't be put off. He had knocked Baranski down and with the help of one of his homeless goons they stretched Baranski's arm over a curb and Rickie stomped on it. The "crack!" was sickening and the pain was instantaneous and overwhelming. Baranski puked all over the homeless guy's shoes and passed out.

When he woke up he was alone but the bone in his arm was protruding from his skin.

Now as he walked around the car his ankle also hurt him. It didn't feel broken but he must have twisted it when they fled from Clawson. With a bad arm and a bad leg he was far from his best.

He opened the passenger door and the woman almost fell out onto the street. He caught her with his good arm and pulled her from the car. She complained and he raised his cast to hit her again but the pain went right through him, all the way down to his toes, so he hissed, "Shut your mouth!" and dragged her across the grass.

"You wanted your park?" he said. "Here's your park. You're going to have your park for the rest of your natural life."

She put up weak resistance but he pulled her along without a problem, bad leg and all. Her raggedy-ass belongings were still where they had been when he had snuck up behind her and jerked the pillowcase over her head. He kicked them out of his way as he dragged her into the trees and threw her down along the back wall of the little building where the bathrooms were. She lay where she fell.

He was loathe to squeeze the life out of her with his own hands . . . as he knew, that got messy and took too long. He needed something fast and effective. He looked around on the ground for something to use, but in the darkness could find nothing suitable.

"Stay there," he ordered. "I'll be right back."

He left her and went back to his car.

Still groggy, Sheila gazed at her stuff. Everything I own, she thought. She was still thick-brained from all the drugs and the rough treatment, but she knew what he had in store for her. She wasn't that far out of it.

She raised herself on her elbows. Her plastic bags were strewn on the ground a few yards away. She crawled over to them and searched through the items. There was her father's wristwatch, broken but still a talisman that reminded her of his loving arms. There were her books, her doll, her photos of her parents, her baby boy who had been taken from her, the houses she lived in . . . everything that was meaningful to her, even the empty glass Coke bottle she kept because it was one of the old-fashioned ones and her father collected them.

Baranski returned. "Hey," he said, "what are you doing over there?"

He approached her, limping, with a tire iron in his good hand.

He knelt next to her and tapped the iron bar against her forehead a few times. She raised an arm to fend off the light blows but he knocked it away. Enough is enough, he thought. "Lights out." He raised the tire iron over his head while immobilizing her with his bad arm. He grimaced from the pain.

He paused as he gathered the strength to bring the iron bar down and crack her head open like an egg. There was a horrible grin on his face. He was going to enjoy this.

The hesitation was her salvation. It was long enough for her to grab the neck of the Coke bottle and swing it hard onto the casted arm that pinned her.

The blow shattered the plaster cast and brought a high piercing animal's cry from him. She pushed him over and he dropped the tire iron and clutched his arm.

Freed from his grasp, she made a brick of her fist and smashed it into his face once, twice, three times.

She scrambled to her knees so she was higher than he was and aimed the bottle at his head. She brought it down hard but he twisted away from the blow and the glass thudded into the ground.

He lunged for the tire iron and got enough of a grip on it to swing it. The edge of the crooked end caught her thigh and took a slice out of it. In an instant she was on her feet and running.

Growling in fury, snuffling and blowing blood, pain exploding through his body, he clambered to his feet and took off after her.

But she knew the park better than he did. He stumbled over the uneven ground and other obstacles he couldn't see in the blackness.

He ran for a minute, then stopped to listen for her. He heard her footsteps running somewhere and heard her harsh panting. He started running again, clutching his arm, and stopped again but couldn't hear her anymore. He couldn't see her silhouette. Everything was so dark.

He stood, panting and with his arm and face and ankle aching like hell. She must have rebroken his arm and broken his nose again. He wiped his good arm across his face and it came away wet and sticky.

What to do? Go after her?

He'd never find her.

Cut his losses and leave?

That was the best idea. If he left now and put as many miles between this place and himself as he could by morning, Rickie would never find him. He had no drugs and no money and he was a bloody mess, but if he could get away with his life he could start again. She could say anything she wanted but he'd be gone.

The main problem was his arm . . . if he could make it to Ohio he could find a hospital where they'd reset it and send him on his merry way.

Baranski went back the way he came until he could see where his car was parked. He stopped to listen but heard nothing. She was gone, he thought.

Good riddance.

He limped out to the street. At the driver's side of the car he set the tire iron on the roof while he wrestled the door open with his good hand. He turned to put his ass on the seat so he could swing his aching leg in. As he turned a wave of dizziness washed over him.

Sheila Hawkins appeared out of the darkness behind him and snatched up the iron bar and clubbed him over the head with it.

Stunned, he crumpled to the ground. He was still breathing but he was moaning and crying and snuffling through his bloody nose. He was at her mercy.

She rolled him over and rifled through his pockets. She found a cell phone.

It took a while to get through, but when she did she said, "Hey, it's me. Sheila."

"Where are you?"

"My park."

Martin Preuss said, "Is Baranski with you?"

"He's here. But he can't talk. He's indisposed."

"Are you okay?"

"I've been better," she said. "But I need a favor."

"Anything."

"Can you come and get me?"

50

Deetz parked the black Camaro behind the building on Second Avenue. The problem with this hidey-hole, he thought as he locked the car and looked around, was the neighborhood. Most of the homes—if you could even call them that—were burnt-out shells. And you never could tell who might be hiding in the shadows.

There was a walkway beside the building that led to the entrance. He followed it and unlocked the front door and climbed the stairs to Larry's fifth floor apartment. He popped the top off a Bud and stretched out on the sofa. In a while he'd try Worm again and make the old bastard wait before he picked him up.

Should have taken care of it myself, he thought. Maybe Worm's outlived his usefulness. Have to find somebody else, one of the younger guys.

Except Marcus. He thought about Marcus and smiled. Got what was coming to him.

After a while his phone rang.

He expected it to be Worm but it wasn't.

"He wants to see you," the voice on the other end of the phone said. "Now."

Deetz closed his eyes. He'd come to dread the sound of that voice . . . so low, so quiet, so placid. So treacherous.

"How about you tell him I'm in the middle of taking care of that thing. He'll know what I'm talking about."

"Not an option."

When there was nothing further except steady breathing, Deetz said, "Lookit, this has been a long day. Can he give me till tomorrow? I'll have everything wrapped up by then."

"Now."

Deetz sighed. "Fine. Where?"

"Usual place."

"Tell him I'll be there in an hour."

"Make it twenty minutes. I'll meet you there. Don't be late."

Deetz disconnected. "I'll get there when I get there," he told the empty room.

Now he was steamed. What am I, his slave, Deetz thought, he can call me all hours and expect me to jump?

He took his time and puttered around the apartment for a good half hour before locking the door behind him and walking down the creaking ancient wooden stairway. Outside he retraced his steps down the walkway and stood beside his car. He looked around, didn't see anybody, just the derelict buildings of the neighborhood.

"Elton."

Deetz turned, recognizing the voice.

That voice.

Relaxed, untroubled, robotic, as if he had all the time in the world. The owner of that voice stood three feet away with his hands by his sides.

"Hey," Deetz said. "I told you I'd meet you there—"

Before Rickie finished his sentence, Ray Bouchard lifted his arm and the gun in his hand made a sharp *crack*!

A spurt of flame. Smoke.

Rickie was dead before he hit the ground.

One down, Bouchard thought.

One to go.

Arthur Campanella lived in a house at the end of a cul-de-sac in Farmington. He was not used to people coming to his door so late in the evening. He had been watching the ball game on television and drinking beer, and he was a little drunk.

He looked through the peephole and was surprised to see Ray Bouchard standing on the stoop in the light from the lantern above the entryway.

Campanella opened the door. "Hey."

"Can I come in?"

"Sure. But why didn't you call? I been home all night."

"I have to talk to you in person."

"Is there a problem?"

"It's about an order that needs to be recalled," Bouchard said, and stepped into the massive front hall.

Wednesday, June 16, 2010

51

Danny Baranski spent the night in Emergency at Providence Hospital. Preuss stayed with him the whole time. They reset his arm and x-rayed his skull but there were no new fractures except for his nose, which they packed with gauze.

Sheila Hawkins was kept in the Short Stay Unit for observation at the same hospital. When Preuss looked in on her, she was sound asleep. "Looks like she's had a rough time," the nurse who was assigned to her said.

"She has. Not just the past couple of days either. She's been living on the street."

"Poor thing's loaded with heroin."

"She's not a user. She was held captive and injected to keep her docile."

"She'll be fine as soon as we get it out of her system. We're giving her naloxone hydrochloride now. She's a tough one."

The nurse went off to see to another patient and he stood in the doorway watching Sheila sleep. Maybe this would help her to change her life, he thought. Though he wouldn't take any bets on it. Who would blame her for wanting to put all this behind her and get back to her park. It even sounded good to Preuss.

Baranski was released in the morning and Preuss took him to the Shanahan, where he charged Baranski with kidnap, adult, to sexually assault; a variety of sexual contact charges; and possession, use, and distribution of a narcotic. He left the young man to sleep on the molded plastic bunk in his holding cell for a few hours.

Preuss went home to sleep but couldn't relax. Instead he showered and changed and returned to the station. Jane Cahill peeked into his office to ask him how he was doing and he filled her in on his previous day.

When he was through she closed his door and wrapped him in a hug. "Glad you're okay," she murmured.

He placed a hand on the back of her head and held her close. After a few moments she pulled away and placed a warm moist palm on his cheek. Her eyes searched his face, and then she slipped away before he could say anything to her.

In the afternoon he woke up Danny Baranski and put him in the large interview room. Baranski requested an attorney and Preuss arranged for a public defender.

There were three in the interview room: Preuss, Baranski, and Baranski's attorney, a young woman who looked around twelve and whose nasal voice was the most grating sound Preuss had ever heard in his life. He hoped she would just listen and not say much. They had pried the tie-dyed shirt off Baranski and stowed it in an evidence bag. He sat looking glum in a Ferndale PD tee shirt. A laptop was on the table.

Preuss advised Baranski of his rights and spun the laptop so Baranski and his counsel could see it.

"I'm going to show you a surveillance video from the parking lot of the Ferndale Cornerstone Community United Lutheran Church taken on the evening of Monday, June 7 of this year."

Preuss pressed the space bar of the laptop and an image from the video appeared. He pressed Enter and the video played, showing Baranski, wearing his tie-dyed shirt, exiting the group home minibus.

"The guy in the hoodie's been identified as Elton Richard Deetz, AKA Rickie Deetz."

In the video the two men went through the motions Preuss knew so well by now. At the point where Deetz returned to the parking lot and dropped off Zach Warranow, Preuss clicked the pause button and sat back.

Baranski kept watching the laptop screen as if hoping it could rewind to tell a different story.

Preuss said, "You're in a jam, Danny. Besides the charges I've already filed, we're going to make a case for GTA, plus we're building cases for one count of murder for Elizaveta Kertész, plus accessory to another count of murder for Billy Simpson. That means you're looking at a long time in prison. Maybe the rest of your life. Tell us what happened on this night, and we might be able to make some of those charges go away."

"I got nothing to say."

His public defender said, "Let me have a few minutes to speak with my client, okay?"

"My client will tell you what happened, on the condition you drop the accessory charge to the death of Mr. Simpson."

"Let's hear what he has to say."

"That was me in the video," Baranski said.

He was silent and Preuss held both hands open. "That's it? We already know that."

When Baranski didn't say anything more, Preuss said, "Here's what else we know. Elizaveta Kertész came looking for your grandfather, and you spoke with her. What did you talk about?"

"She told me she wanted to talk with Gramps."

Gramps. Referring to Kovalenko as *Gramps*, with all the associations the word conjured up with normal happy life, set Preuss's teeth on edge.

"Did she tell you why she was looking for him?"

"She told me he was a big-time Nazi or something during World War Two."

Preuss said, "He was a low-level functionary. But he made a lot of people suffer. He was brutal."

"That's what she said. And I was like, whatever, and sent her away. But then afterwards I started to think if she wanted to get in to talk with him so bad, maybe I'd get some money out of her if I said I'd help her. I needed some serious bank right away."

"What for?"

"I owed this guy."

"Rickie?"

"Yeah."

"How much?"

Baranski looked at his lawyer and Preuss said, "I'm not the narcotics police. I'm just interested in what happened to Elizaveta Kertész."

"I owed him like eight Gs for drugs."

"Why so much? Doing a little dealing yourself?"

"Don't answer that," Baranski's attorney said.

Preuss indicated Baranski's cast. "That how you got a broken arm? Encouragement to pay up?"

Baranski nodded and Preuss said, "So you thought you'd get enough money from Elizaveta Kertész to pay off your drug debt?"

"No, but I thought I'd get enough to buy some breathing space. I didn't have any other way to get money. I tapped out my mother and there was nobody else I could ask."

"So she came to your mother's house. Then what?"

"She left me her phone number, so I called her up and told her I'd get her in to see Gramps for a thousand bucks. She said okay and we set up a meeting and she was supposed to bring the money."

Remembering her Call Detail Records, Preuss thought that must have been the call that came through while she was out with Zach. "Where did you meet?"

"A vacant lot off Hilton, below Nine."

"Why there?"

"I wanted to meet closer to me in Clawson but she said she was working and couldn't take the time. So I picked someplace near her that was out of the way. I figured she could just pull in and keep going."

"After giving you a thousand bucks for nothing. She showed up because she was more anxious to get the information than she was to get her passenger back home."

"When she got there, she told me she didn't have the money."

"Pissed you off, right?"

"Hell yeah! I told Rickie I'd have something for him. I was depending on that."

"What happened when she showed up without it?"

"I go, 'Where's my money?' And she's like, 'I don't have it. But I shouldn't have to pay anyway because you'd be doing a *good deed.*'" He scoffed. "I sort of lost my shit. And then things got out of hand."

Things got out of hand. What a perfect description of how things went with guys like this . . . It wasn't anything to do with Danny Baranski, it was all out of his control . . . Things happened not from any agency of his but because that's what you expect when *things get out of hand.* It took place without any conscious decision by anybody. She pissed me off and she wound up dead.

"What happened then?"

"I guess I started wailing on her and so forth. She tried to fight back and I got my hands around her neck and she wouldn't stop fighting me so I squeezed until she stopped. I freaked out. I moved her behind some blocks in the lot so nobody would see her right away. Then I drove around while I tried to figure out what to do. I knew I had to get in touch with Rickie and give him something because I told him I would and I knew he was expecting something and he'd kill me if I showed up empty-handed. So I called him and asked him to meet me in the parking lot of that church."

"Why there?"

"I had the kid in the wheelchair in the back. I figured if we dropped the kid off near a church, somebody'd find him sooner or later."

"Then what?"

"Then when I got to the church and told Rickie what happened, and told him I didn't have any money, Rickie, man, he went apeshit. He kicked my ass and told me he was gonna take the minibus to make up for my debts. I figured, shit, dude, take it. Ain't mine anyway."

"How did Elizaveta's body get from the vacant lot to the railroad siding?"

"Rickie and me moved her. Along with the other guy who was driving the other van. Rickie thought the cops'd think she was killed near the railroad tracks and there'd be less evidence there than where she died."

Again the agentless action, Preuss thought. The place where she died through no fault of Danny Baranski.

All were silent. From his file folder Preuss removed the photo that Rosa Martinez had given him, the one showing Elizaveta and her daughter happy and smiling with hopes and dreams and plans for the future.

He set the photo in front of Baranski. "I want you to see what you did. The lives you ruined."

"I dunno who that little girl is," Baranski said. "But I didn't do nothing to her."

Preuss stared at him, unable to penetrate the willful ignorance Baranski wore like a suit of old clothes.

52

Preuss left Reg Trombley to process Danny Baranski and called Arnold Biederman, the coordinator of the Evidence Technician Unit. While Biederman assembled his team, Preuss drove to the lot where Baranski said he killed Elizaveta Kertész.

It was east of Hilton between East Troy Street and the railroad tracks two blocks south of Nine Mile, a vacant area where two industrial companies had gone out of business in the recent financial upheaval. They left behind empty buildings and a large patch of land where massive concrete blocks leaned against each other. They were what remained from a construction project that ended when the businesses ran out of money and folded two years ago.

He parked on East Troy and entered the area. Despite Baranski's confession, they would need whatever forensic evidence Biederman's people could find. He searched among the configurations of blocks for confirmation of the struggle that Baranski claimed. The ground was hard-packed dirt speckled here and there with gravel.

Underneath one grouping of blocks he found what he was looking for. He saw a disturbance of the dirt that could have been made by footprints shuffling around and the dragging of a body.

He saw tire tracks too. This was where Elizaveta Kertész had died in her false hope that Baranski would put her in touch with

335

a man who couldn't speak so she could try to rectify a historical cataclysm that could never be made right. Or even understood.

He looked around some more, satisfying himself he had found the killing ground, and went back to his car to wait for Biederman.

"There's not much here," Biederman said. "It hasn't rained since last Monday, so that's a good thing. Looks like most of the activity happened under where the blocks form a kind of steeple." He put his fingertips together. "So the scene's somewhat preserved."

Preuss pointed out the tire tracks and Biederman walked over to them. "They're faint but we can cast them," he said. "There's a little blood, what you'd expect from a beating. We might be able to find some trace genetic material, maybe some fibers. We'll take a sample of the dirt and see if we can match it with anything on the actor's shoes or clothes."

"Well," said Preuss, "seems like he's been wearing the same clothes ever since. We have his shirt, we'll get the rest of it. Do the best you can do, Arn."

"Always do," he grumbled.

One of the techs searching under the concrete blocks shouted, "Got something."

Preuss and Biederman came closer. The tech showed a small evidence bag containing a few colored flecks.

"Found these on the ground. There were just a few of them."

"I've seen these before," Preuss said. They were similar to what he found in Clarence Mueller's pockets at Baranski's apartment. "What are they?"

"Won't know for sure till we get them back and examine them," the tech said.

Preuss said, "Can I see them?"

The tech handed him the bag and he examined them through the plastic envelope.

"They might not even be connected to the murder," Biederman said.

Preuss said, "Mmm, bet they are," and opened up the bag and took a whiff of the contents. He knew what they were.

He closed the bag up. "How soon can you have the analysis?"

Biederman scowled. "I'd say we have another hour or two at the scene. Won't be able to even get to it till then."

"Can you start with these?"

He didn't hear from Biederman till 4:30. As soon as he heard what the evidence tech unit coordinator had to say, Preuss thanked him and hung up.

He punched in Trombley's number. "Who'd you line up?"

"Judge Nussbaum," Trombley said. "He's waiting for me in chambers."

"Perfect. Go for it."

53

When Trombley showed up Preuss was waiting with two uniformed officers in a scout car in front of the barn-like building on Wyoming in Royal Oak Township.

"Did you get them?" Preuss asked.

Trombley handed him the warrants. "Narcotics Enforcement Team's on the way."

The outer work area was empty at this hour. They entered the paint company office without knocking and saw Dolores parked at her desk as usual.

"You can't just walk in here like that!" she said. "I'm just getting ready to go home."

"Dolores, we're here to execute this warrant to search the AAAdvantage Paint Company. This gives us legal permission to search the entire premises. We also have a warrant for the arrest of Alberto Campanella. Is he around?"

"He hasn't been in all day."

She looked from Preuss to Trombley in total confusion. "I don't understand. What's going on?"

Preuss said, "Reg, pick him up at his house."

"On it," Trombley said, and left the search warrant with Preuss.

"Dolores, are all the doors unlocked?"

"No, they're all locked up at this hour. Everybody's gone but me. I stayed late because I was hoping to catch Mr. Campanella but he never came in. He never returned my calls, either."

"Do you have keys to the doors?"

"There's a spare set in Mr. Campanella's desk."

He retrieved a keyring and Dolores said, "Does this mean I have to stay?"

Without answering he gave the keys to one of the patrol officers who was with him and said, "Get started."

He went outside where a pair of Humvees pulled up in front of the building. A half-dozen armed men in body armor piled out of the vehicles. Preuss stepped up to the head of the team. Dan Breen came straight from Central Casting with a military crew cut and lantern jaw set in a permanent scowl. He told Breen what was happening.

Breen spoke with his men and they trooped through the work area searching behind every closed door and under the floor where the hydraulic lifts used to be when this was a collision shop.

The mixing room and the room next to it were the last places to be searched. The mixing room was large, twenty by fifteen, lined with shelves holding covered five-gallon tubs. On a table against the far wall were a trio of computerized mixing machines and screwdrivers and mallets of different sizes. A stack of empty paint containers stood beside the table and a metal sink was in the corner. The floor was a random mosaic of colored drips and spatters and the smell of latex paint was intense.

Preuss pulled a container off its shelf. On the cover was a strip of masking tape with "Dry Dock" handwritten on it and a computerized label with the mixing proportions. He opened the container with a screw driver from the table and beige-colored paint slopped out.

He pulled a long mixing stick from the table and probed the container but there was nothing in it but paint.

He repeated that with six more tubs.

"All I'm seeing here is paint," Breen said.

"I'm certain that's not all."

Preuss pulled a few more containers down from the shelves but all he saw filling them was the opalescence of base paint.

"Are you sure?" Breen said. "This place isn't even on our radar."

"Have your men keep searching these containers. There's one more room to try."

"If we don't find anything there," Breen said, "we're going to stand down."

The door beside the mixing room was locked with a padlock. Preuss tried every key on the keyring but none worked.

One of Breen's men used a pair of bolt cutters to slice through the padlock. They also needed a battering ram because there was a deadbolt on the door that Preuss didn't have a key for. They produced a ram from one of the Humvees and gained access.

It was a smaller room than the mixing room, though with a similar arrangement—shelves containing five-gallon tubs. There was no mixing equipment and no sink. On the floor, scattered like confetti, were hundreds of specks of dried paint such as Biederman's guy found and Preuss found in Clarence's pocket.

"This is it," he said. Breen crowded in to the small room with his men.

Preuss pulled a container from the top shelf and when he pried the cover off they looked into another bucket of paint, this one a deep salmon color. He took a mixing stick and stirred the paint. From the sludge at the bottom of the container rose a dozen quart-sized plastic bags.

He pulled one out and took it into the mixing room to rinse off in the sink. The bag held a dull white powder.

"The mother lode," said Breen.

Left over on the bag were spots of paint. These would dry into the flecks that littered the floor.

Preuss pulled more containers down from the top shelf and found smaller baggies all filled with what looked to be the same powder.

Breen said, "Who owns this business?"

"Alberto Campanella," Preuss said. "I sent Reg Trombley to his house with a warrant for his arrest."

"He's not here?"

"No. Secretary says she hasn't heard from him all day."

"I'd say it's time for a house call."

"I'll tell Reg to expect you."

54

Afterwards Preuss and Trombley sat drinking coffee in Preuss's office. It was priceless, they both agreed. They heard Russo's voice on the phone down the hall crowing about it. NET was organizing a news conference, starring Russo of course.

The catch was that Campanella hadn't been home. "Maybe somebody tipped him off and he decamped," Preuss said.

"But who'd know about it?"

"Possibly Elton Deetz. He was hiding out somewhere so he must have suspected we were after him. Even his girlfriend said she didn't know where he was."

Janey Cahill appeared in the doorway holding a sheet of paper.

"I heard you guys put in a good day's work fighting crime."

"That we did," Trombley said. "Sit down, young lady, and I'll show you a real damn hero."

She sat in one of the visitor's chairs. Trombley said, "You see this guy?" He pointed at Preuss. "He made everybody happy today. The DEA, assorted violent crime task forces, the State Police, the Oakland County Sheriff, the NET, all the local police agencies . . . all in one fell swoop."

Cahill said, "Local boy makes good."

Trombley said, "Bet you have that chief of detectives job sewn up and in. The. Bag."

"Never happen."

Trombley said, "Man, leave it to you to bring everybody down." He laughed and leaned forward and gave Preuss a playful punch on the arm.

Cahill said, "Yeah, well, while you guys were out playing cops and robbers a call came through for you, Martin. From Lieutenant Arthur Jackson from the Highland Park PD. They caught a body, IDed as one Elton Richard Deetz."

Preuss said, "No way."

"Yes way."

Trombley screamed in mock agony. "You mean we can't arrest him?"

"No," Cahill said, "because somebody killed him first."

"What happened?" Preuss asked.

"He was found in a parking lot behind an apartment building. One shot between the eyes, goodbye Elton."

"Why's Jackson calling me?"

"Said your card was in Deetz's pocket."

He thought back to how that might have happened. He had given a card to Louise Simpson, but when would she have seen Elton? The only other person in Deetz's orbit who had his card was Billy Simpson. If Deetz found it then he would have known Billy talked to Preuss . . . and that might have been enough to convince Deetz that Billy needed to be kept quiet . . .

"What's the matter, Martin," Trombley said. "You look even whiter than usual."

"I just had a horrible thought."

"That's not the only thing happened while you guys were out," Cahill said. "A call also came from the State Police post in West Branch. They caught a speeder this morning you might want to know about. Guy by the name of Raymond Bouchard."

Preuss said, "He's Campanella's assistant. I met him at the paint company first time I was there."

"They searched the vehicle and found Alberto Campanella in the trunk."

"Explains why he wasn't home," Trombley said.

"Is he dead?" Preuss asked.

"No," Cahill said. "Mostly dead, though. Bouchard's facing charges for assault with intent to murder."

Preuss said, "Before it's over they'll make him for Elton Deetz, too."

Trombley said, "And maybe Billy Simpson."

"No," Preuss said. "Deetz killed Billy, we know that, probably to keep him quiet about the theft of the minibus. And Deetz tried to have Baranski killed for the same reason, and to cover up Elizaveta's murder."

"So why would Bouchard kill Deetz and try to kill Campanella?" Trombley said.

"Campanella told everybody Bouchard was his assistant, but he was more likely his enforcer for the outfit. I'm guessing he reported to whoever is above Campanella in the food chain. Clarence Mueller's been talking a blue streak. He told us Campanella managed the paint company as a distribution hub for the heroin we've been seeing on the streets. Clarence himself was in charge of one of the drug houses that Deetz ran, where some of the street slingers in Ferndale worked out of."

"Who's in charge of it all?" Trombley said.

"That's still unclear. At the heart of it all was Danny Baranski's debt to Elton Deetz that led to Elizaveta Kertész's death. It all started to unravel once we picked up Sheila Hawkins. Her statement led us to the video, and from there we found Billy Simpson. After that it was a cascade of mistrust and violence as everybody tried to keep a lid on things. When Deetz and then Campanella couldn't handle it and the drug enterprise was threatened, they had to go."

"No honor among thieves," Trombley said.

Five Weeks Later

55

She was waiting for him in front of the Ferndale Cornerstone Community United Lutheran Church. She looked like a different person—her hair was clean and cut to her shoulders, her clothes smelled freshly laundered, and the sparkle was something Preuss did not remember seeing before in Sheila Hawkins's eye.

In the Explorer he asked how she was liking the studio apartment SOS found for her in Ferndale. "So far, so good," she said. "I talked to your friend at the bakery, the one who helps out vets. He said he'll let me do some work around the place."

"Wonderful."

"Yeah, well. We'll see how it goes."

Peggy See and Zach Warranow were waiting in the living room of Zach's group home. Zach was sitting on the sofa. His cast had been removed.

"Look at you!" Sheila yelled.

Zach gathered his long legs under him and stood with a helping hand from the house manager. He tottered toward Sheila and she threw her arms around him.

"Can you stay for a while?" Peggy See asked Preuss.

"I'm due at the station. I'll be back to pick her up in a few hours."

"Don't worry about it. We'll drop her off in our minibus."

Preuss arrived at the Shanahan with enough time to fill his mug of coffee from the machine in Tanya Corcoran's office and push around papers on his desk before the Detective Bureau meeting started. This time everyone was present.

The instant Preuss saw Nick Russo's face he knew what he was going to hear.

It was the first thing Russo said.

"I just got off the phone with the mayor. At the City Council meeting tonight they're going to announce my name as the new chief of the Ferndale Police Department."

All around the table applauded, even Preuss, though his was more a slow clap than congratulations.

"I'll begin my term in two weeks, on August 1. In the re-alignment following my promotion, you'll have a new chief of de-tectives. I'm going to appoint an individual who's served the FPD with distinction for many years."

The pause that followed was tense. Preuss never applied for the position because he knew there was no way he would be appointed, regardless what William Warnock had to say. But he knew Bellamy had applied and been interviewed. People were certain he was the favorite.

"I've worked with this individual over the years, and I know he will serve with excellence. The next chief of the Detective Bureau will be our friend and colleague Lieutenant Stanley Chrysler."

In the stunned silence, Bellamy looked as if his dog just died.

"For those who don't know, Stan is commander of the Southeast Oakland SWAT unit. He comes to us with twenty-three years of service to the Ferndale PD including Day Shift Commander, DEA liaison, and Field Training Coordinator. I'm pleased to be able to call him a friend and I know we'll all make him feel welcome."

Russo straightened the edges of the folder in front of him.

"That's not all my good news," he continued. "I'm pleased to announce that Sergeant Gail Crimmonds has been promoted to the Detective Bureau to fill Tony Tullio's position."

This news at least was received with genuine appreciation.

Afterwards Janey Cahill said, "Nope. Nope, nope, nope, nope."

"It's a done deal."

She read Preuss's two-sentence letter again. "Your last day is August 31st? You're sure about this?"

"Completely."

She huffed. "Oh Martin." She tossed the letter onto his desk. "How am I supposed to go on without you?"

"Maybe you won't have to."

After Cahill left, his desk phone rang. Tanya Corcoran.

"Martin, there's a guy out front to see Reggie but he's not in. Can you take him?"

In the station's reception area a slight man was studying the framed tribute to deceased officers from area police agencies that hung on the wall. "Hello," Preuss said, and the man turned around.

"Detective Trombley?" He had an oval face with a mop of black hair. Chinese, with just a trace of an accent.

"No," Preuss said, "he's not available. I'm Detective Preuss. How can I help?"

"I got a call from Detective Trombley a few weeks ago. I just got back from a trip abroad and this is the first chance I've had to return his call. I thought I'd take a chance and see if he was in."

"If you leave your name and number, I'll make sure he gets the message."

"I'm Evan Chin." He said his number and Preuss had to beg a slip of paper from the officer behind the Police Desk window.

"Can I tell him what this is regarding?"

"He wanted to talk to me about Elizaveta Kertész."

Preuss stopped writing. "Mr. Chin, you know what happened to her, right?"

"I do. Words can't describe how sad it made me."

Preuss heard the liquid pain in the man's voice and he said, "Why don't you come with me."

He led the way back through to his office. Chin sat in the visitor's chair and Preuss offered him coffee, which Chin refused. Preuss took his own seat behind his desk.

"You knew her?"

"Yes. I didn't hear from her while I was away and called her as soon as I got home from China. When she still didn't call me back I talked with one of our mutual friends in our program at Wayne. She told me what happened and I couldn't believe it."

Preuss made some quick notes on a pad on his desk. "I'm sorry for your loss. It's cold comfort, I know, but we caught the man who did that terrible thing."

Chin looked as he was about to say something, then he buried his face in his hands and wept.

Preuss had no tissues but retrieved a Burger King napkin from his drawer and handed it across to the man. Chin dabbed at his eyes and wiped his nose. "Thank you."

"You knew her well?"

"We were engaged to be married. We were planning a future together."

"Everyone we spoke to told us she wasn't seeing anyone."

"We decided to keep it that way. We didn't want anyone to know about us because of all the gossips in our program. She was such a beautiful person. And now—" He choked and couldn't finish the sentence.

"Mr. Chin, if you don't mind my saying so, it was hard to reconcile how people talked about her with the plans she seemed to have once she met the man she was looking for."

"That Nazi guard? Oh no. It was so much like her."

"Really."

"Yes. We talked all about it. It was very much in keeping with the way she lived her life."

"I'm a bit confused, then. Do you know what she was planning?"

"Of course. She wanted to confront the man who had done so many horrible things to her family and to so many people. And she wanted to look into his eyes and tell him she forgave him."

"She didn't plan any kind of revenge for him?"

"Oh no. Never."

"I heard she was looking to get her hands on a gun. I assumed she was going to use it on Kovalenko."

He lowered his head. "That was for me. I just moved to the Cass Corridor downtown and I thought I might feel safer with one. But she talked me out of it. No, Elizaveta knew how damaged her father had been by his experiences in the concentration camps. How much hatred he carried in his heart his whole life for that man who caused so much suffering. And she felt the cycle of hatred had to stop somewhere. She wanted it to stop with her. Her 'revenge,' as you put it, was to let him know she absolved him of all his crimes."

Evan Chin paused to blow his nose in the napkin.

"Because, you see, she wanted her daughter to grow up in a better world."

Epilogue

Preuss arrived at Toby's school just after classes ended for the day. The buses that took the kids home were lined up across the entrance and the teachers were already shepherding their students aboard.

He had called the school and asked them to keep Toby off the bus that would take him back to his group home. Preuss was going to pick him up instead. He had gotten tickets for the baseball game that night and he wanted to spend some time with his son first. So Toby's teacher, Mrs. Rice, kept him out of the line of wheelchairs that were headed toward the buses.

Preuss plunged through the commotion to where Toby sat, reveling in the end-of-the-day hubbub. It took a few seconds before the boy could focus on his father but when he did he raised his voice in a high scream of delight.

When the buses thinned out, he pushed Toby outside to the Explorer. Preuss lifted him into the back seat and buckled him in, then tossed in Toby's travel bag with all his supplies that went to school with him—a few changes of clothes, extra diapers, his feeding pump and cans of the formula the pump sent into his g-tube every four hours.

He hefted the wheelchair into the rear of the vehicle and drove through the Birmingham streets to Woodward. He turned south with the intention of taking Toby back to his house, but on a whim turned right on Maple and headed toward Quarton Lake.

He parked beside the pier that extended into the lake, unpacked the wheelchair, and buckled Toby into it. He pushed his son down the gravel path to the south end of the lake, pointing out the dragonflies that darted around them, the sparrows that flew among the vegetation by the water's edge, and further into the lake the ducklings that followed their mother through the lily pads in a comical straight line.

Toby couldn't see any of it because of his limited vision. He had a deteriorating optic nerve, and in addition when he was a week old he had two cataract operations that left his irises without the ability to adjust to light so in strong sunlight like this he kept his eyes shut. Still Preuss wanted to make sure the boy appreciated the variety of life that surrounded him so as usual he narrated their walk.

When they reached the end of the path they turned around and walked back to the pier. It extended out over the water and made a dog-leg to the left and ended at a rectangular platform with benches. Preuss bumped the wheelchair over the wooden slats and sat with Toby out on the platform.

He rummaged through Toby's travel bag for his Tiger's baseball cap and jammed it on Toby's head.

Toby waggled his head to knock it off but Preuss said, "Sorry, you have to wear this. The sun is too hot to go without a hat."

He found a tube of sunscreen in Toby's bag and slathered it on Toby's face and arms.

After a minute Toby settled down and accepted the cap. It was quiet on the lake, with the twittering of birds on the trees at the water's edge and the occasional buzz of an insect breaking the silence. As before, Preuss narrated for Toby what was happening.

Sitting here with his son, Preuss took a deep breath, let it out slowly. He felt at peace, an unfamiliar sensation of late. He was content to relax with Toby in the aftermath of the decision he had made to begin a new life.

From this point onward there would be a finality to everything he did at work . . . every report he filled out, every investigation he conducted, every regular and unscheduled event at the station would be the last such activity he performed as a detective in the Ferndale PD.

There was even a finality to these stolen hours with Toby. Soon they would have all the time in the world to be together.

And yet . . . As much as he adored the child and knew he would protect him and keep him close for the rest of their lives, Preuss had to keep reminding himself Toby deserved his own life. For all his vulnerabilities and limitations, Toby existed in the world as his own person. He had what Jeanette once called his own "equivalent center of self," a phrase she had picked up from one of her English classes at MSU. Watching his son enjoying the life that teemed around him on his own terms, Preuss realized yet again that Toby possessed a distinct and autonomous individuality that was equivalent to anyone's.

It was a delicate balance, admitting that Toby had his own life to live while having to take care of all his needs—including, as now, the need to mediate between Toby and a world he couldn't see or move through on his own.

And if Toby had his own life, then so did Martin Preuss. Would he pay more attention to himself once he retired and had more time to spend with Toby?

A delicate balance indeed.

Toby began to hum.

Preuss reached out to hold his son's crooked hand.

The boy turned his head and squinted at Preuss from under the bill of the Tigers cap, askew from his head-waggling. He gave a twitchy crooked smile.

"Remember that case I was working on with the group home minibus that disappeared?" Preuss told him how it ended, and what he had learned earlier that day from Evan Chin.

Toby listened.

"What her boyfriend said caught me by surprise. The effects of violence multiply down through generations, until someone like Elizaveta decides to say Stop. By wanting to pardon the man who caused so much suffering, she was going to try and change one corner of the world. Except all the greed and stupidity of the people who stood between her and her intention wouldn't let that happen."

Toby said, "Num."

"You know, don't you. You get it. I wish we were all as wise as you." They lapsed into silence and Preuss switched hands so he could put an arm around Toby and pull him closer in the wheelchair. He smelled the sweet shampoo and young man's sweat on the top of his head. He kissed the flat spot on Toby's temple.

Toby vocalized something that sounded very much like, "I love you, Dad."

"I love you too," Preuss said. He straightened the cap that sat askew on his son's head.

In the end, he thought, this is what we shore against the Kovalenkos of the world.

"Know what else? I'm retiring from the police. I've been thinking about it for a long time, as you know."

Twitchy smile.

"I realized it's time to let somebody else have a turn."

Toby heaved a great and sympathetic sigh and turned his gorgeous face toward his father, a sunflower heliotropically tracking the sun.

They sat together for a while longer, listening to the buzz and rustle of the busy world around them.

Then he trundled Toby back to the Explorer, and they set off for Comerica Park in downtown Detroit, where the Tigers were playing the Texas Rangers.

Acknowledgements

Warm thanks to my grandsons Alex Kril, who suggested the idea for the missing minibus plot thread, and Jamie Kril, whose spirit continues to infuse this series in the character of Toby. For background information I am indebted to Eric Lichtblau's *The Nazis Next Door: How America Became a Safe Haven for Hitler's Men* (Houghton Mifflin Harcourt, 2014); and Dorothy Rabinowitz, *New Lives: Survivors of the Holocaust Living in America* (Avon, 1976). Thanks also to Jerry van Rossum and Peter Chiaramonte for their support, to Rich Carnahan of Publish Pros for his expertise, and to Andy Krieger for one of the band names in Chapter 22. I continue to depend on information from Michael Kitchen, retired Chief of Police of Ferndale, and Michael J. Brady, though all mistakes and errors are my own. As always, my deepest gratitude goes out to my wife Sue for her ongoing love and support.

Also by Donald Levin

CRIMES OF LOVE | BOOK 1

One cold November night, police detective Martin Preuss joins a frantic search for a seven-year-old girl with epilepsy who has disappeared from the streets of his suburban Detroit community. Unwilling to let go after the Oakland County Sheriff's Office takes the case from his city agency, he strikes out on his own, following leads across the entire metropolitan region. Probing deep into the anguished lives of all those who came into contact with the missing girl, Preuss must summon all his skills and resources to solve the many crimes of love he uncovers.

THE BAKER'S MEN | BOOK 2

Easter, 2009. The nation is still reeling from the previous year's financial crisis. Ferndale Police detective Martin Preuss is spending a quiet evening with his son Toby when he's called out to investigate a savage after-hours shooting at a bakery in his suburban Detroit community. Was it a random burglary gone wrong? A cold-blooded execution linked to Detroit's drug trade? Most frightening of all, is there a terrorist connection with the Iraqi War vets who work at the store? Struggling with these questions, frustrated by the dizzying uncertainties of the case and hindered by the treachery of his own colleagues who scheme against him, Preuss is drawn into a whirlwind of greed, violence, and revenge that spans generations across metropolitan Detroit.